TYLER'S UNDOING

A GLOVES OFF NOVEL

NEW YORK TIMES & USA TODAY BESTSELLING AUTHOR

L.P. DOVER

Copyright © 2014 by L.P. Dover
Cover design by Regina Wamba of Mae I Design
Editing by Victoria Rae Schmitz, Crimson Tide Editorial
Formatting by JT Formatting

Printed in the United States of America
First Edition: October 2014
Library of Congress Cataloging-in-Publication Data
Dover, L.P.
   Tyler's Undoing (A Gloves Off Novel) – 1st ed
     ISBN - 13: 978-0-9903964-5-1
     ISBN - 10: 0-9903964-5-2

1.   Tyler's Undoing—Fiction 2. Fiction—Romance
3.   Fiction—Contemporary Romance

http://**authorlpdoverbooks.com**

PROLOGUE

Tyler

FOR ONCE IN my life, I was untouchable.

No more was I the guy who settled for fourth place and moved on. I was determined to be the one everyone screamed for, the one women eagerly fell on their knees for. In the past year, so much had changed. I was finally living the life I'd always dreamt about. I had an agent, an undefeated record, and the women *did* fall eagerly to their knees in front of me . . . literally.

All I ever wanted was to be the best, and now I was here, I didn't want to go back. No one wanted to be the guy who always got close, but could never quite reach the top. Seeing the disappointment on my father's face made me feel worthless. It also didn't help that he had no faith in me whatsoever. He was my coach, and he took his job seriously. Sometimes, I think he forgot he was actually my father as well.

"This is insane," Todd exclaimed, slowly spinning around, beaming at the amount of people sitting in the arena. "They all want you, Tyler. Breathe it in, soak it up. It's only going to get better from here."

You're damn right.

Always the enthusiast, Todd Winfield—with his slicked back, midnight-black hair and expensive gray suit. He was thirty five years old, a born opportunist, and my agent. Thankfully, I was lucky enough to have been found by him after my epic battle last year at the Golden State tour. I had been grappling with UFC's infamous bad boy and Heavyweight champion, Matt Reynolds. He'd kicked my ass, but I sure as hell didn't make it easy for him.

Fast forward one year, and we now found ourselves in Dallas, Texas, at the American Airlines Center. There had to be twenty thousand people sitting around the arena, chanting my name. The sound of the crowd screaming for me as I walked down to the ring, echoed in my ears. Knowing they'd come to see *me,* was the ultimate high. Pumped for the fight, I sauntered down the aisle, keeping my gaze on my opponent.

Countless women raked their nails down my skin, screaming their need for me—what they'd do to my body. My agent and father warded them off, but I fucking loved it. All of it.

It was my time and I was going to live it.

Before I could get into the ring and kick my opponent's ass, my father halted me with a hand on my shoulder. "Concentrate, son," he growled low in my ear. "Cockiness will not win you the fight. It'll only make you sloppy."

Glancing up into the ring, I chuckled. I had nothing to worry about, my opponent was a hard striker, but I was quicker on my feet. "I'm not cocky," I snapped. "I'm confident. This guy's going down."

My father narrowed his eyes and huffed.

I'd been training with some of the best MMA fighters in the league and I didn't only believe I could win this fight, I knew it. Taking off my black and neon green robe, I handed it to my father and jumped into the ring, ignoring the disgusted look on his face.

"When did you get like this?" he argued impatiently, folding my robe over his arm. "I didn't raise you to be an arrogant, self-centered jackass."

Before the announcer made his way to the center of the ring, I leaned over the edge and peered down at my father. His annoyed glare was starting to become permanently etched. Most people agreed we looked alike—he was just an older version of me and also a retired fighter.

"No," I brushed him off, "you raised me to be a winner, and I finally am. Try not to be too overjoyed with the concept." Without waiting for a reply, I strolled to the center of the ring just in time for the announcer to call out my name.

"And fighting in the black shorts tonight, is the one you've all been waiting for! Ladies and gentleman, I give you *Tyler . . . the Terror . . . Ruuussshiiiing!*"

Lifting my arms, I circled around the ring, feeding off of the sound of my name coming across thousands of lips. My opponent—with his navy blue shorts, pale skin, and bright red hair—had a leer on his face the entire time. The combination made him look like a defective American flag. Justin Somers. What a douche. I guess it was Memorial Day weekend, maybe he took the red, white, and blue seriously, except he didn't look to be in a festive mood.

"So were you and Pops arguing over how you were going to lose tonight?" the talking flag sneered.

Scoffing, I planted my feet on the mat and got into stance, clenching my fists tight. I knew the bell was about to ring, and I was going to be ready.

"Actually," I began, "we were just discussing how long it would take to knock that smirk off your face. He said two minutes . . . I disagreed."

Justin opened his mouth, but before he could get one word out, the bell rang and I swung. My fist connected with his jaw so hard, his head snapped to the side, and he flipped backward onto the mat. Total knockout.

I leaned over his limp figure and added, "My mistake, I told Pops it would only take fifteen seconds." I glanced up at the monitor on the wall and smirked. "It was actually under three. Well, thanks for the great fight. I learned a lot."

"Ladies and gentleman, winning by TKO is your champion for the night. . ."

When the announcer held my hand up in the air, I didn't hear anything else. I was too hyped up, endorphins pounded through my veins. *This is what it's all about. This is what being a winner feels like.*

It was a drug and I was on the best fucking high of my life.

"Please tell me we're going out tonight, Ty?" Todd asked, rubbing his hands together. "I think I'm in the mood for a blonde with huge fucking tits, a tight ass, and a strong, Texan accent. Maybe she can show me how she does it cowgirl style."

We were back at the hotel so I could shower and change clothes. Unfortunately for him, I already had my night planned out, and it didn't include Todd reversing his cowboy. "Sorry, but I can't go tonight," I replied, pouring me a shot of Patron. I tossed it back and poured another one; it went back so smooth.

Todd's eyes went wide. "Why not? Come on, these Texas girls are so fucking hot."

"Not as hot as what I have coming to me," I gloated.

Groaning, he ran his hands through his hair and straightened up his gray suit jacket. He knew who I was referring to. "Fine, I'll go see if the twins want to hit the town tonight. Have fun with Gabriella."

Oh, I intend to.

Drinking the last of his whiskey sour, he set the glass down and headed for the door. "I'll see you in the morning, bright and early. Our plane leaves at ten so be ready."

"Got it," I replied. It was a good thing I could sleep on the plane—there wasn't going to be any sleeping tonight.

After Todd left, I fetched my phone out of my gym bag and noticed two missed text messages.

Gabriella: Just landed.

Gabriella: I'll be there in fifteen minutes. What room number?

It had only been one week since she left the note on my pillow saying goodbye. I didn't know if she'd actually come back to me, but when she called two days ago saying she wanted to see me again, I couldn't pass up the chance.

I just hoped she wasn't getting attached to me. I didn't need that. Her brother, Matt Reynolds – former Heavyweight Champion and my best friend – has always tried to keep her from dating fighters. If he ever found out I was fucking her behind his back, he'd kill me. As his friend, he trusted me to watch over her. Regrettably, I couldn't be trusted with her heart.

I texted her back and told her the room number, so she could come right up. I had enough time to pour myself a double shot of Tequila before a gentle knock sounded on the door. When I opened it, Gabriella stood there dressed in a skin tight navy dress, her midnight colored hair falling just past her shoulders, with a small smile on her face.

Now that she'd been training to be an MMA fighter, her arms were toned to perfection and her body was hard as a rock. Yet she still had the perfect amount of curves to get me hard in a fucking instant.

"What's wrong?" I asked, pulling her inside.

Setting down her bag on the couch, she then turned and wrapped her arms around my neck, her eyes troubled. "Tyler," she began hesitantly, releasing a heavy sigh. "As much as I wanted to believe this could work, I don't think we're going to be able to do it anymore."

She tried to look away, but I grabbed her chin and pulled her back. "Why, what happened? In your letter you made it sound like this was what you wanted."

"And I do," she replied, shrugging her shoulders. "But I don't see how I'm going to keep it up with my schedule. Matt's strict with my coming and going, and if I don't do as he says, he'll start asking questions. The last thing I want is for him to be angry with you."

Narrowing my gaze, I stepped back and crossed my arms over my chest. "You weren't too worried about that before. What else is on your mind, Gabriella? Is it because I still fuck other women?"

Halfheartedly, she chuckled and rolled her eyes. "No, jackass. I knew what I was getting into when I agreed to all of this. Honestly, I think it'll be best for us both to keep the other weekend as a wonderful memory. I have too many guy problems right now as it is." She sat down on the brown leather couch and the pressure she was under came out in her sigh.

I never understood why Gabriella wanted someone like me when she could have anyone she wanted, someone who wanted to be with her and only her. I wasn't that guy. I cared about her, but love wasn't what I wanted.

"Who's giving you problems?" I asked, sitting down beside her.

"Well, let's see," she began, "I wouldn't exactly call this a problem, but Bradley wants to see me again. He's actually going with me to Aspen to see Ashleigh. Apparently, things got a little crazy when I arrived home from Vegas that fateful morning."

Bradley was the guy she dated before me. I knew eventually things would change between us, and she would want something more than what I could give her. Hopefully, he could do that for her. She needed something real. As long as she wasn't with another fighter, all would be good.

"What happened when you got home?" I questioned.

Closing her eyes, she tilted her head back and rested

it on the couch. "I honestly don't know the details, Ashleigh wouldn't tell me everything. When I got back to my apartment she wouldn't come out of her room. I called Colin to come help me get her out, but he said he couldn't because she'd broken up with him.

"She said she made a mistake. After that whole baby scare in Vegas, it really messed her up. I think she's in love with Ryley but too afraid to admit it." She finally opened her eyes and looked over at me. "Colin's her safe place, he's someone who won't hurt her. Ryley, on the other hand, is the wild card, the one who ignites the fire deep inside."

I shook my head. "Then why doesn't she just get in touch with Ryley and talk it out? It's obvious they're both miserable."

"You would think, but Ashleigh told me not to say anything to him about her and Colin breaking up. Believe me, it's hard as shit keeping a secret, especially one that huge, from Ryley. Ashleigh said she wanted to be alone for a while. That's why she left for Aspen."

"So basically you don't want me to say anything, is that it?" I confirmed.

Nodding, she looked down at her clasped hands. "Yes, please. I don't know what's going to happen between the two of them, but I figured it's best to stay out of it. Hopefully, she'll tell me what's going on when I get out there."

"And Bradley is going with you," I stated.

Biting her lip, she peered up at me and nodded again. "I guess you can say he's *my* safe place. He keeps a certain someone away from me . . . kind of."

Now that she was training, I knew she was around a

lot of the other fighters. The only other one I knew who was trying to get her was Paxton Emerson.

"Please tell me it's not Paxton," I warned. "You need to stay the fuck away from him. Being with me is one thing, but guys like him are a completely different story."

When Gabriella was in Vegas, my fight had been against Paxton. With the way he looked at her, I knew something was going on. I told him then to stay away from her but obviously he didn't understand what I meant. It looked like I needed to change that.

Gabriella smiled and moved closer, biting her lip provocatively. "Oh, I think I've done pretty well in that arena, don't you think? Plus, he's friends with Kyle. That immediately puts him on my shit list."

Kyle Andrews was my enemy. Now that Gabriella's brother retired, his Heavyweight title was up for grabs, which meant Kyle and I would most likely be fighting for it at the end of the season. That fucker was going down.

"What is he doing to bother you?" I asked through clenched teeth.

Tentatively, she shrugged her shoulders. "He keeps asking me out. But don't worry, I tell him to fuck off every time. It's like he enjoys tormenting me. The part that really pisses me off is that he comes to me when he knows my brother isn't around. I'm pretty sure it's Kyle's way of getting under my skin."

"Do you want me to handle it?"

Mischievously, Gabriella smiled and climbed onto my lap, straddling my waist. "Actually, my body is the only thing I need you to man handle." She squeezed her legs and released, relaxing into my lap. "If this is the last time we're going to be together, I want to make it good.

Pax will eventually get a clue and leave me alone. If not, you are more than welcome to kick his as—if I don't do it first."

I planned on doing it anyway.

Lifting her dress above her thighs, Gabriella rocked her hips against mine. My dick got hard as I watched her lick her lips. She was going to fucking kill me. As much as I hated the fact this was our last time together, it was actually for the best. She knew it, and I knew it.

Gripping her neck, I pulled her down to me and bit her lip. "Making it good is something I *can* promise you."

CHAPTER 1

TYLER

"ALL RIGHT, SON, I'm leaving everything in your capable hands. I trust you to keep everything in order," Jake advised, standing by the front door of his club.

Jake Montgomery was my boss and the Labyrinth had always been a second home when I wasn't in the ring. For years, I'd been a bouncer at the exclusive club. Jake had a thing for the Roman era, so the whole building was made to look like a Roman cathedral. I swear he must've watched *Gladiator* one too many times.

For this particular weekend, I was going to be its owner while Jake left on his business trip. He trusted me, and I wouldn't let him down. In fact, I was ready for him to leave so I could plan the fights.

"Now get out of here before you miss your flight. I

won't let the place burn down," I promised.

Jake was in his early fifties and always pristine in his blue power suits and salt and peppered hair perfectly slicked back on his head. Most night club owners I knew were worthless douche bags who only cared about themselves and making money, but he actually cared about his employees. We were all he had as far as family.

After he met my father and found out about my MMA fighting, he started holding fights at the club because he knew it would help get me noticed. I owed him so much.

Taking one last look at the empty club, Jake picked up his brown leather suitcase and opened the door. "I'll be back Sunday night," he warned, pointing a finger at me. "And no fighting for you this weekend. I'm sure once you see the list you're going to want to partake, but it's your job to run the club."

Incredulously, I gasped and slapped him on the back. "Please, I have a little more restraint than that, old man."

"Whatever you say, son," he chuckled. "Call me if you need me."

Opening the door, he looked back once and smiled before the door slammed shut. Immediately, I went to the list he left on the bar and searched down each line. Halfway down the list there was his name . . . Paxton Emerson. No wonder Jake told me I couldn't fight.

I promised Gabriella I wouldn't go after him, and if he didn't stop, there was no way in hell I was going to keep my mouth shut. She might not be mine, but she sure as hell wasn't going to be his.

Reluctantly, I put my big boy pants on, and matched Paxton up against another fighter, even though I really wanted to put my name beside it. I'd kicked his ass a few months ago when he was fighting in the Heavyweight division. Sadly, he moved down a division this season, which meant he'd no longer be fighting against me.

It didn't matter though. I was going to make sure he left Gabriella alone. If I happened to throw a few punches here and there to get it through his head . . . it wouldn't be that bad. I could control myself.

The club was packed to the brim, with even more people waiting in line outside. Friday and Saturday nights were always busy at the club, but Fridays were the best. In just a couple of weeks, the last half of the UFC season would start and I'd be one step closer to putting my nemesis out of commission and earning the title. *It's a shame Kyle's not in town this weekend.*

"Did you put me down to fight tonight?" a voice behind me called out.

Without turning around, I chuckled and kept my gaze on the newbie fighters warming up. "Actually, I did," I replied. "You're up against, Beckett Miller."

Ryley stepped in front of me, blocking my line of sight. His hair was still dyed dark brown, after coloring it so no one would get him and his twin mixed up. Of course, his usual smirk was still in place.

"And who the hell is that? I've never heard of him," he retorted. He was already in his blue and white fighting shorts and blue gloves, itching to fight.

His opponent, Beck, was a local guy who started training at my gym. He wasn't even in the UFC, but he was one hell of a fighter. Tonight was his first fight and I would rather see him go against one of my friends than one of the other douche bags in the crowd.

"That's because he's never fought before," I told him. "He'll be a good opponent. Just go easy on him, it's his first time."

Ryley's twin, Camden, came up to my side all dressed in his signature red and black fighting gear. "Did you put me down tonight too?" he asked.

Smiling, I pointed over at one of the top upcoming Middleweight fighters in his division. He was about six foot tall, shaved brown hair and a hundred and eighty-five pounds—the ideal weight and height for his class. Never once had I seen the guy smile.

"Landon Baker. From what I hear, he's going to give you and your brother hell this season."

Camden barked out a laugh. "We'll see about that. Have you even talked to the guy? He's like a fucking mute."

"Yeah, when I told him he's fighting you. He just nodded, that's it. All I know is that he's relentless in the ring."

Tilting his neck to both sides, his bones cracked as he stretched. "Not like me," Camden gloated. "I'll take him down."

Before heading over to the ring, he fist-bumped Ryley and watched Landon from across the room—sizing him up. I had no doubt Camden would win, but Landon had the determination. He had the same look in his eyes I had when I first started.

"So I guess you're not fighting tonight?" Ryley asked.

About that time, Paxton walked into the arena. He was by himself, which shocked me, considering he was always surrounded by Kyle's groupies. I hated the fucknut.

"No," I growled, "I'm not."

When Ryley realized who I was looking at, he bumped me in the shoulder. "I take it Gabriella told you about him?"

I nodded.

"I wouldn't worry about it, man. She has Bradley protecting her. I offered to help her out, but she said no. I swear that girl attracts every single cocksucker in a thousand mile radius."

Yes, I know.

"Have you talked to her recently?" I asked.

He shrugged. "Yeah, she told me about you and her calling it quits. Honestly, it's probably for the best. She's left to go visit you know who in Aspen. I'm surprised her brother let her go with the kind of schedule he put her on. I think she trains more than I do."

With a coach like Matt, it didn't surprise me. "What about Ashleigh? Have you talked to her?"

His jaw tensed for a split second, and then he shook his head. "No, and I don't plan on it. She's probably off planning a fucking wedding with her lame ass boyfriend."

If only he knew the truth.

I wanted to tell him, but I respected Gabriella's wishes and kept my mouth shut. "All right, I need to make my rounds. I'll catch up with you after the fights are over."

Ryley shook my outstretched hand and nodded. "Sounds good. Just do yourself a favor and try not to kick

Paxton's ass. The last thing you want to do is cause problems for Gabriella."

"Trust me, I don't plan on it. That's what I have Tex for."

Paxton's opponent for the evening was Tex Montross, a Texan who spent his time fighting and raising cattle on his farm. His real name was Blaine, but only a handful of people knew.

Tex was about six foot two with curly, blond hair he always kept covered with a cowboy hat. I met him about a year ago when I was in Texas for a fight. Needless to say, it wasn't exactly a warm greeting. It was early in the morning and I was in the hotel gym working out when he noticed me, smirking the entire time. It pissed me off. He then proceeded to challenge me and I was more than willing to kick his ass.

We made a bet. He told me I wouldn't be able to handle his workout regime and I bet him that I could. Several of the other fighters in the hotel went along with us to Tex's barn to see if they could handle it too. Luckily, I won the bet–and his money–but even to this day, I considered his makeshift gym to be one of the hardest workouts I'd ever done.

Tex was off in the corner wrapping his hands and putting on his gloves.

"It's not exactly the prairie here is it? Miss your cows?" I teased.

"Ya'll can keep your fancy lights, city boy," Tex jested. "Ya'll don't know what you're missing."

I slapped him on the back and laughed. "Actually, I do and you're more than welcome to keep the cow shit. Hey, listen, I need you to do a favor for me."

6

Tex's brown eyes lit up. "Oh? And what exactly would that be?"

Moving a little closer, I smiled and nodded over at Paxton. "The guy you're fighting is Paxton Emerson. Since I'm not allowed to fight tonight, I need you to send him a message."

Devilishly, he smiled. "You mean like a physical type of message?"

I nodded. "He seems to have a problem with listening. I need to make sure he stays away from this girl I know."

"She your lady friend?"

"No, but we're good friends," I said, keeping my eyes locked on Paxton. "The last thing she needs is to get involved with him."

"Don't worry, city. I'm fixin' to make sure he gets the message loud and clear."

"Good, but I think it'll be fun to give him the message myself. Just get him ready for me."

Tex guffawed. "With pleasure."

Once the club closed, I was free. I could do whatever the hell I wanted.

CHAPTER 2

TyLER

WORD OF MY afterhours fight with Paxton got back to Gabriella pretty quickly. I woke up the next morning to a slew of text messages, and let's just say the ignore button was my friend. Why bring it up, if she didn't want me to fix the problem?

My plan had worked. First, he was pissed because of Tex's message, which provoked him to come after me. When he came up to me, he said he wasn't going to leave Gabriella alone—that she would 'give in' to him eventually. Well, the moment those words left his mouth, I reacted instantly. There were no rules, just full on street fighting out in the parking lot. I think more people enjoyed that than the actual fights inside.

"Do you want to talk about last night?" my father

asked. "You know Jake is going to be pissed as hell."

Huffing, I pounded my fists into the bag, sweat dripping down my face and into my eyes. "I didn't do anything wrong," I snapped. "It was after hours."

"On *his* property, son. What if Paxton pressed charges? You could lose your spot in the UFC."

"That's not going to happen. If you knew the real story, you'd know he was the one who started it all . . . I just happened to finish it."

My father glared at me, his jaw tense. "Either way, you should compose yourself like a normal human being. You may fight for a living, but that doesn't mean you handle real life situations like you're in the ring. I expect better from you."

"Oh, Steven, give the boy a break," my mother chided as she walked into the gym. "I heard what happened and the other guy deserved it. Lighten up on him, sweetheart."

My mother knew what she was doing because my father finally got off my back and started in on her, following her to the front desk. "That's not the point, Mary," I heard him hiss. "The boy needs to learn to control his temper."

"I wonder where he gets it from?" she teased, winking slyly at me over her shoulder.

Since our receptionist left for nursing school, my mother had been taking the day shift answering the phones. She seemed to enjoy it, but it was actually my job to find a replacement. Unfortunately, I hadn't found anyone I liked.

Now that my father's attention was diverted, it was time to put in my hours of training. I had a Heavyweight title to work for.

CHAPTER 3

Kacey

"HOW IS YOUR grandma doing today?" Bree asked as I got into her little silver car.

I didn't think I was being so obvious, but she must have noticed my sadness as I walked out of my grandmother's house. As always, I smiled and tried to stay hopeful, even though I knew there wasn't going to be much time left. "Well, her nurse showed up about an hour ago and we talked for a little while, discussing what the plan was for when . . ." Closing my eyes, I bit my lip and blew out a shaky breath, hoping I wouldn't break into tears. I couldn't even finish what I wanted to say.

Bree reached over and took my hand, squeezing it tight as she pulled out of the driveway. We were headed to the gym to work out because she was a good friend and thought I should get out of the house and spend some time in an environment where I could let my mind go free. I knew she was right, I just needed someone to drag my ass there.

When I came to take care of Nana, I knew it would be difficult when her health went downhill. Knowing, and seeing it actually happen, are two completely different things. At first, she was so full of life, but then the cancer started to spread and slowly took over.

My family, a.k.a. my mother and my older brother, had wanted to put her in a nursing home. This way, they wouldn't have to worry about her. But I couldn't bear to see that happen, so I moved to Las Vegas over a year ago, specifically to take care of her. I had no clue what I was going to do after the cancer took her from this world. Would I stay here or move back home to California? I just didn't know.

For the past year, Cindy James—my grandmother's nurse—always worked the afternoon and night shift, leaving me free to get my errands done before going to work. Nana needed full-time care and it was getting to the point where I couldn't handle it on my own anymore.

Turning to Bree, I saw her chocolate brown hair was pulled off of her face into a low ponytail, and she already had her black yoga pants and pink tank top on. I looked similar in a pair of dark purple yoga capris and a teal tank top. It was just easier to head over in our workout clothes, than changing in the locker room at the gym.

"Do you want to talk about it?" she asked nervously. "You know you don't have to hide your feelings from me."

"I know, Bree. I just want to stay strong for her, even

though it's a battle every day to convince myself I can handle it. She's the closest family I have, and without her, I'll be alone."

She technically wasn't the only family I had, but she might as well have been. Bree Sanderson was my friend and we'd been inseparable since I started working with her in the Venetian Las Vegas resort at the AquaKnox. We were both twenty-five-year-olds, working as baristas until we could earn enough money to get out on our own.

Sometimes I think fate brought us together. Even though we'd only been friends for a year, I considered her family . . . more so than my own mother and older brother.

"What about your family, Kacey? Have you talked to them? Do they know how fast her health is fading?" She was being cautious.

She knew I didn't like talking about my family, nor did she know the specifics of why I wanted to leave them. I figured it was best keeping the details of my dysfunctional family a secret for as long as I could.

"No, I haven't talked to them, and neither has my grandmother."

My grandmother was my father's mother, so my mom didn't give a shit what happened to her. Her worthless ass was too busy using her rich son as a meal ticket. My brother still tried to keep in my life by sending checks every month, but every time one would come, I'd shred it. I didn't need his handout, or anyone else's for that matter.

Money can't buy forgiveness . . . or redemption.

Wanting to change the subject, I blew out a frustrated breath and sighed. I needed something to keep my mind off of my dying grandmother and my worthless family. "Okay, so what's this gym you're taking me to? Are there any cute guys?" I asked, trying to plaster a smile on my face.

Bree chuckled and winked, knowing very well that I needed her optimism. "Of course there are! Why do you think I go there? It's hard to meet guys when we're busy working. What better way than to meet them at the gym? I've met some pretty nice ones there too, but you already know about them. Now that the owners renovated the whole place, it's even better."

I didn't have time to date anyone with my schedule the way it was, which often times made it kind of lonely. So far, I hadn't found anyone worth dating anyway. Still, there was nothing wrong with looking.

"All right, we're almost there," Bree mentioned excitedly. "I figured we could work out for an hour and then rush to my apartment to take showers and change before our shift starts. Sound good?"

I nodded. "Yeah, that sounds great." Pulling into the parking lot, I couldn't believe all of the cars. The place was packed.

Laughing, Bree bumped her shoulder into mine and opened her car door. "Trust me, Kace, the place is a lot bigger than you think. This is nothing. Besides, some of the people aren't even here to work out."

Getting out of the car, I narrowed my gaze in confusion. That made no sense. I followed alongside until we were almost to the door. "Why would people come here if they weren't planning on working out?"

With her hand on the door, she smiled and bit her lip. "You'll see," she sang. "Follow me and enjoy, sweetheart."

Intrigued and excited, I followed her inside and took

one good look around the massive establishment before I wanted to scream. I'd just stepped into my own personal nightmare—a hell which haunted me from years ago. *Will I never get away from my past?* It wasn't her fault, Bree had no idea about my past life.

"Come on, girl," she said, taking my arm and pulling me toward the welcome desk. "Let's get you signed up to be a member, shall we?"

Blowing out a nervous breath, I nodded quickly and plastered a smile on my face. I'd sign up for her, but I had no plans on ever coming back.

Please, God, don't let anyone recognize me.

CHAPTER

4

Kacey

I WANTED TO turn and walk out the door, but I couldn't let Bree down, she was only trying to help me out. I would have to suck this up.

There were fighters everywhere.

My eyes drifted to some guys surrounding a ring on the left side of the gym. It was the same ring my brother fought in, just a couple of weeks ago. I'd also seen Gabriella Reynolds fighting that night. Before then, I had no idea she was a trained MMA fighter. Her brother, Matt, had taken the Heavyweight title away from my brother a couple of years ago.

I'd been involved behind the scenes in the fighting world and wanted nothing to do with it. I left California to get away from this life, and it was all because of my deceptive brother who liked to cheat his way to the top. His friends were exactly the same, and from my experience I'd never met one who fought fair . . . or was honorable for that matter. Well, except for my friend, Pax.

My brother had a lot of enemies and I prayed no one recognized me as his sister. Not that they would, considering I pretty much kept to myself. I'd hate to have to face persecution from those who were victims of his heinous schemes.

It was pretty easy to see that all of the guys around the ring had a bloated ego and a leer of arrogance. If their reputations were the same as those I knew before, then they only had two things on their mind . . . fighting and women.

I wasn't desperate enough to date a fighter. I wanted more, something deeper than a thug who used his fists to earn money and a dick to screw women. I was ultimately looking for Mr. Right, not Mr. Right Now.

All I had to do was keep my distance.

"Everyone here is so nice," Bree whispered before we reached the desk.

The woman behind the desk looked to be in her early sixties, and had sandy-colored hair, mixed with a little gray. Her head was down, looking at a magazine, but when we came into view she looked up and smiled at Bree. "Why hello, Bree, how are you?" She glanced over at me. "I see you brought a friend. Do you want to use one of your friend passes today?"

Bree shook her head. "Actually, Kacey wants to get a membership. Do you mind getting her set up?"

"Certainly." The lady pulled out a clipboard and placed a couple sheets of paper on it before grinning over at me. "Thank you, Kacey, for joining. My name's Mary Rushing and my husband owns the place. I don't usually work the front desk, but as of right now, I'm the only one capable of doing it. I think he and my son would be lost without me."

Grinning, I said, "That's usually how it goes."

With a warm, genuine smile she handed me a clipboard and pen. I took it to the edge of the desk and started filling it out while she and Bree caught up.

After I paid my membership fees, Bree took me over to a vacant corner with several treadmills and some high-tech stair climbers. Give me a road and sneakers and I was good to go. I didn't usually spend my time in gyms, because I knew I could work out just as well at home, if not better—and for free.

"All right, Kace, let's get started on the treadmills. Then we can hop on the stair climbers before we move to weights. Cole gave me some amazing tips on changing up my workouts to give me the ultimate toning."

Cole Bennett was the guy she'd been interested in for the past few weeks, but so far nothing had come of it, much to her dismay. I hadn't met him yet, so I had no idea if he was at the gym or what he looked like.

"Is he here?" I asked, looking around. Climbing on the treadmill, I started off with a brisk walk.

Pursing her lips, Bree glanced around the gym and shook her head. "Nope, he's not here yet. Usually, he comes in around two o'clock, which only gives me thirty minutes to talk to him before I have to leave and get ready for work. Hopefully, he'll be in today so you can meet him. The guys have been dying for me to bring in some of my girlfriends."

I snorted and rolled my eyes. *Yeah, I'll bet.* However, this brought up a question. "So, is Cole an MMA fighter?" I asked. "I don't think you ever mentioned anything about that. Surely, you know better, right?"

Narrowing her eyes, she picked up her pace and glared at me. "What's that supposed to mean? Cole's a good guy and he's funny as hell. Why would I not want to date him just because he's a fighter?"

Because they were all worthless, I wanted to say. "So he *is* one," I stated instead.

"Yeah, and a good one too. I've watched him spar with the owner's son plenty of times." She looked off toward the ring and pointed. "There he is, Tyler. He's the one with the bright blond hair."

I followed her finger and froze. *Holy mother of pearl.* Was he—? Yes. He's the one who fought against my brother in the video that was spread all over the internet.

"I think you'll like that group of guys down there," Bree chimed.

I wouldn't count on it.

"So what does Cole look like again?" I asked. "Does he pump steroids like the other raisin nuts down there?" Not all of the fighters had overly huge muscles, although most were deemed questionable. I loved strong, athletic bodies, but too much muscle wasn't sexy—on men *or* women.

Bree rolled her eyes and groaned. "Kace, they're not allowed to take steroids if they want to compete, and no, Cole doesn't look like that. He has muscles, don't get me wrong, but he competes for the Light Heavyweight title. Also, he has the most gorgeous jet-black hair I've ever seen, and his eyes . . ." She fanned herself with her hand

and smiled. "I have never seen anyone with the same color eyes as his. They're a bright blue with a ring of gold around the pupils. At first I thought they were contacts, but he says they are his real color."

"Yeah, that's great and all," I said, "but looks aren't what's important. Is he nice? Would he be faithful? Because frankly, those types of guys down there aren't what I'd consider relationship material. Dating is one thing, but getting serious with one of them is another."

Shaking her head, Bree chuckled. "I swear, Kace, I don't know what I'm going to do with you. Whatever Cole's intentions are, I honestly think he's a great guy. I have no doubt that you'll think so, too."

After I finished up my two mile run on the treadmill, I moved over to one of the stair climbers and stared helplessly at the buttons. There were so many options I had no idea which one to press. Since Bree was still on the treadmill, I figured if I pressed some of the buttons, one of them would make the machine work.

Before I could start pressing random buttons, a gloved hand reached over my shoulder and pushed one for me. Immediately, I stiffened. Seeing the glove and the tattoos circling up his arm could only mean one thing.

I took in a nervous breath. *Hopefully, he won't know who I am.* The heat from his body radiated across my skin, and instead of moving away from the flame, like I knew I should, I shivered with the sheer closeness, especially when his voice came out right above my ear.

"Not that you needed any help, or anything," he explained cautiously, "but I figured level three would be perfect for someone with your muscular tone. It's a tough routine, but I'm curious to see how you match up against Bree over there. She claims to be the best."

When I turned around, I just barely held in my gasp. It was Tyler. He was standing on the machine next to mine, leaning across the hand rail, smiling at me. Before I could say anything, he winked and hopped off, making his way toward the back of the gym and through another door. If he recognized me at all, he sure didn't give any indication that he had.

As soon as Bree got done with her treadmill run, she rushed over to me with a mischievous grin on her face. I had already started on my routine, so I was trying to concentrate on my breathing when she gasped.

"Oh my goodness, what did Tyler say to you? Isn't he just the hottest thing you've ever seen? Like sex on a stick."

Sure, he was a good looking guy, but I refused to think about him anymore. Rolling my eyes, I shook my head. "Not really, Bree. All he did was show me which button to push. I'm sure a guy like him tries to help all of the girls that come in here."

"Actually, he doesn't. When I first started coming here, I tried to play dumb so he would come and help me, but he never did. Cole ended up being the one to show me what to do. You're the only one I've ever seen Tyler approach."

"Please, you're not here every hour of the day," I pointed out. "I'm sure he *helps* out his fair share of women. Anyway, you're reading more into this than you should. I'm here to work out, not meet guys." *Especially the fighters.*

Bree snorted. "I think what you need is some fun in your life, sweetheart. Even though you have a million responsibilities weighing you down, you still need to take care of yourself in the process. You haven't gone on a single date since I've known you. My company alone can't be giving you what you need."

It was true, there was something missing. I just didn't have time to meet anyone and go on dates. At least, not while I had so many distractions. After I finished the thirty minute stair climbing program, Bree only had a few more minutes left on hers, so I decided to get us both a bottle of water while I waited.

Ignoring the catcalls coming from some of the guys as I walked past, I disappeared around the corner to the drink machines. *I'm so ready to leave this place.* Getting our water, I turned around and jumped in surprise. Tyler was leaning against the wall, arms crossed at the chest, and a huge smirk stretched across his perfect face. I didn't hear him come up behind me.

"I see you survived level three. I knew you could," he announced.

I flashed a fake grin and quickly let it disappear. "Yeah, level three wasn't that difficult," I gloated. "Thank you for helping me, though. I'm sure next time I'll know what to press."

I tipped my head and strolled past him, ready to get out of the vacant corner. Much to my dismay, he followed alongside as I made my way back to where I'd left Bree. When I rounded the corner, I found her happily talking to a guy by the stair climbers. I assumed it was Cole, judging by the dark hair and blue eyes Bree loved so much. He had his shirt off, wearing a pair of navy workout shorts, flexing his muscles as he talked to her.

"This must be your first time here," Tyler guessed.

"I've never seen you before. I know there's no way I could miss seeing that beautiful face of yours."

I rolled my eyes. "Please tell me that's not your pickup line. Because let me tell you, it's not going to work. Yes, this is my first time here, but it's probably my last, too." I didn't want to sound offensive or rude, but I knew it came out that way by the look in his eyes.

Tyler lightly grabbed my elbow and halted me before I could move any further. "Why is that?" he asked, genuine interest appeared in his stormy gray gaze. "If it's what I said, I swear I wasn't saying it to hit on you. You honestly and truly do have a beautiful face. I've been known to come up with some pretty ridiculous pickup lines, but I can assure you that wasn't one of them. Besides, when did it become bad to tell the truth?" He stuck out his hand. "My name's Tyler, by the way."

Shifting both bottles of water to my left hand, I closed my eyes and sighed, extending my hand to his. "Okay, fine, I was quick to jump to assumptions. My name's Kacey," I admitted, "and I guess it's a good thing you weren't trying to use your pickup lines on me."

Curious, Tyler lifted his brows and smiled. "Oh yeah, and why is that?"

"I simply don't date steroid-taking brutes who walk around thinking they're God's gift to women. You're just not my type. Nice to meet you, Tyler. Have a good day." With those last words, I turned on my heel and stalked off, leaving him to stare incredulously at my back.

I had to say . . . his reaction was priceless.

CHAPTER 5

TYLER

"DUDE, I THINK you lost your touch," Cole teased, chuckling loudly. He was standing with Bree, so I walked over and joined them, after I watched the feisty, blonde-haired vixen walk out the front doors. *So I'm not her type, huh? We'll see about that.*

Cole Bennett was one of my closest friends and competing in his second year for the Light Heavyweight title. He also had a smart ass mouth, which I needed to make sure took a hard hit the next time I sparred with him. He was one of the good fighters, but his mouth was sure to get him into trouble one day. Most could say that about me too, especially when I joked around with my friends and their women. Pushing the limits was what I was good at, plus I had fun doing it.

Bree smiled apologetically and shrugged her shoulders. "Sorry about that, Tyler. What did she say to you?"

"Well, let's see," I started. "I commented on how beautiful she was. Then, she basically called me a steroid-taking douche bag. How's that for a recap? I take it she got her heart broken recently?"

"I don't think so," Bree replied, furrowing her brows. "She's never said anything to me about it. I honestly thought she'd go for you, out of all the people here. I guess I was wrong."

Cole chuckled again and slapped me on the arm. "Face it, Rushing. You're just upset she shot you down. You can't always win them all you know."

"That's not what I was doing," I countered matter-of-factly. Then admitted to Bree, "I mean, yeah, maybe I *was* trying to subtly hit on her by giving her compliments, but usually girls go for honesty and all that shit. Also, I figured being your friend and all, she would've heard good things about us."

"I did talk you up," she claimed wholeheartedly. "Kacey has a lot going on right now, so that's probably what her problem is. I don't know if she'd want me telling you her life story, but she has it kind of rough right now. She moved here about a year ago, and she doesn't have many friends."

She paused and quickly glanced at Cole, then back to me, sighing. "We both work in the bar at AquaKnox. That's how I met her. I thought getting her out and meeting other people would be good for her. I hope in time she'll come around and start having some fun. It took me forever to get her to even come here with me."

I wondered what was going on with her. Not that I

ever gave a shit about that kind of stuff, but there was something about Kacey that interested me. Maybe it *was* that she turned me down and I saw her as a challenge. I didn't like to lose at anything.

"Are you working this weekend?" Cole asked Bree.

"Yeah, it's our weekend to work. Why?"

Cole glanced at me out of the corner of his eye and smiled. We were on the same page.

"Because," I cut in, "maybe we could all do something together, after you get off of work. Do you think Kacey would be up for that?"

She bit her lip and peered hesitantly at us both. "I'm not sure. After the way she just acted, I don't know what to think. What exactly do you have in mind?"

Grinning from ear to ear, I quirked a brow. "Well, you said she just moved here, right? Meaning, she probably hasn't seen much of Vegas. I think I have an idea on how to break the ice."

Bree tilted her head to the side. "Hmm . . . I don't know if I like that mischievous look in your eyes, but I'm down for whatever you have in mind. We both get off of work at ten-thirty, so make sure you let me know what's going on."

Cole bumped her in the arm. "I'll text you and tell you what the plan is."

Giggling, Bree reached down to grab her gym bag. "I guess we'll see you both then. Make sure it's something fun." Turning on her heel, she started to walk off, but I had one last request.

"Bree," I called out.

She circled around. "Yeah?"

"Don't tell her I'm going to be there, okay? I'm pretty

sure she'd bail if she knew."

"Tyler, I'm not stupid," she exclaimed. "And believe me, she'd get out of it. Kacey is one of the most determined girls I've ever met. I hope you know what you're getting in to. She deserves a good guy."

Unlucky for her, I wasn't a good guy.

"If you call me tonight maybe we can come up with a plan to break the ice before then. I have some ideas to get her warmed up."

"Sounds good," I replied. "I'll get your number from Cole."

Smiling one last time, she turned on her heel and stalked off. Cole didn't say another word until she walked out of the building. "Okay, Rushing, what's your end game? I've never seen you put out this kind of effort to get a piece of ass, not even for Gabriella."

Obviously, Kacey was going to make me work for it. "I don't know. There's something about her that's different. Maybe it's the outright loathing she has for fighters that turns me on. There's just something about her that's unattainable, and you know how much I like that."

Chuckling, Cole slapped me on the back. "Yeah, we all want the ones we can't have. If you want to work at it, by all means, go ahead. Just don't fuck with this one like you do the others. I actually like Bree, if you mess with her best friend she's going to hate me by association. Don't ruin this for me, bro."

"Wow, you must have it bad for her," I joked.

Cole shrugged and took a sip of water out of his bottle. "What can I say? She's the first girl who actually seems interested in who I am and not what I do. You know how that is. Other than Gabriella, when was the last time you could say you met a girl who wanted you for you?"

"Never," I admitted honestly. Sadly, it was the truth. It was always the same type of girls sniffing around. They either wanted to fuck me or get recognition.

"And that right there, is why I want someone like Bree."

Maybe it was the same reason I had the desire to go after Kacey. She had an innocence about her—something pure. I'd never seen it in any female I'd been with, not even Gabriella. Someone like her had always been un-reachable, unattainable.

Do I really want to taint her innocence with the shit I bring to the table?

"You know what they say, Tyler . . . it's not worth it, unless you have to fight for it. We might have done some stupid shit in our lives, but there comes a time when all of that must come to an end. My time is now. You just need to decide when it'll be yours."

With a sly grin, he punched me in the shoulder and chuckled all the way down to the practice ring. "And if you call Bree tonight, you better not hit on her. I'll serious-ly kick your ass if you do."

"Like you could," I challenged. "I seem to remember every time we get in the ring it's *your* ass that meets the mat."

Cole jumped in the ring and bounced on his feet, practicing his jabs. "That may be so, dickhead, but if you fuck with my girl, you fuck with me. One of these days, you'll know how it feels to be on this end."

Maybe one day I would, but right now I had a chal-lenge to face. Kacey wasn't going to make it easy on me. If it was a fight she wanted, she'd better be prepared to lose. I loved a good challenge.

And so it begins.

CHAPTER 6

Kacey

"KACEY, WHAT'S WRONG with you?" Bree rushed out of the gym.

I felt like an idiot waiting by her car, but I really needed to get out of there. "I'm so sorry," I apologized. "I didn't mean to leave you in there, but it felt like I was having a panic attack." It was a lie, but she knew I had a history of panic attacks.

Bree's brown eyes softened. "Oh, Kace, I didn't realize. I thought it might have been from what Tyler said to you. He asked if you were going to be okay."

"What did you tell him?" I asked, eyes wide.

She shrugged and unlocked the car doors. "I told him you had a lot going on in your life right now. He's actually a decent guy. You should try hanging out with him some time."

"I don't think so. I have no desire to date any of those guys in there," I replied, opening my door and getting into the seat.

Bree started up the car and we headed on our way to her apartment. "Well, maybe you'll change your mind one day," she suggested.

Not going to happen.

Once we got to her apartment and freshened up, we were on our way to the restaurant. It was good money, especially with the tips. Although, working a night job where men hit on you constantly, wasn't exactly what I wanted to do for the rest of my life. Even if I never earned enough money to open up my own restaurant, I still didn't imagine myself working in a bar any longer than absolutely necessary.

"Only two more hours," I groaned, looking at the clock.

Bree chuckled and handed me the limes for my gin and tonics. "It's not that bad tonight. Just be thankful we don't have to work the late shift. Then you really have to deal with the drunk assholes and shitty tips. I did it once, when David couldn't come in for his shift, and regretted every minute of it."

Laughing, I finished pouring up the drinks and turned to her. "Yeah, I remember that. It's a shame he quit to go to medical school. I really liked him. Damn people and their dreams."

"We'll be at that point someday, Kace. Our time will come soon." More patrons started flooding into the bar so Bree quickly smiled at me before strolling to the end of the counter to take more orders.

Grabbing some napkins, I carried my gin and tonics to the two men who ordered them. They were dressed in business suits; one with perfect, combed-over midnight colored hair and green eyes, while the other had really short, dirty blond hair and brown eyes. Both were very attractive and most likely gay, knowing my luck.

"Here you go, gentlemen. Do you want to open a tab?"

"Not for me," the guy with the blond hair said, passing me a twenty dollar bill.

The one with the dark hair smiled and sat down. "I will. I'm meeting one of my clients here shortly." He handed me his card.

"All right, I'll get you set up," I told him.

He stayed at the bar drinking his gin and tonic, while his friend finished his off and left. Once Bree and I caught up on everyone's orders, I was finally able to relax and get a glass of water. Every so often, the guy in the suit would make eye contact with me and smile. *Maybe he's not gay.*

"Would you like another gin and tonic while you wait on your client?" I asked him.

"That'd be great. He must be running a little late." Pulling out his phone, he looked down at it and sighed. "Never mind, he just sent a text saying he's not going to make it. His flight got cancelled."

"Oh no," I replied. "I hate that you've sat here this

whole time for nothing." After I finished making his drink, I slid it to him.

"I wouldn't say it was for nothing. At least I got to sit here and talk to you." He held out his hand. "My name's Liam, Liam Harris."

Taking his hand, I shook it and smiled. "I'm Kacey. It's nice to meet you."

"Likewise."

Bree noticed the interaction and grinned from ear to ear. When a trio of girls came up to the bar, she winked and waved me off, nodding toward Liam. By the look in Liam's eyes and the smirk on his face, he'd cracked her code.

"She's not very subtle is she?" he asked.

Chuckling, I shook my head. "Not at all. She's just happy I'm actually talking to someone of the opposite sex."

That caught his attention. "Do you usually not? I'd think a woman like you would be surrounded by men, especially in a place like this."

"Oh, she is," Bree cut in. "She just doesn't give them the time of day."

Liam laughed. "Well, then I guess I should feel privileged she's talking to me."

My face blushed bright crimson and I could feel the heat flooding to my cheeks. Turning around, I faced the register and ran Liam's card. "Thanks, Bree," I grumbled, glaring over at her.

When I faced him again, he finished his drink and signed off on the receipt, leaving me a three figure tip. *Holy shit!* I closed my eyes and looked at it again . . . yep, three figures.

"So I guess this means you're not seeing anyone?" Liam asked, getting to his feet.

I closed my gaping mouth and cleared my throat.

Bree was the one who replied, "No, she's not seeing anyone."

Liam's brows lifted, waiting on *my* answer.

"I'm single," I said.

Pulling out his wallet, he grabbed the pen off the counter and wrote his number down on the back of one of his cards. "I'm going to leave you my cell number. If you're not busy Saturday night, I'd love to take you out to dinner."

Bree nudged me in the side when all I did was stand there like an idiot. "Answer him," she mumbled under her breath.

"Yes," I blurted out. "Dinner would be nice. I'll give you my number as well." Grabbing a napkin from the bar, I scribbled my phone number on it and handed it to him before taking his card.

"Feel free to call me anytime, Kacey."

Looking down at the card, I nodded then looked back up at him. "I will . . . thanks. Have a good night."

"You do the same." Turning on his heel, he made his way out, looking back once before disappearing out the door.

"I must say, you sure do know how to snag the good looking ones," Bree teased. "At least he's not gay."

His card only had his name on it and a phone number which must've been the one for his work. There was no description of who he was or what he did as far as business. He was a mystery.

"Or so you think," I chuckled, putting his card in my

pocket. "He could be gay and just want to pick my brain on the newest fashions."

Bree snorted. "I don't think so, babe. Not with the way he was checking you out all evening."

Rolling my eyes, I peered up at the clock and breathed a sigh of relief. We only had fifteen minutes left until the end of our shift.

"Are you going to call him?" she asked.

Shrugging my shoulders, I pulled out his card again and bit my lip. "I don't know. He could be a complete ass for all I know."

"True, but he could also be pretty cool too." Her phone buzzed in her pocket. Pulling it out, she tapped away, smiling from ear to ear. It had to be Cole.

"I'm assuming that's Cole. Are you two going out tonight?"

Finishing up her text, she nodded and put her phone in her back pocket. "Yeah, he wants to see me later. For a guy, he's actually been taking it kind of slow. I never thought he'd be like that, given the reputation some of the fighters have."

"Which is exactly why I stay away from them," I remarked dryly. "The last thing I want is to be just another fling for a day."

"That's not how Cole is, Kacey. Tyler might be a little different, but he's still a good guy. I think you need to give him a chance, or better yet, just be friends with him. He's actually pretty cool to hang around with and he's funny as hell. It'd be great to have us all go out together some time."

Clasping her hands in front of her, Bree pouted her lips and whimpered pleadingly. She was the only friend I had and I would do anything for her because I knew she would do the same for me.

"Okay, let me think about it, Bree. Just because I'm considering it doesn't mean I want to have anything to do with Tyler. I can tolerate just about anyone, but if he gets in my space, it's not going to be pretty."

Bree snickered and shook her head. "Um . . . you know he's a lot bigger than you, right?"

"I don't care," I exclaimed. "I'm a lot stronger than I look. Besides, there's one thing he doesn't have that I do."

"And what's that?"

"My refreshingly charming wit. He won't even know what hit him."

"I'd like to see that," she teased.

I wouldn't, because then that'd mean I was actually going to be around him. I just had to hope and pray he didn't want to have anything to do with me after our time at the gym today.

7

TYLER

AFTER COLE AND I sparred, he left to get ready for his date with Bree while I continued my training. Much to my surprise, my father had basically been leaving me in charge for the past couple of months. The only time he was really in the gym was during my training sessions, which happened to be starting right now.

"All right, son, let's see what you got," my father called out. "Make sure to concentrate."

Anticipating another fighter's moves was one of the most important things you needed to learn in the ring. If you could anticipate their moves, you could hit them in their weakest spots. I was good at everything but that, and it pissed my father off more than anything. He was an expert at it. Every time I failed his approval, I had to hear how unfocused I was and how I would never win the title.

Padded up with his boxing gloves, my father circled the ring and I countered him, trying my best to concentrate on his movements. He was good at psyching people out, including me. I would give anything to move like him, but I had strengths he didn't possess. Sometimes, I wondered if he even realized that.

Once his posture shifted I knew his strike was coming to my left. When I dodged, he smiled and nodded his head. "Good, son," he praised.

He struck again and again, each time I deflected his attacks. "See, I'm not so bad?" I remarked excitedly. It was the first time I'd thwarted every single attack.

The second I let my excitement get the better of me, my father swung and snapped my head to the right side with a hard punch. Out of every single fighter I'd fought against, my father had the hardest hit. Head ringing, I rolled my neck and cracked it, massaging my jaw.

"Maybe I spoke too soon," I grumbled.

Sighing, my father slipped off his gloves. "That's your problem, son. You get too cocky and it gets to your head. Stop letting it control you."

"It was only one hit," I challenged. "I've taken plenty of hits and still came out on top."

"Yeah, but it only takes one to make all the difference. You fight Kyle in three weeks for the title. He's gotten ruthless with his fighting. I just want you to be ready."

"I will be," I promised.

"I sure hope so, son. The last thing the league needs is Kyle taking the title again. Everyone's counting on you."

Yes, I know. I wasn't going to let anyone down.

Once I closed up the gym, I started on my way home and called Bree. She was on a date with Cole, but he knew I was going to call.

"Why hello, Tyler," she answered the phone.

"Hey, Bree. Are you still with Cole?"

"Yes, I'm here cocksucker," Cole called out. "You're on the speakerphone."

"Okay, I'll make this quick so you two can get back to . . . well, whatever it is you were doing. Anyway, I wanted to see if there was anything you could tell me about Kacey. Something that'll help me out."

"Honestly, I don't know if anything will," Bree confessed. "She was pretty adamant on keeping her distance. She did, however, say she would *maybe* hang out with all of us one day. Knowing her, she'd still try to avoid it if I asked her to go."

"That's a start though. Make sure not to tell her about Friday."

"I won't."

"What about hobbies? What does she like to do?"

"She likes to play golf. Her father taught her when she was a little girl. She talks about it all the time, but I don't play. I usually just go with her and drive her around in the golf cart. Do you play?" she asked.

"Of course," I lied. "Maybe I'll see if she'll do that with me."

"That would be amazing," Bree squealed. "She'll

love to play with someone."

I had never even set foot on a golf course before, other than the local putt-putt when I was a kid. I mean, how hard could golf be?

"What else does she like to do?" I inquired.

"Um . . . she likes to go running every morning. If I could get up early enough, I'd go with her, but she always goes at like six in the morning. That's too much for me."

Now that was something I honestly did as well. I just usually went running around my neighborhood. "Where does she run?"

"She goes to the local high school by her house, to run on their track. If you show up there tomorrow, you better not mention I had anything to do with it," she warned.

"I won't." I chuckled. "Just tell me which school she goes to and I'll pretend this phone call never happened."

She sang like a canary and we hung up. Kacey was going to be pissed.

CHAPTER

8

Kacey

BREE HAD DROPPED me off a little after ten o'clock last night and I was up again at half past five for my morning run. It was my daily routine: run, take care of Nana, eat, work, and sleep. By the time I got out of the house at six, the sky was already pink and gold with the rising sun. It was beautiful.

Cindy's shift ended at seven, giving me just enough time to wake up, put on my black workout shorts and bright yellow T-shirt, and get my running done before my grandmother woke up. Sitting at the kitchen table in her scrubs and her auburn hair pulled in a low bun, Cindy was busy documenting my grandmother's chart when I walked past.

"Be careful, sweetheart," she murmured.

Grabbing my iPod off of the kitchen counter, I slipped it into the holder on my arm and placed the ear buds in my ears. "I will. I'll be back in about forty-five minutes."

Time to run.

The local high school was only a quarter of a mile away, so it never took long to get there. It was the end of the school year, but there were always a couple teachers who did their morning runs there as well. I was never alone, which was comforting.

Before taking off on the track, I scrolled through my albums and picked one of my favorite bands, Avenged Sevenfold. Usually, I listened to pop, classical, nineties music, and even songs from the sixties, but when I ran I wanted something harder, more untamed.

Once my favorite song came on, I took off running, enjoying the tension release of just letting go. Other than playing golf on the delicate green grass of a golf course, running was my other secret pleasure. It gave me time to think, to pretend I was somewhere else, where I didn't have responsibilities weighing me down.

I wasn't exactly a fast runner, but I could get at least three miles done in thirty minutes. I thought that was pretty good. With one lap down, I made sure to keep my pace steady so I wouldn't lose my momentum—which was promptly thrown out the window when I felt a presence close behind me. A little too close.

Quickly, I glanced over my shoulder and lost my footing. Before I could fall on my face, Tyler scooped me up and twisted me around so that he took the blow when we landed on the ground. Breathing hard, I lied on top of him while my mind caught up with what just happened.

"What the hell are you trying to do, give me a heart attack?" I snarled, smacking him in the arm so he'd let me go.

Guffawing, Tyler let me go and got to his feet just as I did, his face alit with humor. "You're welcome for taking the fall, beautiful. I can't help it you're clumsy."

Humiliated, my face turned blood red, cheeks burning. "I am not clumsy," I shouted. "I can't help it you snuck up on me like some creeper." Brushing off my legs, I huffed and started back on the track, hoping to get away from him. It didn't work.

"Okay, so you're not clumsy," he gave in a little. "It must've been the sheer pleasure of seeing me again."

Picking up my pace, I gritted my teeth and kept on running. I didn't care if my lungs burned like fire. "Can you please go bother someone else? I'm going to call the police and tell them you're stalking me if you don't."

The only people who knew I ran at the high school in the mornings were my grandmother, Cindy, and Bree. I was pretty sure I knew which one had told him.

"Ooh . . . I've never been in handcuffs. I might like it," he teased.

"I am so going to kill Bree for this. You have a lot of balls coming here, knowing I have no interest in you."

He kept up his pace beside me, not even breaking a sweat. I envied his stamina because I felt like I was about to pass out.

"You may not have interest in me, but I'm interested in you. I'm not going to leave you alone until you give in."

"Then be prepared for disappointment, Tyler. I told you before, you're not my type and I sure as hell am not yours. See, I'm a *real* person, not just some whore who'll ride your cock and leave when you're bored. I'm better than that. So do us both a favor and stay away from me. I don't want to be one of your many conquests."

His pace slowed and eventually he fell back, letting me go. I hadn't finished my laps, but I needed to get out of there. Especially after I saw his disheartened face just before he dropped back; he was genuinely upset with what I'd said. In my heart, I wanted to turn around and apologize. Maybe he wasn't what I accused him of, but in my experience, almost all of the fighters were complete asshats. I couldn't be sucked into that trap.

Besides, he wouldn't even be talking to me if he knew my brother was Kyle Andrews.

CHAPTER 9

Kacey

IT WAS FRIDAY—two days had passed since my encounter with Tyler—and I hadn't heard a word from him. Either I'd spoke the truth and he gave up on me, or I'd really hit a nerve. I was hoping he gave up on me, because if I really hurt him, I'd feel bad about it.

"Girl, what's wrong with you?" Bree asked. "You've been moping around here all day. Cheer up, our shift's about to end."

"I know. I guess I just have a lot on my mind," I replied.

"Yeah, I'll bet. I heard what you said to Tyler. Cole told me he's been in a shitty mood ever since. You were right when you said your words would knock him down. Do you feel good about your win?"

"Dammit," I hissed. "I didn't think he'd even care. I feel terrible now."

"As you should," she remarked, pursing her lips. "However, being the friend that I am, I won't hold it against you."

"Gee, thanks."

Chuckling, Bree put her arm around my shoulders and squeezed. "I'll tell you what'll make you feel better. Cole and I thought about doing something fun tonight. Why don't you join us? There's so much you still haven't seen of Vegas."

"Don't you want to spend time with Cole by your-self?" I asked. "I don't want to get in the way." I did want to see more of Sin City, but I also didn't want to encroach on her time with Cole. I hated being the third wheel.

Bree rolled her eyes and grabbed her bag from under-neath the bar. "Oh, whatever, Kacey. You're not going to get in the way. Let me run to the restroom really quick to get changed, and when I come back I'll wait for Pandra while you go."

Before rushing off to the back, she squeezed my arm and smiled. If it wasn't for her, I didn't know how I would've made it past these last few months. She always had a way of making things better. Now that my grand-mother was steadily getting worse, I missed having the support of a family.

"Hey, Kacey, what's up?" Pandra called from behind. "Have you guys been busy tonight?"

"You know it," I replied, turning to face her.

She had on a black corset-style top and a black leather skirt. Her white blonde hair was cut short in a pixie style, with one hot pink strip on the left side of her face. Each month, she changed the colors—last time it was blue.

I knew better than to try to color my hair again. One time, I had some hot pink streaks put in my hair and it bled all over my blonde. I'd walked around for a week looking like the Pink Panther had tried to fuck my hair.

Setting her purse underneath the bar, she grabbed a bottle of water and clocked in. Pandra always worked the night shift and loved it, which made me happy because that meant I never had to do it.

"All right, lovely, you can go," she said to me. "Be safe. Bree told me in the break room that you two were going out tonight."

"Yeah, her and this guy she's dating want to show me around. I figured what the hell, right?"

"You have to live your life while you're young, Kacey. Sometimes you need to put yourself first."

I wish I could actually do that.

After fetching my purse, I clocked out on the computer and said my goodbyes before rushing off to the back, where Bree stood talking on her phone.

"Hey girl, hurry up and get dressed. We need to meet Cole in fifteen minutes. This is a date I do not want to miss."

"Where are we going?" I asked curiously.

Her smile grew wider. "I can't tell you . . . just trust me. It's something even I haven't experienced before."

For once, seeing her excitement actually had me feeling it for a change. Maybe I could forget my troubles for at least for a couple of hours, before the real world came back to bring me down.

"Why are we at the Stratosphere?" I asked as Bree pulled into the parking lot.

Once she parked, she checked her makeup in the mirror and squealed. "We're here because we're going all the way to the top."

"Don't they close pretty soon? I don't want to spend the money to go up there and only get an hour. That's a waste, don't you think?"

"Not tonight, it's not. Come on, let's go," she commanded. "Everything is taken care of."

After grabbing our purses out of the backseat, we got out of the car and sauntered inside the busy hotel, straight for the elevators. There was a middle-aged woman at the elevator and as soon as we approached she smiled, ushering us inside.

"What floor ladies?" she asked politely.

Bree smiled and bounced on her feet. "We're going to the indoor observation floor first, please."

The doors to the elevator closed and once inside, Bree couldn't keep still the whole way up. I was glad she was happy about going out with Cole, but I wanted her to be careful. I was, however, happy to be able to see Las Vegas from the top of the Stratosphere. He'd made a good choice.

When the doors to the elevator opened, I expected to see a slew of people milling about, but there was no one except a couple of employees. "Uh, Bree?" I called hesitantly, turning to see the elevator doors shut. "Are you sure we're allowed to be up here? Where is everyone?"

Before she could reply, one of the employees – a young man who looked to be about my age with short, red hair – came over with a tray and handed Bree a glass of wine and me a Tequila Sunrise.

"If you need anything just let me know. My name's Trey," he said, acknowledging us with a nod before walking away.

Pursing my lips, I held up my drink and peered over at Bree, lifting my brows. How did he know that a Tequila Sunrise was my favorite drink?

"How is this possible?" I asked. "Not many people know that this is my favorite drink."

Nervously, Bree took a sip of her wine and chuckled. "I might have told Cole what you liked. Speaking of which, he's around here somewhere. Why don't you go look around and enjoy the view? As soon as I find him, I'll come over and join you."

"Okay," I breathed in awe, gazing excitedly at the windows all around. "Don't rush on my account."

Giggling, she strolled off in search of Cole, while I walked toward the windows. Why wasn't there anyone around? As soon as I looked out at the sea of lights, all thoughts of everyone else ceased to exist.

"Wow," I murmured. It was amazingly breathtaking. Alas, my moment of enjoyment quickly dissipated at the sound of a particular voice behind me.

"If you think this is awesome, you need to check out the observation deck upstairs. It's a different experience when you're outside."

When his reflection showed up in the window, my

heart sped up at the sight of him. Tyler was dressed in a pair of faded jeans and a light blue T-shirt. I blamed my reaction on the adrenaline from being so high up in the sky.

"So I guess me blowing you off at the track was too subtle for you?" I remarked dryly.

His chuckle made me shiver. "No, actually I got the message loud and clear. I just chose not to listen to it."

Rolling my eyes, I huffed. I didn't want him to know he affected me. "You're a fool then."

In the window, I watched him smile and shake his head before coming to stand right beside me. I didn't want to appear weak, so I stood my ground, even when his arm lightly brushed up against mine.

"I'm not a fool, Kacey. An ass, most definitely, but never a fool. I don't think there's anything wrong with trying to get to know someone. Even after your harsh words at the track, I still want to try. There has to be a reason you detest people like me and I want to know why."

"Like *that's* what you're doing," I blew out. "I know what guys like you are about and talking isn't one of them."

Tyler nodded his head and watched me through the reflection in the window. "And you're right. Most guys like me only want one thing. Tonight, however, isn't about that."

"Then what is it about?" I asked boldly, glaring at him.

His hands closed over my shoulders and I reluctantly let him turn my body toward him, his fingers slowly sliding down my skin. "It's about you," he murmured gently. "I don't know who you are or what's going on in your life, but Bree's been worried about you. She said you hadn't seen much of Vegas and I thought this would be a good place to start."

"It was *your* idea to come here? I thought it was Cole's?"

Tyler's eyes twinkled and he chuckled, which actually made me smile. "Nothing against Cole, but his idea of seeing Vegas would be visiting the casinos. I figured you'd appreciate the true beauty of it all."

Gazing out the window, a genuine smile splayed across his lips as the lights below sparkled in his gray eyes. "How long have you lived here?" I asked.

"My whole life," he replied. "It's my home."

I wish I had a place that felt like home. My grandmother was all I had and now that her health was failing, it would only be a matter of time before I'd really be alone.

"What about you?" he asked. "I know you just moved here. Where did you come from?"

"California. I moved out here to take care of my grandmother," I responded. "I don't know how much longer she has left."

"So is that what Bree meant when she told me you had a lot going on?"

I shrugged. "Yeah, among other things. I honestly don't know why I'm even talking to you about this." Turning on my heel, I started toward the elevator, my heart thumping wildly.

Grabbing my arm, he turned me around before I could go any further, his demeanor heated . . . almost angry. His hold on my arm wasn't tight, but he wasn't about to let me go either. "Your preconceived notions about me are starting to piss me off. If there's one thing you need to know about me, it's that I tell it like it is. If all I wanted was to fuck you I would've told you that at the very beginning. I'm honestly trying to do the right thing for once."

We stood there staring at each other, neither one of us backing down. "So you're saying that at the end of the night you're not going to try to hook up with me?"

Lips tilting up in a smirk, he chuckled and shook his head. "Not unless you wanted to. I know when I'm not wanted, Kacey. All I want to do tonight is have a little bit of fun."

"What kind of fun?" I asked nervously.

Tyler winked and grabbed my hand. "I think it's time you found out."

CHAPTER 10

Kacey

I HAD NEVER laughed or screamed so hard in my life. At the very top of the Stratosphere, they had three thrill rides as well as the sky jump—there was no way in hell I was doing that. The adrenaline coursing through my veins was phenomenal. For the first time in a long while, I actually let myself enjoy having fun.

"So what did you think about that?" Tyler asked as we got off of the Insanity thrill ride.

Through my tears from laughing so hard, I looked at him and wiped them away. "If I don't throw up I'll let you know. Other than that, it was awesome."

"See? I knew you would have fun," Bree squealed excitedly, holding onto Cole's hand. "But it's getting kind of late. Don't you need to get back home?"

Glancing down at my phone, it was closing in on two in the morning and I knew I needed to get some sleep before Cindy's shift with my grandmother ended. "Yeah, I probably need to get back."

Bree nodded. "All right, let's go."

Side by side, Bree and Cole walked in front of me and Tyler, completely mesmerized with each other. Cole seemed like a nice guy. I just hope he stayed that way.

"As soon as I take Kacey home, I'll come over to your place," Bree murmured quietly to Cole. She didn't want me to hear it because she thought it'd make me feel bad.

Before getting on the elevator to travel the hundred and eight stories down, Tyler leaned in close and whispered, "If you want me to take you home, I am more than willing. If not, I completely understand. It's your choice."

Much to my dismay, I'd actually had a great time with him. He didn't overstep any boundaries and he also didn't talk about himself or fighting the entire time. It'd been different than hanging out with most of my brother's friends.

"Okay," I said, hoping I didn't regret my decision. "You can take me home."

Once inside Tyler's shiny, new black truck, he turned the music down so we were riding in silence. "If you don't mind my asking," he began, "what is your grandmother suffering from?"

Clearing my throat, I leaned my head back on the seat. "She has stage four colon cancer. When I first moved out here, her mind was still sharp as a blade. Now it's spread to some of her other organs and some days I don't think she even knows who I am."

"Who's taking care of her right now?"

Out of the corner of my eye, I could tell he was looking at me so I swallowed hard and met his stare. "I have a nurse who comes in and works the night shift while I'm at the bar. During the day, I'm the one who takes care of her."

"That's a lot of responsibility on your shoulders," he murmured. "Do you not have any other family to help?"

If he only knew who that family was.

"No, I don't. Or at least no one who is willing to help. That's why I left them to come out here."

"What are you going to do when your grandmother passes? Are you going to stay in Vegas?"

"Most likely," I replied. "I don't want to go back to California. Besides, I have Bree here and we have our own dream to pursue."

Once we got off the highway, I gave him the directions to my grandmother's house. When he pulled in the driveway, he put on the brake and turned to face me.

"So what are your dreams? Did you go to college?"

"You sure do ask a lot of questions," I teased. "What about you? Did *you* go to college?"

He chuckled and shook his head. "No, school was never my thing. My father was a boxer and ever since I was old enough to get in the ring, that's where all my focus has gone. College didn't interest me."

"What about after you retire from fighting? Will you be taking over the gym?"

"Mmm-hmm," he said with a nod. "My dad can be a pain in the ass, but when he retires it'll all go to me. I hate to say this, but I'm ready for that time to come."

"Why is that?" I asked. "You seem to have a pretty good life from what I can tell."

"Now look who's asking all of the questions," he flirted. "I think I've answered my limit for the night. But if you want to know more, you can ask me tomorrow."

Laughing, I crossed my arms and tried to ignore the excitement coursing through my veins. "Is that your way of wanting to see me again?"

He smiled. "Maybe. Are you interested?"

Closing my eyes, I let my mind decide even though my body wanted something else. "Actually, I don't think it's a good idea."

"Why not?" he asked, his smile dissipating. "I thought we had a good time tonight."

"I did, but it's only been one night. Just because you appeared to be a good person for a few hours doesn't mean that you are one."

"The same can be said about you as well," he countered in all seriousness. "What if you only wanted to be around me because of my money or because of my name? You have no idea how many women want to be with me for those superficial things. It's hard to find someone real."

Biting my lip, I sat there speechless. He got me again. "Touché," I muttered, defeated. "I didn't think about that. Don't you have a fight tomorrow night though?"

"I do. Would you like to come? I'm sure Cole can persuade Bree to go as well."

I actually enjoyed watching fights, but it was the people who were going to be there that might be a problem. If any of Kyle's friends saw me, they would tell him. Swallowing hard, I opened the door and slid out of his truck, meeting him in front.

"I can't go. I have a dinner date tomorrow night."

For a split second, Tyler's gaze darkened before he nodded and looked down at the ground. "I see. I didn't think you were dating anyone."

"I'm not," I said. "I made these plans before going out with you tonight."

He reached for my hands, and I let him hold them, even though I knew it was wrong. What the hell was I doing? Nothing about being around Tyler was safe.

"What about breakfast?" he offered. "Can you do that with me? That way I'll be the one on your mind when you go out tomorrow night."

Shaking my head, I laughed and squeezed his hands before letting go. "You sure are full of yourself, aren't you?"

"Sometimes," he admitted. "So what do you say? Breakfast in the morning? I know you'll be taking care of your grandmother, but I can cook a pretty decent omelet. That is, if you let me come over."

My heart pounded so loudly in my chest I was sure he could hear it. I didn't know what to do . . . should I say yes? Bringing his hands up to my face, I stood there frozen in place, as he lowered his lips achingly close to mine. I should've pulled back, but that's not what I did.

The answer was decided when he took matters into his own hands and kissed me.

I was going to see him in the morning..

CHAPTER II

Kacey

I ONLY GOT about four hours of sleep before Cindy tapped me on the shoulder. "Kacey, it's time for me to go. Your grandmother is still asleep."

Sitting up, I rubbed my eyes and yawned. She was in her dark green scrubs and her tired hazel eyes stared back at me.

"Thank you, Cindy. I'll take a quick shower and get ready before she wakes up. Did everything go okay last night? I got in kind of late."

Quietly, she chuckled. "Yes, I saw that. The gentleman who brought you home looks like a nice young man. I'm glad you're taking the time to date."

"We're not dating," I clarified. "Trust me, that's the last thing I need."

Cindy smirked and shook her head. "Okay, child, keep telling yourself that. As far as your grandmother is concerned, I think she's finding it more difficult to think clearly. All you can do now is go along with it, which will keep her confusion and anxiety to a minimum."

"I understand," I said. "I know what to do."

Once Cindy left, I rushed to the bathroom and took a quick shower. Tyler was supposed to come by for breakfast, but I had no idea what time, or if he was even going to show.

Hurriedly, I put on a pair of denim shorts and a pink tank top before putting my wet hair in a side braid; once it dried, it would be wavy. When I got out of the bathroom, my grandmother was in the living room, sitting by the window.

"Hey, Nana," I greeted warmly. "Did you sleep okay? I'm about to make us some breakfast."

Just a few weeks ago, we were told her chemo had stopped working. Needless to say, we stopped treatments and ever since then, her health had rapidly decreased in a short amount of time. She was pale and sickly skinny, with no hair whatsoever. When she was younger, she had the most beautiful, thick blonde hair I'd ever seen. She was happy that I had inherited my hair from her.

"It was the best sleep I've had in a long time, sweetheart," she replied. "I got to see my, Matthew."

"You did?" I asked nervously. "What did he say?"

My grandfather had died twelve years ago from a heart attack. She'd been heartbroken after that and we all thought she wouldn't live through it, but she had my father who needed her. She lived for him.

My grandmother looked to me and smiled. "He said

he was going to see me soon, and he missed me. Oh, honey, I would give anything to be with him again."

Blinking quickly, I tried to keep the tears from falling down my face. "I know, Nana."

It won't be long now.

About that time, the doorbell rang. "Good heavens, who's coming by this early in the morning?" my grandmother asked.

"Nana, he's a friend of mine. He wanted to eat breakfast with me. Try not to tell him embarrassing stories about me, okay?"

Slowly, she got to her feet and followed me into the kitchen where she took her seat in the corner. She always sat there while I cooked breakfast, so she could talk to me.

Taking a deep breath, I licked my dry lips and opened the door. With a sly grin on his face, Tyler stood there wearing a navy baseball cap with a fitted white T-shirt and khaki shorts. His tattoos went down both arms, but they weren't full sleeves like I'd seen on some of the other fighters. They actually looked really good on his tanned skin and bulging muscles.

"Tyler," I greeted. "Would you like to come in? I'm about to start breakfast." I didn't realize my grandmother was right behind me, until I stepped back into her. "Oh, Nana, I'm sorry I didn't know you were behind me."

Her expression was surprised as she looked at Tyler with tears in her eyes.

"Nana, are you okay?" I asked, taking her hand.

"Yes, child," she whispered. "I think I just got something in my eye. I'm okay now."

Tyler held out his hand and she took it, never taking her eyes off his. "I'm Tyler. I'm a friend of your granddaughter's."

Not letting him go, my grandmother held his hand and led him to the chair beside hers in the kitchen. "Well, Tyler, thank you for coming over. Be prepared though. My little angel cooks the best food I've ever tasted. You get kind of spoiled after a while."

Tyler sat down and winked at me. "I think I could get used to that."

"You wish," I teased.

While my grandmother talked nonstop to Tyler, I pulled out everything I needed to get breakfast started. The eggs, bacon, and French toast were easy to whip up. After I was done, I made my grandmother and Tyler a plate and set them down in front of them, along with a glass of freshly squeezed orange juice.

Tyler looked down with wide eyes. "This looks amazing, Kacey."

"Well, it should," my grandmother stated. "She had the best teacher around. Not to mention, she went to the top culinary school in the United States."

"And by the best teacher around you know she meant herself, right?" I remarked, winking at my grandmother.

To be on her death bed, Nana still had a sense of humor. I was glad that through all of her suffering, she was still able to hold onto that part of herself.

"So that's what you went to school for?" Tyler asked. "Why aren't you utilizing your talents?"

Shrugging, I sat down at the table and took a sip of my juice. "I plan to someday, when I earn the money. Bree and I want to open up our own restaurant. Working at the bar is just a means to an end. One day, I'll be out of there and doing my own thing."

"How much do you need to save up?" he asked.

Sarcastically, I laughed. "A lot. Bree and I have about half. When my father died, I saved the money he left me and ever since then, I've been working my ass off. We're hoping to earn the rest in the next five years or so. Until then, I'll keep working long hours."

My grandmother finished eating, and yawned, gazing sleepily at me. She spent most of her time sleeping these days.

"Nana, do you want to go lie down?" I asked as I took her empty plate.

"I do, child. I can barely hold my eyes open."

"All right, let me put our plates in the sink and I'll help you to your room."

Tyler stood and put a hand on my shoulder, halting me. "I'll take her, if that's okay."

Before I could say anything, my grandmother smiled and grabbed his hand. "Why that would be very kind of you, young man. I think I'd enjoy that."

Chuckling, I rolled my eyes and cleaned off the table while Tyler helped my grandmother to her feet. "Ah, I see what you're doing now. You're trying to flirt with my friend."

On her way by, she placed her hand on the side of my face and kissed my cheek. "He only has eyes for you, my child. Be good to him."

Tyler winked at me and disappeared around the corner with my grandmother at his side. I never would've thought that a hard-core, muscular fighter like him would ever have a soft side. I'd never seen it with any of the others, but then again it was my brother and his friends we were talking about.

When Tyler came back, his odd countenance caught my attention.

"Is everything okay? Does she need me?"

Shaking his head, he came over to the sink to help me, so I passed him a clean dish and a towel. "No, she closed her eyes as soon as she laid down."

"Then why do you look like that?" I asked, passing him another dish.

He dried the towel and looked down at me. "Who's Matthew?"

I turned away and sighed. "He's my grandfather. Nana claims she's been talking to him in her dreams. What did she tell you?"

"She said that Matthew had told her I was coming to take care of you and that everything would be all right."

Oh hell, she's really losing it. I tried to keep my voice from shaking, but I failed. "Tyler, I'm so sorry. I know you didn't come here to deal with all of this. She's never said anything like that before. I know it has to be weird."

Taking my soapy hands, he pulled them around his waist and held me tight with his hand on the back of my neck. Instantly, I relaxed and held my head to his chest, listening to his heart beat as I breathed him in.

"It's okay, Kacey. I know it's not easy to witness her health failing. I saw a picture of her in her room. She was a beautiful woman . . . much like you."

For a split second, I smiled and enjoyed the feel of him touching me, but then reality hit and I realized my feelings were changing toward him. It made me uncomfortable, and I needed to get away. Pulling back, I went to the sink. "I'm sorry, I need a moment."

After drying off with a towel, I walked out of the

kitchen to my room. It was the largest one in the house, with soft green walls, almost pistachio colored. I had an antique dark cherry headboard for my queen sized bed, covered with my favorite cream wool comforter. I sat on it and couldn't deny that I wondered what it would be like to have Tyler in this bed with me.

I heard a knock on the door frame and looked up to see him standing there.

"Can I come in?" he inquired.

I didn't know how to answer him, but I knew I didn't want him to go, so I nodded.

"What just happened?" he asked, shutting the bedroom door lightly behind him. "Are you still worried about me pretending just to get in your pants? Because, let me remind you, what you see is what you get. We may not know much about each other, but I'm hoping to change that. I can't do anything about it if you keep pushing me away."

Slowly, he approached me, his gaze guarded.

"I'm about to lose the only family I have. My heart can't take anymore. I don't know if I can take this leap of faith you're asking of me," I whispered sadly.

Kneeling in front of me and taking my face in his hands, Tyler gently rubbed his thumbs under my eyes to wipe away the tears. "Pushing people away only adds loneliness to the pain. I've been hurt a lot, Kacey, but you know what?" He tilted my face up higher. "I keep on going. Sometimes you have to let the bad in with the good. There's no other way. It's what makes us stronger."

"I'm just tired," I murmured. "Sometimes I feel like all I get are the bad things."

Gently, Tyler brushed his thumb across my lips before placing his on mine. He waited on me to respond, and when I kissed him back, he opened my lips further with his tongue, slowly and deeply. It felt like it'd been forever since a man truly kissed me, but I knew not to move fast with him.

Reluctantly, I pulled away and placed my fingers to his lips. "I need you to be honest with me, Tyler. You said you would tell me the truth so I want to know . . . why me? What makes me so different from the other girls?"

Tilting his head to the side, he smirked and stared at my lips for a few seconds before meeting my eyes. "Honestly, it was your mouth," he confessed. "I have never had a girl talk to me the way you did. It was startling, and refreshing."

Laughing, I playfully smacked him on the arm. "So, basically calling you names and telling you to go to hell, turned you on?"

Biting his lip, he grabbed my wrist and placed a gentle kiss on my palm. "Maybe. You were fucking sexy in the gym the other day. I can't promise you that I don't come with any problems, because I'm sure as hell not perfect. I *can* promise you this though. . . what I want is not the same type of girl I'm used to being with. I want something real and I didn't even know it until I saw it in you. All I'm asking for is a chance to see what happens."

If he only knew that my problems were bigger than any of his combined. Would he still believe I was something real?

"Tyler, I'm not perfect either. Being with me will only cause you more problems."

Standing up, he leaned into me, guiding me back on my bed, covering me with his body. "It's a risk I'm willing to take."

Spreading my legs with his knee, he slid his hand along my bare leg up to my thigh. "Before you stop me, I already know you're not ready for this. I know you don't want to move too fast."

"You would actually wait for me?" I asked.

He held his body above mine, with his arms on either side of my head. "For you . . . yes. It'll be a new challenge."

Wrapping my legs around his, I smiled and bit my lip. "Well, in that case I think I need to make it a little more challenging." I rocked my hips against his, and then my phone rang in my back pocket.

Groaning, Tyler bent down to kiss my neck, trailing his lips down to my collarbone while keeping hold of my wrists. "Do you want to answer it?"

"No, but I need to," I told him.

Reaching underneath my ass, he grabbed the phone out of my back pocket and handed it to me. I didn't recognize the number.

"Hello," I answered, trying not to sound breathless.

"Kacey, hey it's Liam."

"Oh, hey, how are you?" Tyler's stubble tickled my skin as he kissed my neck, and it took all I had not to giggle.

"I'm doing well. I wanted to call and make sure we were still on for dinner. You haven't changed your mind have you?"

"No, but if I go I want to make something clear. I'm not . . ."

Liam chuckled and finished my sentence, "Not ready for something serious. I get it, Kacey. We can go as friends. All I want is to go out to dinner with you and get to know you."

"Okay, great. Friends it is."

"Do you want me to pick you up at your house?" he asked. "I can be there by six."

"That'll be great." I gave him the address to my house and said my goodbyes.

Tyler lifted up on his elbows and stared down at me. "I know you already told this guy you'd go out with him, but I have to say I'm not liking it."

"He knows we're going out as friends," I reiterated. "And besides, I didn't know I wasn't allowed to go out with other people. It's a little too soon to be exclusive, don't you think?"

Furrowing his brows, he pursed his lips. "Kacey, don't get me wrong. You can do whatever you want. It's just the thought of sharing you with other men gets my blood boiling."

"What about you?" I challenged. "I know your reputation. If I were to invest time in whatever we have going on here, I have to tell you, I don't like to share either. You're not exactly a one woman kind of guy."

His face was a stony mask. "There's only one way to find out isn't there? You will just have to trust me."

"We'll see," I whispered.

He nodded his understanding and glared over at the clock on my bedside table. "Are you sure you don't want to come with me to the fight tonight?" Sliding off of me, he pulled me up to my feet.

"I can't, Tyler. I'm sorry. You can call me afterward and let me know if you won."

He tapped my chin with his finger. "Are you sure

you're not going to be too busy with your date?"

Rolling my eyes, I pushed him out of my bedroom and chuckled. "No, I can promise you I'm not that kind of girl."

"I'm glad to hear it."

Opening the front door, I walked Tyler out to his truck in silence, my mind a jumbled mess. What was I doing getting involved with him? It was the stupidest thing I'd ever done. Yet, it was the one thing I wanted more than anything at this moment.

If my brother found out about this, he would make it his life's mission to keep Tyler away from me. He would ruin everything.

"What are you thinking about?" he asked, pulling me closer. "Are you having second thoughts?"

I shrugged. "Kind of. It's just, there's a lot you don't know about me. If you knew what my life was like, you'd run as far away from me as possible."

He chuckled. "The same could be said about me, but you seem like a tough girl. I have no doubt that whatever it is we'll be okay."

"Do you honestly believe that? What if it's something *really* bad?"

"Trust me," he murmured, bending down to kiss my lips. "Whatever skeletons you have in your closet probably don't come close to the ones I have. Have a little bit of faith in me, okay? I'd rather not divulge our deepest, darkest secrets on only our second date."

"Okay, but as long as you have faith in me . . . wait, did you just call this our second date?"

He kissed me one more time. "Just think, the next time we get together will be our *third* date," he wiggled his

67

eyebrows and slapped my ass.

I giggled as he walked around his truck. "In your dreams, buddy," I called out.

Laughing, he said, "Just don't forget me tonight."

That wouldn't be possible. I really wanted to go to his fight, but there was a huge possibility my brother or his friends would be there. I couldn't take that chance . . . at least, not yet.

Not until I tell Tyler who I really am.

CHAPTER

12

Kacey

ONCE INSIDE, I quietly opened the door to my grand-mother's room and noticed her queen-sized bed was emp-ty. Her white, quilted comforter was folded down perfectly on her bed like it was every day after she got up from a nap.

"Nana?" I called, opening her door the rest of the way. I found her sitting at the desk, scribbling away on a piece of paper. She hadn't sat at that desk in months.

"Nana, what are you doing?" I gasped, strolling into the room. "I thought you were asleep?"

She slid her papers to the side and turned around, her warm chuckle making me smile. "Oh, dear child, no. I was never sleepy to begin with. I pretended to be so you and your friend could have some *alone* time."

"Nana," I shrieked. "It's not like that with him. I only met him a couple of days ago."

"That doesn't matter. I met your grandfather one day, and then the next—"

I held up my hands, stopping her. "Okay, I don't need to hear about your escapades with Granddaddy."

She was trying to get up out of her chair, so I helped her by quickly grabbing her arm and leading her over to the bed. With as weak as she's been, I'm thankful she hadn't fallen and broken any bones.

"I'm just saying, honey, that you can't put a timetable on love. Some people fall in love after one day, and for others it doesn't happen for months or even years. Once you get over your fears, it'll happen."

"You don't understand, Nana. Tyler knows who Kyle is . . . they don't get along at all. Once Tyler finds out who I am, he's not going to want me anymore."

My grandmother reached over and patted my cheek. "You have to have faith, Kacey. You're not like your brother. Good things happen to good people. Tyler will see it in you and it won't matter. He'll still love you."

"It's a little too soon for love, Nana," I teased. "Besides, other than you and daddy, no one's ever loved me. I wouldn't know the first thing about it."

Smiling, my grandmother laid back in her bed and I covered her up. This time she wasn't pretending. She took my hand and held it over her heart. "It comes naturally, sweetheart. There's no handbook telling you how to love someone. Soon, you're going to have your own life and I need to know that you'll be okay. Let him in, Kacey. Can you do that for me?"

My eyes burned but I refused to cry. I always tried to

stay strong for her. "I promise," I whispered. "I'll be okay. Now get some rest. I'm going to finish cleaning the kitchen."

Tugging on me, she placed her cold, frail hands on my cheeks and gently kissed my forehead. "I'm so proud of you and the woman you've become. I love you so much."

I smoothed my hand over her dry skin and let the tears fall; I couldn't hold them back anymore. "I love you too, Nana."

She smiled at me once before closing her eyes and falling asleep. This was probably the last time I'd speak to her until the following morning. Maybe I could get Tyler to have breakfast with me again . . . she'd like that.

"I can't believe you're going out with that other guy when you could've come with me on a road trip with Tyler and Cole," Bree scolded. "Just think of all the fun we'd be having right now."

The fight was a little over three hours away in Los Angeles at the Staples Center, and my brother was most definitely going to be there. My family and I were mainly from the Sacramento area, but we moved around a lot. San Francisco was my favorite place, and I would love to go back—I just couldn't risk it.

"I know it would be fun, but I told Liam I'd go out with him. You know I like to keep my word. Tyler can't hear you right now, can he?"

Chuckling, her voice echoed in the background. "No, silly, I'm in the bathroom. All he's talked about on the way out here is you. Even Cole said he's never heard him talk like that about anyone other than—"

Abruptly, she stopped and tried to talk about something else, but I caught it. "Other than *who*, Bree?" I demanded.

She sighed. "Cole told me not to say anything because it was like this huge secret, but Tyler and Gabriella Reynolds had a thing going on for a while. Apparently, they both decided to stop seeing each other."

They were both in the video that was taken just a few short weeks ago with the fight against my brother at Tyler's gym. If they had something going on, it apparently wasn't that long ago.

"How long ago did they call it quits?" I asked, clenching my teeth. I wasn't about to be the rebound girl.

"Cole didn't exactly say, but I know it was recent. I wouldn't worry about it though. He's obviously really into you. Cole said that Tyler was glad they called it off."

"Yeah, well let's see how long that lasts," I remarked dryly. "Is she going to be there at the arena tonight?"

"No, I don't think so. If she is, I'll see how they are together. I have a good eye for that kind of stuff. I'll be able to tell if they have feelings for each other."

"Thanks, Bree. I know he wasn't too thrilled about me going out with Liam tonight."

"You got that right," she laughed. "He hasn't shut up about it. It also didn't help that Cole was pushing the knife in a little bit deeper. I thought they were going to fight it out at one point. My guy wouldn't stand a chance."

No one could stand a chance against Tyler . . . not even my brother. At least this way, Tyler would be ready for the fight tonight and kick some ass.

"All right, Bree, I need to go. Liam will be here in about ten minutes."

"Okay, girl. Be careful tonight. I'll call you later."

After we said our goodbyes, I rushed to put on my white flared skirt and light blue sleeveless top, before putting the final coat of lip gloss on my lips. I felt guilty going out with Liam, but I already knew it was going to be a one night thing.

It wasn't long before I heard the sound of a sports car revving its engine down the road. When I looked out the window, a red Jaguar XK convertible pulled in beside my Camry. That sure put everything into perspective. Tyler didn't flaunt his wealth, nor did he act like he had a lot of money. With Liam getting out of his car in his tailored suit and his hair all gelled to perfection, I could see I was out of his league.

Cindy met me out in the hallway and smiled. "Is that Tyler? Your grandmother told me all about him."

"No," I admitted regretfully. "This is Liam. I agreed to go out to dinner with him and I didn't want to break my promise. We're just going as friends."

"Well, make sure he knows that. Your grandmother is a good judge of character. If she likes Tyler, I kind of have to side with her. Just be careful tonight. This one looks like trouble."

After she disappeared down the hall, I opened the door just as he was walking up the front steps. His eyes went wide and he smiled. "You look amazing, Kacey."

"So do you," I replied. He was wearing a pale green

button down under his suit, and the green matched his eyes perfectly.

"Are you ready to go?" he asked.

No, but I was going anyway.

CHAPTER 13

TYLER

ONCE WE GOT to the Staples Center, Cole walked with Bree to her seat and I went to the dressing rooms to get ready. I was angry as hell knowing Kacey was with another guy. I just wanted to fight and get the fuck out of there.

"Tyler!"

Turning around, my agent rushed up to me. Todd was dressed in a black, MMA Pride T-shirt with jeans and a huge smile on his face.

"What's with the grin?" I asked as I kept on walking.

"Because you, my friend, are going to want to thank me big time for what I'm about to tell you. Where's your dad?" He caught up to me and blocked my path.

Aggravated, I stopped and gritted my teeth. "He couldn't come. Cole's in my corner tonight."

"I see. So . . . aren't you going to ask me what's going on?"

Knowing him, it probably had to do with a club and a shit ton of women. "If it's about plans for after the fight, I can't make it tonight. I'm going back home."

Todd chuckled and shook his head. "Damn, Ty, calm down. I actually have my own plans for the night. I wanted to give you the good news." He paused for a second, waiting on me to show interest. When all I did was stare deadpan at him, he shook his head and laughed. "Guess whose face is going to be all over every single cover of the *Physique Sports and Fitness Magazine* next month?"

"Are you serious?" I asked, mouth gaping open.

"You're damn right, I am. Shelby's going to do the ten page spread on you."

Physique was the most well-known fitness magazine in the world, and Shelby was one of the best journalists around. She also happened to be Gabriella's sister-in-law. For months, I'd been waiting on this opportunity.

"Did Gabriella set it up?"

"No," Todd replied. "Shelby contacted me and asked when you'd be available. She wants to meet with you sometime next month. Since she's working from home with the baby, she asked if you'd be able to fly down to San Francisco for the interview."

"Yeah, of course," I agreed. "I'd do anything for this opportunity."

Todd slapped me on the back. "That's what I thought. Now, do you want to tell me what's going on with you? Is it Gabriella?"

Shaking my head, I started off down the hall until we got to my room. "No, it's not her. We're not seeing each other anymore."

He sat down on the brown leather couch in my dressing room and sighed. "I kind of thought that when I saw her with that baseball player the other day. They looked awfully close. Do you know about him?"

When he said it, I expected to feel some pang of jealousy, but I didn't. "Yeah, she told me. We mutually agreed to end it. I'm actually seeing someone else, or at least trying to."

"Trying to? Since when do you have to try?"

Halfheartedly, I chuckled. "Since I met this girl who's unlike any other woman I've ever met. She's not making it easy on me."

"How so? Is she here tonight?"

"Nope, she's out with another guy."

With a loud belly laugh, Todd slapped his knee and shouted, "So that's why you're all pissed off! I never would've guessed it'd be over a female. Why don't you find someone else?"

Because I didn't *want* to find anyone else . . . I wanted her.

When I didn't answer, Todd whistled and got to his feet. "Well, I'll be damned. I never thought I'd see the day when Tyler Rushing actually gave a fuck about someone, other than Gabriella."

"This girl is different. I would choose her over Gabriella any day."

"Well, whoever she is, I pity her for having to deal with your crazy ass," he joked. "But for now, get her out of your mind. If you win this fight and Kyle wins his, you'll only be two fights away from battling each other. That's what you need to focus on."

"Oh, I'm focused. You don't have to worry about that."

My opponent was going down tonight.

"*Tyler! Tyler! Tyler!*"

"All right, man, let's see if you can beat my record tonight," Cole exclaimed. "I knocked Jamie out in the first round."

His right eye was swollen from his fight earlier in the night, but he'd still won, advancing closer to the Light Heavyweight title. It was the beginning of the first round and the crowd was screaming my name. It wasn't Bastian Tober's, it was mine.

"What do I win if I beat you?" I asked.

Slyly, he looked down at the seats where Bree sat, smiling up at us. "It's not necessarily something to win, but it's probably something you'll want to know. It'll make the ride home more bearable for all of us."

"What the hell are you talking about?"

"Fighters, take your positions," the announcer called out.

Before I started forward, Cole winked and nodded toward Bastian. "Trust me. Now go out there and kick his ass."

Bastian Tober had only been fighting for about a year, but he was one of the best up-and-coming fighters in the league. Not to mention, he wasn't a fuckwad like a lot of the other guys. He was about the same height and build as me, with long, brown hair pulled into a ponytail. I used to do the same thing before I had mine cut.

Grinning, I bumped Bastian's gloved hand with mine. "Good luck tonight," I told him.

He chuckled and put his fists up in defense. "Same to you. I promise to go easy."

Ding, ding, ding.

Usually Bastian waited on his opponent to attack, but tonight he struck first. I dodged it easily. "Switching it up tonight, I see."

He winked and struck again. "I like to keep you on your toes. Dance monkey, dance." He swung and I avoided his fist again.

Looking at the clock, thirty seconds had already passed. I had to take him down soon. All it would take is one hit and I'd have him knocked out. "That's a good strategy, B. However, tonight it's not going to work."

He jabbed and I ducked. "Oh yeah, why is that?" he asked humorously.

"Because," I stated, pretending to go for his stomach, "of this." As soon as his arms lowered to protect his body, I swung hard and fast to the right side of his head. His legs fell out from under him and he went down . . . completely limp.

The crowd screamed as the announcer lifted my arm in the air victoriously. "And the winner by TKO after one minute and ten seconds. . . *Tyler* . . . *The Terror* . . . *Russsshhhiiinnnggg!*"

After my arm was let go, I reached down and helped Bastian get up on his feet.

Unstable and shaking his head, he opened and closed

his jaw, rubbing it with his gloved hand. "Damn, Rushing, I didn't expect to get knocked out that fucking fast. Next time give me a little bit more time."

"Sorry about that, bro. Cole said I couldn't knock you out in under two minutes. I had to prove him wrong."

Chuckling, he looked over in my corner and flipped him off, which only made Cole laugh. "Payback's a bitch, Bennett," Bastian joked. "You guys going to the party to-night?"

"No, we're heading back home. Maybe we'll catch you next time."

"Sounds good, Rushing. I'm sure I'll see you around next weekend."

The crowd was still going wild, so I made my rounds around the ring and climbed the fence, raising my arms in the air. I fucking loved the sound of them hollering my name. I'd waited years to hear it.

Waving at the crowd one last time, I jumped down and followed Cole out of the ring to where Bree stood waiting on us.

"You did amazing, Tyler," she gushed. "I wish Kacey could've been here. I sent her the video of you fighting though. She absolutely loved it."

"So you're texting her while she's on her date? I bet the guy loves that," I stated with a huge smirk.

Bree bit her lip and looked sheepishly over at Cole before turning back to me. "Actually, she's having a terri-ble time."

Was it bad that I was happy about that? *Fuck no.*

"She's still with him?" I asked. "What the hell have they been doing for the past four hours?"

She looked down at her phone and scrolled through

her messages. "They went out to eat and now they're at one of the bars in the Bellagio. She says she's ready to leave, but he ran into some people he knew. Apparently, he's busy talking to them."

"Tell her to call a cab and go home," I hissed. "What fucking asshole takes a girl on a date and ignores her?"

"Uh . . . you?" Cole teased.

"Correction, cocksucker. I never took girls out on dates. I just fucked them, *then* ignored them." When Bree's mouth dropped open in disgust, I held up my hand to stop the enraged words from flying out of her mouth. "I'm not like that anymore, Bree, so stop looking at me like that."

"It's just I never thought you'd be that way," she admitted. "I mean, I knew you had a lot of women following you around, but I never thought you'd treat them like shit. I must be an awful judge of character because when we met Liam at the bar last night, I thought he was nice and really interested in her."

When she said the name Liam my hackles rose. Surely, it couldn't be the same Liam I knew. If so, then Kacey needed to get the hell away from him fast.

"What's his last name, Bree?" I asked, grabbing her by the shoulders.

Her eyes went wide, especially when she saw Cole looking just as nervous as I was. "Why, what's wrong?" she shrieked. "I don't know his last name. He has dark hair and green eyes, and he's a sharp dresser . . . that's it."

"Holy fuck, do you think it's him?" Cole asked, exasperated. "Out of all the people Kacey could go out with, how the hell did it wind up being him?"

"Guys, tell me what's going on," Bree demanded.

It was too loud in the arena, but I had to try to get in touch with her somehow. "I need your phone," I said to Bree. She quickly handed it to me and I dialed up Kacey's number. When she answered, I could barely hear her over the noise on both ends.

"Bree?" she answered, screaming into the phone.

"No, it's Tyler. What's Liam's last name?"

"What? I can't hear you."

"What's Liam's last name?" I yelled into the mouth piece.

"Hello? Are you there?"

Fuck! This wasn't working. Reluctantly, I hung up the phone and texted her.

Me: What's Liam's last name?!?!
Kacey: Tyler?
Me: YES, it's me. What's his last name?
Kacey: Harris, why? Is everything okay?

When I saw his last name I thought I was going to go in-fucking-sane. I was four hours away, and if anything happened I wouldn't make it there in time. "Goddammit!" I shouted, taking off for the dressing rooms. Cole knew exactly what was going on, so he grabbed Bree's hand and pulled her quickly along.

"It's him?" Cole asked.

"Yes," I growled. "I need to get to a place where she can hear me. I can't believe she's with that fucker."

"Guys, please," Bree begged. "I need to know what's going on."

When we got to my dressing room, I rushed inside and immediately changed out of my gear, putting on my khaki shorts and black MMA Pride T-shirt. Grabbing all my shit, I hurried out the door with Cole and Bree following closely on my heels.

"Liam Harris has to be one of the dirtiest motherfuckers on the goddamned planet. He's Kyle Andrews' agent and just as bad as he is. Do you know who Kyle is?" I asked her. She'd been around enough of the fighters to get an idea on who the cocksucker was.

"Yeah, I've heard stories about him. I also saw the video of you two fighting a few weeks ago."

Getting in the car, I started it up and headed straight for the highway, bolting down the road at least twenty over the limit. "Okay, so you know who Kyle is. Liam, on the other hand, is even more fucked up, if that's possible. He's even been accused of rape a couple of times, but the courts have always let him off due to no evidence.

"It's the same bullshit that happens with Kyle. The slimy motherfucker never gets in trouble for any of the shit he's done. All I know is, if Liam touches one hair on her head, I'm going to fucking kill him."

Bree's eyes filled with tears. "Oh my God, if something happens it'll all be my fault. I'm the one who pushed her to start dating. Do you know for a fact he's guilty of the charges?"

"I do," I growled furiously, gripping the steering wheel so hard my fingers went numb. "One of the girls was someone I worked with at the Labyrinth, and I know she wouldn't lie. Her name was Sadie."

Shortly after it happened, she left Vegas to get away from the ridicule of her family and friends, who thought she made up the story just to get revenge on Liam for turning her down. He had told the courts she was angry because he wouldn't go out with her. In the end, he was made out to be the victim.

Relentlessly, my heart pounded as I dialed Kacey's number again . . . she didn't answer. "Goddammit, Kacey, answer the fucking phone," I shouted. Over and over I dialed her number, only to hear the sound of her voicemail.

Please, God, let her answer the phone.

CHAPTER 14

Kacey

"WHAT THE HELL is going on?" I said as I typed out the text message to Tyler. Why did he want to know Liam's last name? I tried to get away from the noise so I could hear what he was saying, but it didn't help.

It wasn't until I was walking out of the restroom when a new text message came through. As I was looking down to read it, I was stopped with a set of hands grasping my shoulders.

"There you are," Liam chuckled. "I've been looking everywhere for you."

"Funny," I snapped. "I didn't think you noticed when I walked away. You were a little preoccupied with your friends."

Not that I cared, but it was rude the way he left me

sitting there, bored out of my mind. During dinner he'd asked me questions about my job, my grandmother, and if I was seeing anyone exclusively. I didn't tell him about Tyler and I sure as hell didn't want to tell him about my grandmother. I made it seem like my life was perfect. After that, he spent the rest of the evening texting on his phone and talking about himself.

Putting his arm around my shoulders, he peered down at me with a devilish smirk splayed across his face. "Oh, baby, did I make you upset? We can go to my place, and I'll make it up to you."

Disgusted, I pushed his arm away and stormed off. "Actually, I was just leaving." My phone buzzed again, but I couldn't take the time to look at it—I needed the first cab out of here.

Catching up to me, Liam grabbed my elbow and pulled me toward the door. "Well, at least let me take you home."

I tried to jerk out of his hold, but he held on tighter. "Liam, what the hell are you doing? Let me go."

"Sorry, princess, but I can't. I was told to make sure you got home safely."

"What? What are you talking about?"

Once out to his car, he opened the door and nudged me inside. "I'm talking about my neck being on the line if something happens to you. That's all you need to know."

The guy was fucking insane. Quickly, he marched to his side of the car and got in, squealing the tires as we flew out of the parking lot.

"There's something truly wrong with you," I hissed, pulling out my phone.

Chuckling, the corner of his mouth tugged up. "You

have no idea, doll. It's just a shame you won't get to see that side of me."

"Whatever. Just get me home."

The look in his crazed eyes had me trembling in fear. When I was younger, my brother always told me not to show my fear, to look at it head on and conquer it. It was easier said than done.

My phone buzzed yet again. With sweat dripping down my back and clammy hands, I typed in the password to my phone so I could read my messages . . . and to possibly call the police.

Tyler: Get away from him as fast as you can.
Tyler: Why aren't you answering?!?
Tyler: DO NOT let him go into your house.
Tyler: Call me!!

Even if Tyler hadn't warned me about Liam, I was pretty sure I'd have figured out not to trust him. Just as I was about to call him back, his name appeared on my screen with an incoming call.

Heart pounding, I swallowed hard and collected myself, answering the phone as if nothing was wrong. "Hello?"

"Thank fucking God," Tyler snapped. "I've been trying to call you, but it kept going straight to voicemail."

Liam looked over at me, his eyebrows raised, but I turned my head and looked out the window. I was almost home. If I knew he wasn't taking me home, I'd have already tried to call the police.

"I must've had bad service in the bar," I replied coolly, hoping Liam couldn't hear the hesitation in my voice.

"What's up?"

A horn blared in the background along with a few curse words from Tyler before he responded, "You need to get the fuck away from that sleazy son of a bitch, that's what's up. Whatever you do, do *not* mention my name. If you do, it'll only cause more problems. Where are you?"

"I'm only a couple of minutes away from home. Liam is with me. Why don't . . ."

Before I could finish my question, he interrupted me, "Don't ask questions, Kacey. Just listen to what I have to say. I don't know why he targeted you, but I know who that fucker is and what he's all about. He's an agent who represents my biggest nemesis."

I stopped breathing. "And who would that be?"

"Kyle fucking Andrews."

The moment he said Kyle's name, I felt bile rise in my throat, burning like acid. It was totally something he would do, and now it all made sense. Kyle had gotten Liam to spy on me, to find out what I'd been up to and how I was doing. That must have been who he was texting during dinner; giving him the play-by-play.

Tyler continued, "I thought Kyle was bad, but Liam is much worse. You do *not* want to be alone with him, Kacey. Do you see where I'm going with this?"

Oh my God, how could my brother want me around someone like that? I knew what Tyler was referring to and I got shivers thinking of how different this would be if it wasn't for my brother telling Liam to keep me safe.

Swallowing hard, I licked my dry lips and cleared my throat. "Yes," I murmured hesitantly. "I understand."

"All right, Kacey. We're about an hour away from Vegas. I'll be there as soon as I can. If that cocksucker so much as touches you, I'm going to rip his fucking dick off and shove it down his throat." I could hear the venom dripping in his words.

"I'll see you soon though. Be safe."

"You too, Kacey."

By the time we hung up the phone, I was no longer scared of the guy sitting beside me—I was furious. Liam knew who I was when he approached me at the bar. It was a set up. My brother had tried calling me for weeks, leaving me messages and asking how I was doing . . . and every single time I ignored him. So, of course, why wouldn't he have a perv come take me out for a night on the town?

Finally, we pulled into my driveway and I hastily grabbed my purse, hand on the door ready to get out.

"Who were you talking to?" Liam asked, shutting off the ignition.

Snarling in disgust, I opened the car door and got out before storming up the front porch steps. "I don't think that's any of your business," I snapped angrily, glaring at him over my shoulder. When I turned around to face him, he stopped on the bottom step and smiled up at me. *What an arrogant ass.*

Crossing my arms over my chest, I glared down at him. "Or are you just trying to find out so you can report it to my brother?"

Immediately, his smile faded. "How did you know about that?"

"I have my ways," I retorted. "But right now, I want you off my property."

Slowly, he walked backwards toward his car and opened his door. "All right, I'm leaving," he said, holding up his hands in defeat. Before getting in, he peered up at me and winked. "I have to say it was definitely a pleasure, Kacey. It's a shame we couldn't have more time together."

Gritting my teeth, I waited on him to leave before pulling out my phone. Kyle would be getting a lot more than just information from me this evening.

CHAPTER 15

Kacey

MY HANDS SHOOK with rage as I dialed Kyle's number and waited on him to pick up. Over and over it rang, most likely because he was on the phone with Liam. Finally, after calling him five times, his amused voice came over the line. I could see him now, sitting in the living room of his three story mansion, in front of the movie theater-sized television.

Kyle was three years older than me and we were both born with the same color hair, but now he bleached his to look white. He looked like our mother, with the same permanent sneer that made him look evil. What really made him a scary were his eyes; one was so dark brown it looked black, and the other was a pale green. Thankfully, I took after our father, and inherited his sea green eyes.

"Before you get all pissed at me, you have to understand why I did it," he greeted calmly.

"Are you serious?" I snapped. "How could you do this to me?"

"If you'd answer my calls, I wouldn't have to take such measures. I figured it'd be easier to do it this way than come out there myself. How did you find out who Liam was anyway?"

"That doesn't matter," I growled. "In the end, I found out. Not to mention some vile things about his past." I didn't exactly know what he'd done, but I could guess. "How could you put me into a situation like that? What if he'd done something to me?"

"He knew not to touch you, Kacey. If he did, I would've killed him. I just wanted to know how you were doing. You're my sister, and believe it or not I care about what happens to you."

Incredulously, I burst out laughing. "You can't be serious right now. Since when do you care about someone other than yourself?"

"Don't be like this, Kacey," he warned.

"If you don't want to hear the truth, stop calling me, Kyle. After tonight, I have no desire to ever talk to you or see you again. Just stay away from me!"

As soon as I hung up the phone, I sat down on the steps and let the tears finally fall down my cheeks. Was I ever going to be free from my brother's clutches? The simple answer was no. The guy who used to be my brother wasn't there anymore.

"Kacey, are you okay?" Cindy asked, joining me on the front steps. "I take it from that phone call you were talking to your brother."

Sighing, I set my phone down and looked over at her. She smiled and handed me a steaming mug of hot chocolate . . . my favorite when I was stressed. Cindy knew me well.

"I don't know what his problem is. That guy I went out with tonight is his agent, and I had no clue. It was Kyle's way of getting close to me."

Furrowing her brows, Cindy bit her lip and shook her head. "I'm astounded at the kind of things going through your brother's head. He's truly unstable."

I snorted and took a sip of my hot chocolate. "You think? As much as I want to stay here after Nana passes, I think it might be a good idea to disappear. It's the only way to know my family can't find me."

"What about Tyler? Have you told him about the issues with your brother?"

Setting my cup down, I leaned on my elbows and ran hands through my hair. "They already know each other. Tyler's an MMA fighter."

"Oh dear," she remarked, eyes wide. "I take it they aren't friends?"

"Not exactly. What's worse . . . Tyler doesn't even know I'm Kyle's sister. He'll hate me when he finds out."

"He won't hate you," she murmured softly. "If he's as

good of a guy as your grandmother believes he is, then he'll know you aren't like your brother. It's best to be honest and up front with him."

As much as I didn't want to do that just yet, I knew I needed to. Nodding, I turned my attention toward a set of headlights coming into view. It was Tyler.

"I'll tell him tonight," I agreed. "It's better to do it now before things get too serious."

Cindy patted my hand and got to her feet. "All right, child, I'm going to go in and finish separating out your grandmother's medicines for the week. I'll check on her before I leave."

"Thanks, Cindy. I appreciate you doing that."

Sadly, she smiled and started for the door, but then stopped and reached for something in her pocket . . . it was an envelope. "Oh, before I forget, your grandmother wanted me to give this to you."

"Thanks," I said, taking it from her. It had my name scribbled on the front in my grandmother's writing. It must've been what she was working on earlier at her desk.

Cindy smiled and nodded toward the black truck entering our driveway. "Good luck tonight, Kacey. I'm sure he'll understand."

I had severe doubts about that.

Disappearing inside, Cindy left me alone with Tyler who bolted out of his truck, his temperament wild and black. He had on a baseball cap that hung low on his head, making his eyes look even darker. I got to my feet and met him halfway, my stomach in knots. *He's going to hate me after tonight.*

"Are you okay?" he asked, putting his hands on both sides of my face, searching.

Swallowing hard, I nodded my head and licked my dry lips. "Yes, I'm fine. He didn't give me any problems when I told him to leave."

Tyler grunted his uncertainty and took my hands in his, leading me up to the front door. "That's surprising. He usually doesn't give up so easily. I've seen him with women at the club all the time."

"And you said he's an agent?"

He nodded. "Yeah, to Kyle Andrews. Be glad you don't know that motherfucker."

And there it was . . . the opening that was going to change the course of the evening.

"Actually," I began, letting go of his hands. "There's something I need to talk to you about."

I knew that once I confessed to him, he'd turn his back on me and leave just as fast as he came. Taking a deep breath, I looked up into Tyler's unsure gray gaze.

Cindy interrupted by opening the front door and I jumped. Her lips were trembling.

"Cindy, what's wrong?" I asked, rushing over to her. Tears were streaming down her face when she clutched me so tight in her arms, I could barely breathe.

"She's gone, child," she whispered, her voice pained. "I went to check on her because I just had this feeling. When I noticed her chest wasn't moving, I rushed to take her pulse . . ." She trailed off, shaking her head.

Taking off inside the house, I ran straight to Nana's room, bursting through the door to her bedside. Even though my grandmother was destined for death, it still didn't make it any easier. She was the only person who truly knew who I was, the only one who was always there to take care of me. Just gone.

I had no one now.

She had a small smile on her face, like she would open her eyes any moment and say 'I fooled you.' Yes, that was morbid, but my grandmother loved to tease. Her hands were perfectly clasped together on her stomach, but I kneeled down and undid them, cupping one inside of mine. They weren't cold, but they weren't warm either.

Holding her hand to my face, I closed my eyes and hung my head, listening to the sound of my tears thumping as they hit her bed. "I love you, Nana. I didn't even get to say goodbye."

"And she loved you," Cindy said behind me.

Lifting my head, I placed my grandmother's hand back on her stomach and stood, secretly hoping she'd open her eyes and talk to me. "What do we do now?" I asked hoarsely.

Cindy put her hands on my shoulders and turned me around, her warm hazel eyes full of tears. "You, my dear, are going to go outside with your friend and let me handle the details. He's really worried about you."

Nodding, I turned and looked at my grandmother one more time. "Okay," I murmured. "I'll be outside."

"Are you going to call your mother and brother?"

"No," I answered automatically. "It's not like they care."

My mother was probably hoping she was in the will to inherit money, but little did she know, it all went to me. Nana didn't want my mother getting a dime, and I didn't blame her. Turning on my heel, I slowly walked out of my grandmother's room, knowing that everything was about to change.

CHAPTER 16

Kacey

I WALKED INTO the living room and found Tyler sitting on the couch, holding his head in his hands. Immediately, when he heard me enter the room he lifted his head and got to his feet.

Silent tears streamed down my face as I went to his side and took his hand, pulling him back down on the couch with me. His warmth seeped into my body as I curled in against him, laying my head on his shoulder. I breathed him in . . . his scent was comforting. I didn't even have to ask him to hold me because he already had his arm sliding across my shoulders, pulling me closer.

"I'm sorry, Kacey," he murmured, kissing me gently above my ear. "If there's anything I can do, I'll do it."

"Thank you. Right now I don't think there's anything

you can do."

"Do you need to call anyone else to let them know?"

As much as I wanted to tell him about my family, I just couldn't do it right now. I didn't want to let him go yet. "No," I lied. "There's no one else who needs to know. Everything goes to me."

"What about the house? Are you going to stay here?"

Noncommittally, I shrugged my shoulders and took in all of Nana's things around the room. The house was paid for, so it'd be stupid to put it on the market. I didn't want to sell her stuff or leave, but for the time being I needed to get away.

"I think I'm going to find somewhere else to stay for a while, after everything gets settled. Leaving Vegas isn't an option though. Bree and I still have to open our restaurant."

Gently, Tyler brushed the hair off my face and turned my chin so I'd have to face him. "If you need a place to stay, you can always stay with me."

Abruptly, I shook my head. "Tyler, that's really not a good idea. We barely know each other."

"Well, if you'd let me explain, you might change your mind. Just listen okay?"

He only wanted to help and I could see it in his eyes. Nodding, I took a deep breath and motioned for him to continue.

"I have a pool house that's separate from the main one. It has a bathroom, small kitchen, and a bedroom—it's more like a studio apartment. If you'd prefer, I can even charge rent."

The offer was intriguing, but it was too much to think about at the moment. I just needed to get through the next few days without breaking down. "Thanks, Tyler. Right now I'm going to stay here for the week, until all of the affairs get taken care of. Can I let you know?"

"Of course. Take all the time you need."

About that time, Cindy came into the room and hung up her phone. "The coroner will be here in just a couple of minutes," she explained. "Do you want to stay at my house tonight?"

"No, that's okay," I told her. "I'll be fine. I need to get used to being alone anyway."

She nodded her head and strolled off into the kitchen. It was the sad truth . . . I was alone.

"I can stay with you if you want," Tyler murmured. "I don't want to leave you by yourself. Especially after the kind of night you had."

Tilting my head, I sighed. "I'd appreciate that. I can't say I'll be good company, but you're more than welcome to stay."

Tyler squeezed me around the shoulders and then let me go before getting to his feet. "I'll be right back then. I need to get my phone out of the truck and make some calls."

When I nodded, he walked into the kitchen and said something to Cindy and shook her hand. They talked for a few minutes, but I couldn't hear what they were saying. I didn't have the motivation to get up and join them, so I laid down on the couch and felt my back pocket crinkle.

The letter. I'd almost completely forgotten about it.

Pulling it out of my back pocket, I slid my finger underneath the flap and tore it across. My heart thumped harder and louder as I reached in and lifted out the piece of paper containing my grandmother's last words. Swallowing hard, I unfolded the letter.

My lovely Kacey,

There is so much I want to say to you, but sometimes I feel as if my mind has already left me and I can never remember what I wanted to say. Thankfully, God has helped me today. In fact, I feel like I'm twenty-four again, just not with the long blonde hair and the perfect body. If I could choose any one thing I want you to know, it's that I have never been more proud of anyone, as I am of you.

The day I visited you in the hospital after you were born, I knew you were special. I could see it in those precious eyes of yours. Please remember this, Kacey. You're strong and you're genuinely kind. You left your entire life behind, just so you could take care of me. This is just one of the many reasons why I've left you something (not even your grandfather knew I had). I was always told to make sure I had a plan for a rainy day, and I know you're about to have plenty of them.

In the spare bedroom, underneath the third floorboard to the left, there will be a notch to where you can slip your finger under it. Once you lift it up a little ways, you can pull the whole board up. Inside you'll find a box that will help you through the hard times. Follow your dreams, sweetheart.

If there's one thing I ask of you it's to live your life to the fullest. Your grandfather told me last night that your new beau will take care of you. I believe him, which is why it's easier to finally let go . . . but I'm also a firm believer on taking care of yourself. Spend your nights doing things that young kids do, instead of slaving away to earn your keep. You don't need to do that anymore. You took care of

me, now I'm going to take care of you. I love you, Kacey.
   Love always,
   Nana

"Kacey, are you okay?" Tyler asked, kneeling in front of me.

I hadn't even realized he was standing there. Wiping away my tears, I quickly nodded and jumped off the couch, heading straight for the spare bedroom. "Come with me," I offered.

When I got into the spare room, I looked down at the third floorboard to the left and got down on my knees. The notch she spoke of was tiny, so I stuck my pinky inside and lifted as hard as I could—the board moved. Once I had it in my grasp, I moved it to the side and took a deep breath . . . she was right, there was a box. It was a golden encrusted jewelry box that looked to be older than my grandmother and her mother before that.

"What are you doing?" Tyler asked softly.

"Here," I said, passing him the letter. "My grandmother wrote it today. She told me she left me something here, and I came to check it out. Her mind had started to get worse these past few weeks so I didn't know if it was true or not."

Furrowing his brows, he took the letter and peered down into the hole. "What's in it?"

Gently, I lifted the jewelry box out of the hole and set it on the floor. It was dusty from years of not being moved.

"I don't know," I replied. "I guess it's time I found out."

My fingers shook as I lifted the top of the jewelry box, revealing its many contents inside. Eyes wide, I shut it back and peered up at Tyler, completely in shock.

"Holy hell," was all I could say.

CHAPTER 17

TYLER

One Week Later

NOW THAT HER grandmother's affairs had been settled, things had finally started to calm down. She quit her job at the bar, much to Bree's dislike, but she was determined to live her life according to her grandmother's wishes. Besides, what she left in the box helped ease Kacey's worries and put her ten steps closer to reaching her goal. She was *so* close.

Kacey was completely different from any of the girls I'd met. She let me see her pain and wasn't ashamed, she owned it and fought when it threatened to drag her down. That was the kind of person I needed in my life. Kacey was a born fighter, strong-willed and genuine. If only I could get her to stop being so stubborn and let me help her.

It was infuriating how hard-headed she was, but then my father said I was the same way.

Today, however, I showed up at Kacey's house and told her to get in the car, along with her grandmother's ashes. There was something she wanted to do and I was going to make sure it happened for her.

"Did you know she had that much money saved up?" I asked as I drove down the deserted, dusty road.

Dressed in a pair of denim shorts and a small green T-shirt, she was so fucking beautiful with her blonde hair thrown up in a ponytail and no makeup on. I wouldn't say she was completely innocent, but she was close. She was also way out of my league. I had never attracted girls like her, and for the first time in my life, I couldn't treat her like I did with every other female I'd been with—nor did I want to.

This whole week I'd spent every free moment with her, helping her sort through her grandmother's things. Never in a million years would I have imagined ever doing that for a female. Even at night when we were alone in her room sleeping together, I kept my distance and held her, trying so fucking hard to keep my dick from poking her in the back. I wanted her . . . but it wasn't the right time.

"I had *no* idea. If she hadn't said anything, it would've stayed under the floor, untouched."

In the box, there wasn't just an insane amount of cash, but also some jewelry, including the antique sapphire ring she currently had on her ring finger. There were also some old photos of her grandparents, as well as pictures dating back hundreds of years. Apparently, the ring she wore was not just antique, but ancient. It was passed down from mother to daughter for centuries.

I was pretty sure if she sold that ring, she would get the last amount of money she needed to open her restaurant and then some. It was important to her—as it should be—so it didn't surprise me when she said she wanted to work for the rest of the money. She was looking for a day job and it just so happened I had the perfect one for her. I just needed to wait for the right time to ask her.

It wasn't long before the air field came into view and I turned into the parking lot, passing dozens of commercial planes, gliders, and helicopters, until we reached the one we were going to be flying in.

"What are we doing here?" Kacey asked, clutching the black and silver urn in her lap.

"We don't have to go if you're not ready to, but I know you said that your grandmother wanted her ashes to be spread across the Grand Canyon."

Gazing down at the urn, she nodded and smiled. "I'm surprised you remember that. I didn't think you were paying attention." She talked a lot in the past week and I made sure to listen to every detail.

"So what, us fighters don't have compassion now?" I asked, opening the car door. "Don't you think it's time you put those preconceived notions out of your head? I'm not completely worthless you know." I winked at her to let her know I was kidding, but she'd been around me enough this week to start feeling more comfortable.

"Oh, I know you're not worthless," she teased. "I think it's a good idea to go ahead and get this over with. It'll finally be the end. She would want me to move on and concentrate on myself."

"And by concentrating on yourself, I hope you mean to let me take you out on a real date. I'm still waiting for that third date."

Elbowing me in the side, she chuckled. "Yes, I promise. I know you've been patient with me on all fronts, but after today it'll all be different. You'll see."

I couldn't wait.

While Kacey scattered her grandmother's ashes through the Grand Canyon, we all sat in silence until every last trace of her grandmother fluttered out into the wind. I honestly thought she would break down and cry, but she never did. In fact, she surprised me when she wanted to see more of the canyons. For over an hour, Larry flew us around in his helicopter.

"That was so amazing," Kacey exclaimed, jumping up and down on the tarmac. "Not exactly the part about spreading my grandmother's ashes, but the rest was simply breathtaking. Can we go up again sometime?"

Larry smiled at her and then to me. "Certainly, I'd be happy to take you both up again. Just let me know when."

Larry Briggs was a retired military general and also a good friend of my father. His white hair was shaved down close to his scalp, but he made sure to keep a scruffy white beard on his face. When I was younger I used to think he was Santa Claus, just a skinny one.

"Will do," I replied, shaking his outstretched hand.

Instead of shaking his hand, Kacey wrapped her arms around his neck. "Thank you for doing this for me. I really appreciate it and I know my grandmother would too. She loved the Grand Canyon."

Larry's face was red when Kacey let him go. "It was my pleasure, darling. Don't be a stranger now, okay?"

"I won't."

Kacey started toward the truck while I stayed behind with Larry. As soon as she was out of earshot, he whistled and slapped me on the shoulder. "How in the hell did you manage to get that one?"

I turned to look at her as she got in my truck. "Lucky, I guess. I don't deserve her at all."

"That's not true, Tyler. You're a good guy. You've just let success go to your head a little bit. I know your father's been worried about you."

"More like pissed," I grumbled. "The man doesn't know how to give me a break. Everything I do isn't good enough."

"He only wants the best for you, son. Since he never won a title in his boxing days, I think he has a lot of regret weighing him down. Take it easy on the old man."

"I have to keep him on his toes," I chuckled, heading back to Kacey. "He wouldn't know what to do if I didn't." I waved over my head and got in the truck.

Larry waved at us as I slowly backed us out of the parking space.

"I take it you and your dad have a couple issues?" Kacey asked.

I turned to look at her with my eyebrows raised.

Sheepishly, she smiled and shrugged her shoulders. "I heard. The window was down—it was kind of hard not to."

"It's not that we have *issues* per se, it's just that he

likes to ride me hard. Nothing I do is ever good enough. I could win a fight and all he'd do is bitch about what I did wrong."

"He's your coach," she murmured. "I'm sure he only wants the best for you, especially if he never won a title himself. Imagine how he must feel after fighting for so long and never making it to the top? You are so close to winning the Heavyweight title, and if you win it'll make your father's dreams come true, for him and you. My father was the same way."

"What could he have possibly gotten on you about?" I asked curiously. She was smart and a hard worker. There was nothing for her parents to be disappointed about.

Turning her head, she gazed out the window. "It wasn't me. Unfortunately, I have a brother who is very good at disappointing people."

"I didn't know you had a brother. Why didn't you mention it when I asked about your family?"

She shrugged and looked down at her hands fiddling in her lap. I could tell she was uncomfortable talking about it. "I guess because I don't consider him family anymore. The same goes for my mom. I try not to talk about them."

"Do they know about your grandmother?"

She bit her lip and shook her head. "No, I haven't called them. It's not like they care anyway. They wanted to put her in a nursing home and leave her there. My father wouldn't have allowed that to happen."

"I'm sorry, Kacey. Here I am, complaining about my dad, when I know you miss your father." Other than her grandmother, her father was the only other person she talked highly about.

"More than anything," she murmured, smiling off in

the distance. "But at least I have Bree. She's been the only thing holding me together."

Taking her hand, I brought it up to my lips and kissed her palm. "Well, now you have me . . . that is, if you want me."

"I'm still deciding on that one," she teased. "But I'll let you know."

Little did she know, but her smile gave me the answer I needed. She was mine.

CHAPTER 18

Kacey

"WHAT ARE WE doing at your gym?" I asked curiously.

Tyler parked his truck and turned to me, chuckling. "You weren't really being serious last week, when you told me you weren't coming back, right?"

"Kind of," I confessed. "Especially now that I know Liam is part of the fighting crowd. He and his clients don't come into your gym do they? They are the last people I want to be around."

It was an underhanded question, but at least it would give me peace of mind about hanging out in his gym. If I knew Kyle's friends wouldn't be there, I'd be safe. Immediately, he growled low, "They know not to step foot in my gym, unless I've given specific permission. You have nothing to worry about."

"Then I'll go in there," I replied, breathing a sigh of relief. "Is there a reason we're stopping here?"

Tyler grinned sheepishly and opened his door. "Actually there is. I need help with something and I was wondering if you'd be able to do it."

"Do what?"

He winked and slid out of his truck. "Come and find out."

After everything he'd done for me, I'd be more than happy to help him out. His smile, on the other hand, had me suspicious. He was clearly up to something.

Once inside, it was like every person in the room instinctively turned their heads toward him, especially the women. I waited for his eyes to linger . . . but they never did. He kept them solely on me.

"Okay, so what do you need help with?" I asked.

Taking my hand, he pulled me over to the front desk and pointed to the seat. "I need you to sit right there for a minute."

"O-kay," I muttered, sitting down in the chair. "What now?"

"Just wait there. I need to check on something."

What the hell was he doing? Even some of the patrons in the gym were wondering, as their looks bounced between the two of us. Tyler hopped up into the practice ring where his father stood coaching two teenage boys. Words were exchanged between them, ending with his father glancing up my way and waving with a grin on his face. Unsure of what was going on, I smiled and waved back.

Before Tyler could get back up to the desk, his mom, Mary, beat him to it. Her sandy-colored hair was pulled back in a low ponytail and she looked to be in her sixties. Although, her body was well-toned, with defined muscles. That didn't surprise me, considering she owned a gym.

"Kacey, right?"

Quickly, I stood and moved away from her seat and around to the front of the desk. "Yes, ma'am," I replied, holding out my hand.

Instead of taking my hand, she laughed and pulled me into a hug. It was awkward for me, so I just stood there until the next words came out of her mouth. "Dear girl, there's no need for such formalities. Tyler told me about your grandmother. I can't begin to express how sorry I am for your loss. I'm glad he was able to stay with you and help you through the worst of it."

"Thank you," I murmured softly, returning her embrace. "It would have been unbearable without him."

Letting me go, she smiled and stepped back. "So did Tyler ask you yet?"

Furrowing my brows, I didn't even get a chance to reply before Tyler interjected, grinning mischievously.

"Not yet, but I was about to," he said to his mother, coming to my side. "I wanted to make sure she was comfortable coming back here, before I threw the question at her."

"Well, then I'll excuse myself so you two can get down to business." His mother winked at him and then smiled at me one more time. "I'm sure I'll be seeing you around, Kacey."

I nodded. "I'm sure you will, Mrs. Rushing."

"Mary," she corrected. "I want you to call me, Mary."

"Okay . . . Mary. It was good to see you again."

Once she walked away, I watched her walk out the

door and disappear around the corner. *I wish my mother could be more like her—heartwarming and loving.*

"Kacey? Are you okay?" Tyler asked, bumping me in the shoulder.

"Yes," I answered hastily, glancing up. "Sorry, I was just thinking. Your mother is pretty awesome. I've never met anyone so genuine and approachable." I looked away and smirked to myself. "Too bad you didn't take after her."

"What?" he asked incredulously, head whipping around.

Turning to him, I shrugged. "I'm just sayin' . . ."

His eyes bulged, mouth opening and closing like a fish.

Breaking into a laugh, I pinched his side. "Yes, yes. You're the same way, dear. I'm positive you got it from her. So what is it that you needed to ask me?"

Pushing me away and then immediately taking my hand and pulling me back, he chuckled. "You're the devil." Kissing just above my ear, he pulled me behind the desk and pointed to the chair. Once I sat down, he locked me in with a hand on each arm rest and sank down to his knees, caging me in.

"You're looking for a job, right?"

Pursing my lips, I crossed my arms at the chest. "Yeah, why?"

"What would you say about working for me?"

"For you?" I gasped. "Doing what? And please don't tell me it's to be your maid."

"No," he chuckled. "Although I have to say that thought is very tempting. You in a maid's uniform would be fucking hot. I'd never let you leave my house."

Just the thought made my temperature rise. We'd basically been together non-stop for the past week and a half, with zero physical contact other than a few kisses here and there. Each day was obviously more difficult than the last for him to keep his distance, but he did it without getting frustrated—it was a test many men had failed. Out of my twenty-five years of existence, I'd only slept with two men, both of whom I was in love with. One was my high school sweetheart, and the other was a guy I met in college.

"Okay, fine, I accept," I stated boldly, sliding forward in the chair, playing with the front of his shirt. "Where's the outfit, and when do I start?" I was just teasing, but the prospect was kind of exciting. I knew being his maid wasn't what he wanted from me.

His mood grew dark. "Don't tempt me, Kacey. I'm liable to say to hell with everything today and take you to my house right now. You have no idea how hard it's been to give you your space."

"I didn't ask for it," I whispered.

He brushed the hair off of my face and slid his fingers down the side of my cheek. "You may not have asked for it, but I gave it to you, beautiful. Your mind was on other things."

"You're right, it was," I agreed, "but seriously though, what exactly do you mean by working for you?"

Smiling, he stood and turned toward the room, opening his arms wide. "Here," he offered. "I want you to work here with me, until you save up the rest of the money for your restaurant. I know you're not far from your goal."

Which was true, I wasn't. Between me and Bree, we only needed about twenty thousand more. After the extra money from Nana we actually had enough to get started, but we wanted to make sure we had plenty of money to keep us comfortable. We didn't want to be bankrupt before we even got off the ground.

"What will I be doing? Answering phones?" Working with him could quite possibly be the smartest, or the stupidest decision ever. Seeing him every day would definitely be a perk.

Tyler smirked and winked at me. "Yeah, that . . . among other things. I figured you could also help some of the females who come in here, if they need help."

"What about the men?" I interrupted him, teasing. "They might need help too."

"Not from you they don't," he snarled, his jaw clenching tight.

"But what if they strained a muscle and needed it massaged? Am I supposed to just let them suffer? What kind of person would I be if I didn't help?"

It took all I had not to smile or laugh, at least until the topic backfired and his mischievous grin came back. "Well, then I guess if one of the ladies comes in and needs a massage I'll just have to rub them down, won't I?"

"Ugh . . . fine, you win. I won't touch any of the men."

"Now that's what I like to hear. So are you in?"

"How much will I get paid? I have to know you're not going to be using me for free labor," I joked.

Taking my hand, he pulled me up to my feet and put his arms around my waist, drawing me in. "Well, we might want to talk about that. I'm sure there's going to be times when I need you to stay after hours to help me train."

"Oh wow, then I'm going to request at least a thousand dollars a week. Not to mention the fifty extra dollars an hour I'm here after hours. Are you sure you can afford that?"

"Is that what you want?" he asked seriously.

When he didn't smile, I felt like an idiot. "No, I was kidding. I don't expect you to pay me that much. I want you to pay me what you would with any other employee in the same position."

His deep chuckle in my ear sent shivers down my body. "Don't worry, beautiful, you'll be more than happy with the pay. And if not, I'll personally make sure to supplement with some extra perks." He bit his lower lip and pressed into my hips.

"And that right there has me sold. Something tells me I'm going to like your perks." I stared at his lips and wiggled my hips against him. "So, are you going to show me what to do, you know, how you *like* things? I don't want to screw up on my first day."

Sliding his hands up and down my back, he smiled and let me go. "Don't worry, I'll train you well. Tonight, however, we'll finish the afterhours stuff at my house. That is, if you're ready. Does that sound good?"

My heart thudded unbelievably hard in my chest as Tyler stared down at me, with the promise of a passion-filled night in his eyes. Everything inside of me clenched, even the spot between my legs that hadn't been touched by a man in almost two years. I was nervous and terrified, but also excited to take the next step. I wanted him and he wanted me.

"Yes," I breathed. "I'm ready."

CHAPTER

19

Kacey

TYLER SHOWED ME around the gym, where they kept their supplies, and how to work all of the exercise machines. So now, if anyone needed help working them, I knew exactly what to do. The fun started when Bree and Cole showed up. Cole smiled and said hello before strolling off to the practice ring where Tyler stood, wrapping his hands and getting ready to train.

My man was dressed in a pair of green and black fighting shorts, completely bare-chested, showing off his tattoos, and definitely drawing the attention of every female in the gym. I waited on him to acknowledge the ogling stares, but he never once did. Instead, his gaze landed on mine . . . all mine.

"Girl, what are you doing? I've been trying to call

you all afternoon," Bree scolded, snapping her fingers in front of my face. "I guess you've been too busy with lover boy to remember lil' ol' me."

Breaking our stare, I batted my eyelashes innocently and smiled. Her pigtail braids looked cute framing her glowing face. She was still a little angry about me quitting the bar, but once I told her about the money my grandmother left me, she lightened up quite a bit.

"Tyler's been a big help, Bree. He and I took a helicopter ride over the Grand Canyon and scattered my grandmother's ashes today," I told her somberly.

Gasping, she covered her mouth with her hand. "Oh, my goodness, Kace. I know that couldn't have been easy. I didn't mean to sound like a bitch. It's just I haven't seen you very much in the last week. I've missed you."

"I've missed you too, Bree. Look on the bright side, I got a new job and I'll probably be seeing you every day."

"Really? Where?"

"Here," I chuckled. "Tyler asked me to work for him today."

"I thought you didn't want to ever come back here again?" she teased.

"I didn't, but things have changed now. I can't describe it, but it honestly feels like things are looking up for once. Not to mention, by the end of the year, we'll have the money we need to get our restaurant up and going."

Bree smiled and placed her hand over mine. "I can't believe it's about to happen."

I know.

Over her shoulder, I watched Cole get into the ring with Tyler. Other than watching him on the video a few weeks ago and with his last fight, I hadn't actually seen him fight in the flesh.

"Your boyfriend's about to get his ass beat," I stated, pointing behind her.

Bree groaned and peered at them over her shoulder, shaking her head. "They do this every single day," she complained, "and every single day, Cole gets hammered. When he fights some of the other fighters he kicks ass, but against Tyler he loses. I don't know when he'll ever learn."

I had yet to formally meet Mr. Rushing, but he was walking around the ring, studying Tyler and Cole's moves, tapping his finger against his lips in deep thought. When Bree and I approached, Tyler quickly glanced down at me and winked before taking Cole to the mat, grappling with him.

"Come on, Cole!" Bree yelled. "I'll give you a blow job if you beat him!"

Instead of fueling him to win, it caught him off guard and Tyler took that moment to lock him in an arm bar. Cole reluctantly tapped out and collapsed onto the mat.

"No BJ's for you," Tyler joked, picking on him. "Maybe she'll give you a consolation hand job, bro."

"Oops," Bree mumbled, "Cole's going to be pissed now."

Snarling, Cole got to his feet and got into position. "Again," he snapped. "One of these days I'm going to make you tap out."

Sweaty and looking sexy as hell, I couldn't look away from Tyler even if I wanted to. He was so confident in the ring, focused. Watching him fight was thrilling and erotic. I could picture those bare arms wrapping around my naked body, holding me on him . . . claiming me.

My center clenched just thinking about it.

"Do I need to pick your mouth up off the floor?" Bree whispered, chuckling. "Haven't you had sex with him yet?"

"No, not yet. I think it's about time though. He's been patient with me. Besides, after watching him fight just now, I think my vag would disown me if I didn't give her something to play with."

"Oh my God, girl! You are so bad." We broke out in laughter, leaning on one another. After calming down, she continued, "Yeah, Cole's been really shocked with the way Tyler's been around you. He says Tyler has *never* been like this with a girl, not even Gabriella. I think you've got something there."

I think so too, but . . .

"What about his past? I can only imagine the types of things he's done. Do you think that kind of stuff really molds a person? I mean, you don't think he'll want to go back to fucking a bunch of women for fun?" I asked hesitantly.

"Not if he finds the right girl, Kace. And it's looking like he's already found her."

It still didn't help with my situation. I hadn't slept with a bunch of men, but I had a brother who was Tyler's ultimate enemy. Would he be able to look past that and still believe I am who I am? That I'm not the same as my brother.

Tyler's father, Steven, kept his trained eyes on the guys but also managed to meander over, side by side with me and Bree. He was dressed in a pair of dark denim jeans and a navy T-shirt with the gym logo on it. *I wonder if I'll have to wear those when I really start working.*

Taking his eyes off of the guys, he smiled at me, extending his hand. "Kacey, it's good to finally meet you. Tyler's been telling me all about you."

Firmly, I took his hand and shook before letting go. "I hope it's all good things," I replied with a chuckle. "Thank you for the opportunity to work here. I really appreciate it."

"You're welcome. I'm assuming he's told you about his fighting?" he asked, pointing up into the ring.

"Oh yes, of course. He looks good up there."

"That he does," he remarked. "For the past week he's been doing even better than usual. I don't know if it's because of you, or if he's finally getting his head on straight. Either way, it's a good thing. Make sure he keeps it up, would ya?"

I wish Tyler could've heard those words. "I will," I promised. "He's an amazing fighter. I have no doubt he'll win the title this season." Steven stared longingly at the ring and then at his boxing gloves hanging like a shrine where the trophy cabinet sat. There were at least fifteen trophies in there, all glistening and shiny underneath the soft glow of the lights.

"I hope so," he murmured, smiling over at me. "I truly hope so."

As if the moment was over, Steven shook his head and climbed up into the ring. "Come on guys, stop being pussies and attack. *Attack!*"

Tyler chuckled and rolled his eyes. I could tell he was trying to take it easy on his friend.

Steven, however, smacked Cole on the head. "Wake up, Cole! If you ever want to beat my son, you have to work harder than this, *smarter* than this. Focus!"

Cole was spent, breathing hard, and just trying to keep up with Tyler's movements. It was all over when Tyler took him down to the mat. Two seconds later, Cole tapped out. They both got to their feet and smacked gloves, laughing now that all was said and done.

If that was my brother up there, he'd be looking for the easiest way to land a cheap shot. He wasn't a fair fighter with his opponents, or his friends. It was refreshing to see Tyler and Cole be able to beat the shit out of each other and stay on good terms.

While Tyler stayed behind to talk to his dad, Cole jumped out of the ring and scooped Bree up into his sweaty arms, giving her a quick kiss. "I'm going to hit the showers really fast and then we can go if you want."

"But I haven't even worked out yet. I was too busy watching you," she exclaimed.

Cole squeezed her ass and then smacked it. "No worries, babe. Your ass is perfect the way it is. In fact, it could probably stand to be a little bigger. More cushin' for the pushin'."

After smacking him on the arm, Bree pushed him away and gasped with mock surprise, "I don't think so. Is that why you keep bringing me those homemade apple turnovers?"

Taking her arm, he pulled her back to him and captured her chin, tilting her face up. "I buy them because I know you love them." Not caring who was around, he kissed her. "I'll be out in just a minute."

Why couldn't my relationships be as easy as they made it seem? In a way, I was jealous of what they had— they didn't have the secrets that I did. When Cole left to head to the locker room, Bree watched him the entire time with a sparkle in her eyes.

"My God, I love him, Kace."

"Yes, I can see that. It's been so long since I was in love."

Bree nodded up into the ring at Tyler with a smirk on her face. Even though his father was talking to him, Tyler kept sneaking glances my way. "Well, it looks like you're about there again, but Tyler definitely beat you to it. The way he looks at you is unreal."

Rolling my eyes, I bumped her in the shoulder. "Oh whatever, Bree, it's only been a week and a half."

"So?" she objected. "It was just last week when I figured out I was in love with Cole, and it's been less than a couple of weeks since we officially started dating. Guys like Cole and Tyler are used to getting what they want—they've never had to work for a girl. While you were taking a break dealing with your grandmother's affairs, I made Cole do something that ultimately proved he would do anything to make me happy."

"What did he do?" I asked curiously.

Snickering, she moved in closer to make sure no one could hear her. "He'd kill me if I told anyone about this. Anyway, I made a comment about going to see the Disney on Ice show and then just last Friday he shows up at my place with tickets. It was the sweetest thing ever."

Yes, it was, but I couldn't imagine Tyler ever doing that.

"What are you two whispering about?" Tyler asked, jumping out of the ring. He put his arm around my waist and pulled me in to his side.

"Oh, just the usual," Bree remarked, looking around at the other people in the gym.

Tyler furrowed his brows. "And what would that be?"

Bree chuckled and started off toward the treadmills, answering him over her shoulder. "Just talking about how hot some of these guys are in here. I think you need to hire me, so I can look at them all day." She winked at me and burst out laughing.

Tyler didn't think she was too funny.

"Lighten up," I told him. "You know that's not what we were talking about. I couldn't take my eyes off of you to even look at someone else. You were amazing up there." His body was slick with sweat and hot to the touch, but I didn't care. I leaned into him and breathed him in. "It actually kind of turned me on," I whispered in his ear.

"Now that's what I like to hear. Let me go change clothes and then we can leave and get something to eat. Afterward, we can go to my place."

Biting my lip, I glanced up at him and nodded. "Hurry."

I didn't want to wait any longer..

CHAPTER 20

TYLER

THE LOOK IN Kacey's eyes when she told me to hurry had me so fucking hard. I couldn't wait to get her to my house and lay her out on my bed. However, as soon as I changed and met her back in the gym, all hopes of getting out of their fast completely diminished. My mother had shown up with dinner, like she always did each night. I was about to pass on it, but then she put her clutches into Kacey. We weren't going anywhere.

It was strange to see my parents so interested in Kacey. I didn't know if it was because they felt sorry for the loss of her grandma, or if she just captivated them like she did with everyone. Then again, they'd never seen me interested in just *one* girl; it was always dozens, which pissed my mother off. She always made sure to tell me she raised me better than that.

My mother was an amazing cook and with Kacey being one as well, they had a lot in common. Especially when my mother told Kacey about my great-grandparents and how they owned a thriving restaurant in the nineteen-twenties. Even during the depression, they were able to stay afloat.

Kacey took notes as my mother went on and on about the do's and don'ts of running a business. It was the happiest I'd seen Kacey since her grandmother died. She had that spark, a passion to succeed. It made me want to be better, to be the fighter I knew I could be.

Once dinner was over, Kacey and I bolted out of the gym to my truck.

"I was afraid we weren't going to get the fuck out of there," I muttered, opening the car door for her. She'd enjoyed the time spent with my mother, but I could tell she was just as impatient to leave as I was after a while. "I love my mother and everything, but she sure as hell can talk. She seemed to be pretty taken with you though."

Kacey hopped in the truck and snickered. "Is she usually not like that?"

"Honestly, I don't know. I've never introduced her to any of . . . you know . . . the girls I've been with," I sputtered hesitantly. We hadn't exactly talked about all of the women I'd been with, but I was sure she had a good idea.

"Not even, Gabriella?"

I stiffened. "How did you know about her? That's not something many people know." I had a good guess though . . . Cole.

Instead of answering, Kacey bit her lip and sat there, warring with herself on what to tell me. Obviously, she was told not to say anything.

"So it is true?" she asked. "You two were seeing each other?"

Releasing a heavy sigh, I shut her door and walked around to my side of the truck and got in. Through her tone, I couldn't tell if she was worried about something or if she was angry.

Once I started down the road, I reached for the hand laying in her lap and squeezed it. "Did Cole tell you?" I asked, glancing over at her. "You can tell me if he did."

"Actually, no," she replied, shaking her head. "He didn't tell me, but I kind of figured it out on my own."

How the hell could she do that? She wasn't even around me during that time. "How could you figure something like that out?"

"It was in the video that went viral," she stated. "It was the one where you and that other fighter started battling it out and then Gabriella and the other female finished. The way you two looked at each other wasn't just a 'friends' look . . . it was much deeper."

It had to be a female thing to notice something like that because no one else ever made any comments about it. "It's not like that anymore," I admitted honestly, staring straight at her. "What we had is over. We're just friends now." I hadn't even talked to Gabriella since I'd been with Kacey.

"That video was shot just over a month ago," Kacey stated adamantly. "You're trying to tell me feelings just disappear?"

"A lot has changed in a month, Kacey. Look how far you and I've come in just the last week. There's nothing going on. Besides, we were never even exclusive."

She nodded, clearly uncertain by the rigidity in her body.

"How did you know about that video anyway?"

"Google will give you everything," she replied. "All I had to do was type in your name and voilà. My only concern is that she'll be at the fights with you. I just want to make sure I don't have to worry about something happening between you two when I'm not around."

"Nothing's going to happen," I promised her, tapping her on the chin to get her attention. "She's moved on and so have I. I'm happy where I'm at . . . with you. It was a mutual understanding to end things. What I need from you is to trust me. Can you do that?"

"I do," she murmured wholeheartedly. "Nobody likes to get their heart broken. I guess I've spent a lot of my time guarding mine."

Bringing her hand up to my lips, I kissed it gently and locked my gaze onto hers, hoping to erase the doubt on her face. "I don't want to get hurt either, but it's a risk you take when you let people in. I can't promise I'm not going to do stupid shit and piss you off, but I *can* promise I will always be honest and straightforward. If there's something you want to know, I'll tell you the truth."

Her face instantly lit up, a mischievous smirk splaying across her lips. "So if I ask you *anything*, you'll tell me the truth?" she inquired curiously.

"Yes, but I'm warning you. Be mindful of the questions, because you might not want to hear the answers."

Turning her body completely toward me, she grinned and rubbed her hands together. "I think I can handle that. All right, let's see . . . were you in love with Gabriella?"

Of course it had to be about her. In all seriousness, I

looked her in the eyes and answered, "No, I was never in love with her. She's a good friend and I care about her, but that's as far as it goes."

Furrowing her brows, she stared at me for a moment before nodding her head, hopefully satisfied with my response. I was beginning to think I should've given her a five question limit.

"Have you slept with anyone since you met me?" she asked.

"No. Have you?"

Deep down, I knew she hadn't because she wasn't like that—she wasn't like me. Hell, I used to love fucking different women almost every night, or at least three times a week. I could get anyone I wanted, but I had yet to fully get the one I truly wanted.

"Hey, these aren't my questions. I don't have to answer that," she teased. "But since you're answering mine, I'll at least be nice enough to answer one of yours. No, I haven't slept with anyone since you met me. In fact, I haven't had sex in almost two years."

Two years? Hot damn, that was a long time. "Why? Is it because you were taking care of your grandmother?"

"Yes, it was mostly that, and also I've never been the type of girl to give it up to just anyone. I don't even want to know how many people you've been with."

Ouch. In her eyes I could see that dealing with my past wasn't going to be easy. "So, I'm assuming that's not your next question?" I asked hesitantly.

"Oh, God no," she shrieked. "I prefer to be ignorant on those details. Besides, it's not about our pasts, or the things we can't change. We have to look forward, right? I mean, what if there was something about me you couldn't change? What if I had a family member who was basically the spawn of evil?"

I laughed, I couldn't help it. "The spawn of evil? That's probably a little extreme don't you think?"

"I wish it was, but unfortunately it's true." Nervously, she fiddled with her fingers. "I just wouldn't want you to think badly of me because of my family. You wouldn't would you?"

"No," I exclaimed incredulously. Why would she even think that? "I don't care what other people in your family do. It's you I care about." Turning into my driveway, I shut off my truck and reached for her hands.

Almost instantly, that seemed to appease her. She breathed a sigh of relief, her fingers relaxing in my grasp.

"I have one more question for you," she murmured, leaning her head against the seat and biting her lip provocatively. Her skin tight green T-shirt hung so close to her skin I could see her nipples peeking through the fabric. I wanted to taste them, to roll my tongue around them and make them pucker more. I wanted to taste all of her.

"What's the question?" I growled low, watching her tongue slide across her lips.

Slowly, she moved forward and stopped only an inch away from me, her mouth so achingly close. It killed me to keep my calm, to not pick her up, carry her into my house, throw her on my bed, and just fuck her like I'd been dying to do since the day I met her. I had never wanted someone so bad and not be able to have them.

"I'm ready for you, Tyler. Are you ready for me?"

Grasping the back of her neck, I brought her closer and gently nipped her bottom lip making her gasp. "You have no fucking idea."

CHAPTER 21

Kacey

AS SOON AS Tyler pulled into the garage and we got out of his truck, it was like we couldn't get back to each other fast enough. He wrapped his arms around my waist and lifted me up, kissing his way down my neck to the tops of my breasts.

With my legs around his waist, he carried me inside and slammed the door, ripping my shirt off before we could even get to the stairs. Giggling, I looked down at the tattered garment on the ground and then up to him, his gaze was raw.

"I'll get you another one," he assured me.

Leaning me against the wall, Tyler lifted my bra and cupped my breast in his hand, shifting me up so he could suck my nipple between his teeth. Closing my eyes, I moaned and held him close, my insides tightening. I could feel the blood rushing to the spot between my legs that ached to feel Tyler's touch. Only one gentle stroke and I would be completely lost and at his mercy.

"Tyler," I breathed, arching my back.

Chuckling, he reached around behind my back and unclasped my bra, letting it fall to the floor. He stood back and looked up and down my body as I straddled him. His cock getting harder between my legs.

"You are so beautiful, Kacey," he murmured, sliding a strand of my hair off my forehead. "I promise to go slow with you tonight. I don't want to hurt you."

From the feel of him below, it didn't take a genius to figure out he meant he didn't want to hurt me physically. No matter how turned on I was, I knew it would hurt once I had sex again. It had been too long.

"I know you won't," I answered him softly. "I'll be okay."

Slowly, he leaned forward and placed his forehead to mine, breathing me in. He was a dangerous man in the ring, yet so gentle in his touches. His hands were used to hit and fight, but with me they caressed and smoothed away my fears.

My God, I was falling for him. I shouldn't have let it happen, but I couldn't fight it.

Carrying me up the stairs, I couldn't even see anything in his house because it was so dark. It didn't matter because the only place I wanted to see was his bedroom.

"If it gets to be too much, just tell me to stop," he whispered.

I nodded, understanding his concern, but really wanting this to happen. Plucking at his shirt, I demanded, "Off, please."

He smirked and lifted one arm. I promptly tugged his shirt over his head and he let it fall to the floor. I ran my hands over his tattoos and inspected his body as he opened a door and turned on the light, carrying me into his room, and lying me down gently on his king-size bed.

Starting at my lips, he trailed his finger down my neck, in between my breasts, on to my shorts where he slid them down my legs and tossed them to the side. His hands were warm as he ran them up my legs to spread them, caressing my thighs. I watched him slink along like a tiger, all sleek muscle and predatory eyes as he took me in, laying completely open to him.

Sliding off the bed, he glanced around his room, pursing his lips. This gave me a chance to look around. His room wasn't what I expected. The walls were painted a dark gray with framed black and white abstract photos on his walls, and his bed was perfectly made, covered with a black comforter and gray sheets. It was all dark and masculine, just like Tyler, but the paintings gave his room an edgy yet sensual feel.

Tyler turned off the overhead light, covering us in nothing but darkness. Then he opened his balcony door wide, letting the wind blow, the sheer, white gossamer curtains flowing inside his room. The moon was positioned just right, basking the room in a soft, gentle glow.

It was all so perfect.

"You didn't take me as the kind of guy to like art?" I mentioned, pointing to the paintings on his walls.

Smirking, he lowered his shorts to the floor and slowly climbed back on the bed. Biting my lip, I spread my legs as he slowly crawled up my body. He rested off to the side, his thick length pressing into my thigh as he turned me to him.

"Most people don't know the real me, Kacey. But with you . . . I want you to see all sides of me . . . I need you to."

"Well, I'm very pleased you showed me the real Tyler. I love this side of you," I murmured wholeheartedly.

Spreading my legs with his knee, he smiled down at me and covered my body with his, leaning on his elbows to keep his full weight off of me. I was small underneath his body, utterly at his mercy. It was an archaic feeling, but I wanted him to take me, to claim me for his own— leave his mark on me.

"I love the way you look when you're happy, it's breathtaking the way your face glows," he claimed, brushing his fingers down my cheek. "However, your eyes are what I love the most."

"Why is that?" I asked, kissing his fingers as be brushed them over my lips.

He looked deeply into my eyes. "When I look at you, I see that light, beckoning me closer. It's that light I've been so afraid will burn out if you let me in, but the more time I've spent with you, it's only gotten brighter. I'm addicted to it . . . to you. These days I can't seem to think of anything else."

I felt the same way.

"And once you make love to me it'll only get worse," I admitted tenderly. "Is that a risk you're willing to take?"

He lowered his lips to mine and I closed my eyes, loving the way my lips tingled every time they touched his. "Yes," he answered. "I'd risk just about anything for you."

Looking at him, I smiled and wrapped my legs around his waist, feeling his cock jump in anticipation as I rubbed against it. "Then make love to me. I'm ready to take the risk."

Ever so gently, Tyler unhooked my legs and slid his hand up the inside of my thigh, opening my legs further. Lowering his head, he flicked his tongue across my clit. I gasped.

When he chuckled, his breath fanned across my body making it even more sensitive. I'd only had one guy go down on me in my lifetime and it actually sucked, but Tyler . . . his tongue worked wonders. Every time he pushed his tongue inside of me, he rolled it around, tasting me while nuzzling my bud with his nose, keeping me stimulated.

"Tyler," I moaned, fisting my hands in his hair. I was so close.

"That's right, beautiful. Let me make you come."

I screamed out his name as the force of my release had me arching off the bed, my hands still tangled in his hair. Slowly, I released my hands and brought them to my chest, where my heart thumped wildly. That was the best orgasm I'd had in years.

"I think you're ready now," he claimed, licking his lips.

Reaching over to his bedside table, he pulled out a condom and opened it up. Before he could slide it down his length, I lowered my hand and wrapped it around him. I hadn't told him I was on the pill, but it was probably for the best right now. As I glided my hand up and down his cock, Tyler pushed his length through my hand, biting his lip as he watched me. I loved seeing that wild, primal look in his eyes.

"Mmm . . . that feels so good, beautiful."

The more I rubbed him, the more he trembled and started losing control.

"That's enough, Kacey. I'm a little too worked up to be played with."

"Next time, then," I teased.

Slipping on the condom, he lowered himself onto my body and bit my lip, tugging on it. "I look forward to it."

He rocked his hips against mine and his arousal moved between my legs, rubbing along the slit, getting nice and wet. Then, the tip found its mark, pushing inside, stretching me. Taking a deep breath, I closed my eyes and felt a tender kiss before he slowly pressed in the rest of the way. The pain of it made my eyes water, but it was a good pain. In fact, I needed more.

"You can go harder, Tyler. I promise I won't break."

"Are you sure?" he asked.

Capturing his face in my hands, I bit his lip and sucked on it as hard as I could. He growled low and gripped the edges of the pillow beneath my head. I loved that he was worried about me and it made me care about him more, but I really needed to feel the heat I knew he was restraining deep inside of him.

"Yes, now stop holding back."

Almost immediately, his breathing picked up and his eyes darkened, the intensity building in the room. I shivered in response and gripped my legs tighter around his waist, rocking my hips hard against his. That was his undoing.

Fisting his hands in my hair, he pulled my head to the side and bit down on my neck, his thrusts growing deeper and faster. I screamed out in pleasure, but Tyler silenced me by closing his lips over mine. The harder he pushed his body into me, the closer I was to losing control. I could tell he was close. As soon as I started to clench down on him, he released my hair and brought his hands down to my face, keeping his eyes locked on mine.

Digging my nails into his skin, I rode wave after wave of pure bliss as the longest damn orgasm of my life rocked through my body. It only intensified when Tyler growled in my ear, biting down on my lobe as he too released, pulsating inside of me.

Breathing hard, he lifted up on his elbows and smiled down at me.

I smiled back. The night was everything I could've wanted and more.

"Are you okay?" he asked.

I was more than okay. However, looking down at his lips, he definitely wasn't. His bottom lip was red and swollen. "I'm perfectly fine, but I can't say the same about you," I pointed out slyly, chuckling.

"What are you talking about?"

Biting my lip, I looked down at his and cringed. "I kind of left a mark on your lip. I hope it goes away before we go to the gym tomorrow."

He didn't seem to care by the grin on his face. "Is it bad?"

"Not really, but I'd hate for you to have to explain it to people."

With a smirk, he tilted my head to the side and said, "Well, it can't be any worse than your neck. Looks like we're even."

Great, now everyone will know we did it. I guess it

was bound to happen at some point.

CHAPTER 22

Kacey

IT WAS FRIDAY morning, the day after our first night *together*. I was a little sore, but I made sure to soak in his bathtub afterward. He made fun of me for walking funny this morning when I met him in his kitchen for breakfast. Needless to say, I've been consciously paying attention to the way I walked.

Since I didn't have any clothes at Tyler's house, and I couldn't go to work with the same clothes from the night before, I had gotten him to take me home.

"I didn't get the chance to ask you last night, but will you come with me to my fight tomorrow? I actually want to head out tonight. We're going to Phoenix."

Shit! What if my brother's going to be there? I hadn't looked at his schedule to see where he'd be fighting at.

"I don't know," I replied, dodging the question. "What if your father thinks I'm a distraction?"

Tyler scoffed. "Please, he knows better than to say that shit to me. Besides, even he's noticed that I've been fighting better than I ever have."

Which was true, but still . . . I had to check to make sure my brother wasn't going to be there before I could give him an answer. Glancing down at the clock, my eyes went wide when I noticed it was closing in on eight o' clock. Tyler always started training with his father at eight.

"Tyler, you need to be at the gym, like ten minutes ago. We can talk about your fight later. Right now, you need to go before I get fired."

"No one's going to fire you, Kacey," he chuckled as he pulled into my driveway. "Are you sure you don't want me to wait on you?"

"No, because I still want to take a quick shower and change clothes. I'll be at the gym in thirty minutes, I promise."

Grasping my chin, he kissed me. "Fine, I'll see you later. And don't think I haven't noticed you avoided my question." He lightly bopped me on the nose with his finger. "I expect an answer about Phoenix when you get there."

Swallowing hard, I slid out of his truck, forcing a smile on my face. My secrets were going to be the death of me. Why couldn't I just tell him the truth? I could explain why I never told him, or anyone for that matter, that Kyle was my brother. Surely, he would understand why I didn't want to tell anyone that shit. I was ashamed.

I waved at him as he pulled out of my driveway and slowly trudged my way to the door. The house was lonely now that my grandmother had passed. It was quiet, and not the least bit inviting anymore.

When I got inside, I set my purse down and pulled out my phone, turning it on. It immediately beeped from missed messages. Most likely from Bree. Sadly, only one message was from her, while the others were my brother. Why couldn't he just leave me the hell alone? The one from Bree was basically her demanding that I was going to Phoenix with them, whether I liked it or not.

While booting up my laptop, I listened to the few messages. The first two were nothing, only the sound of Kyle hanging up the phone. The third one, however, was him.

"I'm assuming since you're not answering your phone, you're still pissed at me. You know, you could avoid all of this if you'd just talk to me. I don't know why you're making things so difficult. So listen, I'm going to be in Vegas this weekend for my fight. I want to come by and see you and Nana, maybe grab something to eat. As much as you hate me right now, you're still my sister, my family. I'll be there tomorrow around lunch time."

Groaning, I shut my laptop. There was no need to see where he was fighting anymore. Sitting on my bed, I ran my hands through my hair and stared at my phone. If I ignore him, he'll do something stupid to get my attention. If I call him and tell him about our grandmother, he'll get pissed because I kept it from him. Situations like this shouldn't be difficult. At least, they're not supposed to be.

I should be able to call my mom and go shopping, like normal mothers and daughters do, but instead all she wants to do is talk about herself. Never once in the last eight months has she called me to see how I'd been doing. Knowing there were real mothers out there like Tyler's, made me realize how lonely and sad my life really was— especially now that Nana was gone.

Basically, I only had one option. Taking a deep breath, I sat on my bed and dialed his number, secretly hoping he wouldn't answer.

"Well *hello*, Kacey. I'm glad you called me back," he answered.

I snorted and rolled my eyes. "Yeah, it was either that, or wait on you to do something stupid. I'd rather deal with you, than put up with your dirt bag friends."

"Damn, Kacey," he chuckled. "My friends aren't going to mess with you. I only had Liam get close to you to get information on your well-being. I'm just worried about you out there by yourself, taking care of grandma. Especially since you don't cash any of the checks I send."

"It's because I don't need it, Kyle. I'd rather work for it myself instead of taking your blood money."

"Kacey, you're being ridiculous, but I guess we both get our stubbornness from dad. So anyway, I'm going to be in town. Let me take you out to lunch tomorrow. We can go anywhere you want."

Here we go.

"I'm sorry, Kyle, but I'm not going to be in town. Bree and I are going away for the weekend. We leave tonight."

"Tonight? What about Nana? I thought you were taking care of her?" he replied.

I closed my eyes and hung my head. The pain of my grandmother's loss was always going to hang heavy on my soul. I don't think there will ever come a time when I don't feel that pain.

"Kyle, I think you should know. . ." I started, but then stopped to take in a calming breath. "Nana passed away last week."

The phone went silent, at least until Kyle's angry outburst tore through the phone. "Are you fucking serious? Why didn't you tell me?"

To avoid a screaming match, I calmly responded back, "Can you honestly tell me you give a fuck? You never once called her or talked to her—neither had mom. I didn't see the need in telling you. Everything is taken care of and she's put to rest. It's all over."

"Yeah, it appears that's not all you hadn't told me," he grumbled.

Immediately, I stiffened. "What do you mean?"

"I'm talking about your job at the bar, Kacey. I found out that you stopped working there. Liam went to check on you and was told you quit. What are you doing for money?"

"I find that working the corners in Sin City is very lucrative," I replied sarcastically, rolling my eyes. He didn't seem to find that funny by the growl in my ear. "Don't worry, I have plenty of money saved up. I'll be fine until I open up my restaurant."

I wasn't about to tell him I worked for Tyler. He'd show up in a heartbeat to drag me out. "How much more do you need?" he asked curiously. "I can loan it to you if you want."

"I don't think so," I scoffed. "I don't need your help. In fact, I really need to go." Looking at the clock, I had already wasted ten minutes on the phone with him.

Kyle huffed. "All right, I get it. Just so you know, I'm going to be back in Vegas in two weeks for the title match. We're going to have to celebrate when I win."

Instantly, I felt sick to my stomach. I had known the title match was coming up, but I didn't realize it was in two weeks. "Who are you fighting?" I asked, already knowing the answer.

"Tyler fucking Rushing," he sneered.

"What is your problem with these other fighters? Are you jealous of them?" I snapped. "What did they ever do to you? I hate hearing stories of the things you've done to screw with people."

"It's just part of the business, sis. Besides, the guys I have a problem with always think they're better than me. You should see the way they look down their noses at me, like I'm no better than a pile of shit. Tyler's the same way. He's going down. I have a plan and it's going to tear him apart."

Holding in my gasp, I swallowed hard and closed a hand over my mouth. "What are you going to do, Kyle? You need to stop doing this."

"Oh, don't you worry about it. I just hope I get to see it all take place."

Before I could even form a coherent thought, Kyle chuckled and hung up the phone.

Oh my God! What would he do? Quickly, I threw off my clothes and hopped in the shower, holding back my tears. I had to make sure Tyler was ready for anything, but I had a feeling he already knew to be on guard.

My choice for the weekend was made . . . I was going to Phoenix.

CHAPTER 23

Kacey

I THOUGHT VEGAS was hot, but Phoenix was hotter. Even in my strapless, pink sundress I was burning up. Hopefully, I wasn't getting sick. I could usually handle the heat, but today it was proving to be quite difficult. Tyler, in his dark blue tank top and khaki shorts, appeared to be comfortable and not overheated at all.

As soon as he'd finished training with his father, I'd followed him to his house so he could pack his bags. Mine were already packed and ready to go. In fact, I'd made sure to put extra clothes in there so I'd have them in case I stayed at Tyler's when we got back. Mostly, I didn't want to go home for fear that my brother would be there waiting on me.

When we pulled up at the hotel, my mouth flew open

at the sight. I loved playing golf and the hotel was right smack dab in the middle of a course—an amazing one at that. "Oh my God," I breathed. "This place is gorgeous. It's a shame I don't have my clubs."

I used to play with my father every weekend, and even played in tournaments with him. We were the best team. Tyler had won trophies for fighting and karate as a kid, but I had ones for golfing.

He smirked and parked the truck; probably thinking I was kidding.

"I'm being serious, Tyler. I used to golf all of the time. I was actually pretty good."

"Oh, I know," he stated, turning to me. "Bree told me you played. I have a tee time scheduled for us in an hour."

"Are you shitting me?" I gasped wholeheartedly. "This is amazing. I can't believe you'd do that. Do you even know how to play?"

Opening his door, he guffawed and shook his head. "Not exactly, but I figured I could give it a try. That's why I wanted to stay here, so you could play."

We were staying at the Camelback Inn, which was only about twenty minutes away from the arena. It worked for me because I knew it was a place where we could have some privacy and not be around the other fighters. Bree and Cole would be joining us later, since Bree had to work the day shift to make up for being gone.

"And then, after you kick my ass in golf, I figured we could go skinny dipping," Tyler announced, waggling his eyebrows. We unloaded our bags from the truck, and again, only I was drenched in sweat.

Wiping my brow, I smacked him on the arm, giggling. "And how are we going to do that? I don't think I want to get naked around the other guests at this hotel." Although, right now, I would probably jump in a frozen lake if I could.

"Oh, you don't have to worry about the details, beautiful."

"And why is that?"

He winked and kissed me on the lips. "You'll see."

Knowing him, he wanted us to sneak into the pool area after hours. I could be adventurous, but I sure as hell wasn't going to do that. When we got inside, Tyler checked us in and we started off toward our room. He smirked the entire time and I had no idea why until we got to our floor and he opened the door. Our room wasn't just ordinary. It was a gigantic suite, with a living room that had a couch and two chairs, a separate bedroom with a king-size bed, and a door that led onto our own patio.

And on that patio . . . was our own *private* pool.

"So that's why you mentioned skinny dipping, huh?"

We both set our bags down and waltzed onto the patio. I was in awe because I didn't live the upscale life like my brother and mother, or Tyler for that matter. I just wasn't used to all of this. It sure was nice though. Sliding off my sandals, I brushed across the top of the water, sighing when it felt cold to the touch.

"If you want the water warmer, we can turn on the heat," Tyler said, sticking his hand in.

"No, it's perfect, we don't need it. As soon as we get done playing golf, we'll want to cool down. I've never been skinny dipping before."

Taking his hand out of the water, Tyler dried it on his shorts before putting his arms around my waist, his mischievous gray eyes sparkling. "It'll definitely be something to remember. Now let's go before we're late."

Once we were done golfing and back at the club-house, I sat down to untie my shoes. I briefly thought I was going to pass out from heat exhaustion, but thankfully it passed. The adrenaline of playing golf again—and thoroughly kicking Tyler's ass—helped me feel better. Not to mention the amazing gift he gave me.

"I can't believe you did this, Tyler. I don't know how to thank you."

He took off his shoes and put his tennis shoes back on. "I think you already did about twenty times in the last three hours." He flashed a smile.

"Yes, but it's not enough," I countered. "I need to repay you somehow."

When we left to check in for our tee time I had no clue what we were going to do as far as golf clubs and shoes. I never brought them with me to Vegas because I didn't think I'd have time to play. Anyway, there waiting for me with a giant ribbon around them, were a pair of brand new golf shoes and a golf bag full of clubs. They were mine. Tyler had bought them for me and they weren't cheap either. They were top of the line. I couldn't begin to imagine how much he spent on me.

"I'll tell you what," Tyler began, getting to his feet. Now that my shoes were off and tucked under my arm, I was waiting on him. He stalked closer, biting his lip. "Why don't we go to the room and you can show me your appreciation in there. I think we both would enjoy that, don't you think?"

Taking my hand, we started out of the club and straight to our room, his grasp assertive as he held onto me.

"It's still not enough," I pointed out. "There's nothing I can give you that you don't already have. I have nothing to offer in return."

When we got to the room, he opened the door and pulled me in, capturing my face in his hands as soon as the door shut. He wasn't smiling or his usual playful self. He was nothing but serious as he looked at me, the intensity taking my breath away.

"Kacey, if there's one thing I don't want to hear come out of your mouth, it's what you just said. You give me more than I could ever want just by being with me, by being you." He brushed his fingers over my cheek and down to my chest, where he placed his hand over my heart. Immediately, it beat harder and he smiled because he could feel it. That was when he took *my* hand and placed it over his heart. The second I touched him, I could feel his pulse thumping hard.

"This is what you do to me, Kacey. Every time I see you, every time you touch me, I feel like I'm going to go insane. I can never get enough of you. Even last night after you fell asleep, I wanted to wake you up and make love to you again. You're constantly on my mind and when you're not around, I fear something's going to happen and I'll never see you again; that you'll get tired of my lifestyle. I have to make sure you stay with me. I . . ."

With my heart beating out of control, I licked my dry

lips and felt a bead of sweat pour down the center of my back. "You what?" I asked, whispering the words.

Sighing, he leaned over to kiss my lips softly. There was nothing soft about the man before me, but deep down he had the biggest heart of anyone I knew. "I was going to say that I love you," he murmured against my lips. "I am so fucking in love with you."

I slid my hands up his chest to hold his face, and smiled up at him. I had been in love before, or at least I thought I had, but nothing compared to the way I felt about Tyler. We had a forbidden love, but he didn't know that. He didn't know that what we had would have me disowned by the only family I had left. The truth was, I didn't care. What Tyler and I had was strong, stronger than blood.

"I love you too," I whispered.

"And that right there, is the one thing you've given me that no one else in this world can do. So you see . . . as long as you love me, there is always something you can offer me."

Smiling, I bit my lip and let my hands trail to the top of his shorts, where I slipped my hand inside and gently grabbed his growing cock. It didn't take him long to get rock hard once I started massaging him, leaving me hardly any room to move my hand.

"I think there's more I can give you," I tempted. Sliding my hand out of his shorts, I grasped the hem of his shirt and lifted it over his head, letting it fall to the floor. Next, I unbuttoned his shorts and with a light push, they fell down his legs. Kicking them to the side, he stood in only his boxers and tennis shoes.

"On the couch," I commanded. "I need to warm you

up first before we get in the pool."

Doing as I said, he situated himself on the brown leather couch while I got down on my knees and unlaced his shoes. He kept his gaze on me as I removed his socks and shoes, but when I spread his legs so I could move my body between his, his eyes got darker . . . almost possessive. I loved seeing that look in his eyes, like I was his and no one else's. It was the way I felt about him.

Gripping the top of his boxers, I slowly lowered them down, but Tyler had to lift his butt so I could slide them down his legs. His cock laid thick and heavy on his stomach, making my insides ache to straddle his body and ride him hard. *Not yet, Kacey.*

Instead, I cupped his balls in my hand and massaged them, enjoying the groan that escaped his lips. When he closed his eyes and his head fell back on to the couch that was when I lowered my mouth to his dick, wrapping my lips tightly around the head. His body jerked and he groaned even louder as I sucked him off, taking him in as far as I could go.

"Kacey," he growled. "Holy fuck."

Over and over, I licked and sucked the tip of him, tasting the saltiness of his body as I drove him toward the edge. His hips were rocking into my face and his abs were contracting. He was so close.

"Stop, beautiful. I want to be inside you when I come."

I gave him one last swirl and suck, removing my lips with a popping noise. He lifted me onto his lap, where I straddled his waist. I took my dress up and over my head, exposing my strapless pink bra and thong. He pushed his cock against the aching spot between my legs and it was my turn to groan. All he had to do was move across my clit and I would explode right where I sat. I was more than ready to have him inside me. My drenched thong was proof enough.

Sliding the offending thong to the side, Tyler rubbed me with his thumb and breathed deeply when he felt how wet I was for him. "You're not sore from last night are you?" he asked gently.

Moving his hand to the side, I sat up and then lowered onto him, until I had him seated completely inside of me. His fingers dug into my ass and he held on tight as I grinded my hips against his, riding him slow and deep. Pulling me to him, Tyler unclasped my bra and tossed it aside before latching onto one of my nipples and pulling it with his teeth.

I hissed with pain, until he circled his tongue where he'd bit and it felt so amazingly good I almost exploded around him.

"I'm not wearing a condom, beautiful," Tyler growled low. "We can't take any chances. I know I'm clean, but we don't need any little ones running around just yet."

"You have nothing to worry about," I murmured, biting his bottom lip. "I'm on the pill."

"Why didn't you tell me that last night?"

I pulled back and grinned down at him. "You didn't ask."

Getting to his feet, he grabbed my thin, lacy thong and ripped it off my body before walking us outside. He did all of this while still inside me.

"What are you doing?" I shrieked, holding onto him.

"We're going skinny dipping, baby. Besides, your

body is on fire and if you keep riding me like that, I'm not going to last. It's my time to make *you* suffer."

"I think you made my thong suffer. You're going to owe me some new underwear, Mr. Rushing," I exclaimed.

He slowly walked down the steps into the pool and once the cool water touched my legs I sighed in relief. "I'll buy you some new ones. Maybe I could go with you and you can model them for me in the store."

Most places didn't allow that, but with his charm, I was sure he'd find a way. "Sounds good to me," I murmured, clenching my legs tighter around his waist.

Now that we were all the way in the pool, the water came up to my shoulders. He backed me up against the pool wall and held onto the edge before lowering his lips to mine, they were so soft and firm. Willingly, I opened for him and he pushed his tongue inside with demand, like he *needed* me . . . I loved it. I'd never been needed by anyone.

"I love being able to feel you like this," he groaned, pushing inside of me. "But I think it's time to heat things up a bit."

"How so?"

Without answering, he gripped my waist with his strong hands and lifted me off his length, turning me around. I gasped with how quick he moved me, my heart thumping wildly in my chest when he lowered his lips to my ear, biting down.

"You're going to want to hold onto the edge, beautiful."

Instantly, my insides tightened in anticipation and my nipples grew more sensitive. I held onto the edge of the pool as he snaked his arms around me, pushing his rigid cock between my legs, and pinching my nipples between his fingers. I squeezed my legs around him, and he used my breasts to pull me up and down, his length sliding along my slit. I could feel my orgasm beginning to build and the moment my body clenched down, Tyler changed angles and slammed his cock inside of me.

I bit my lip to keep from crying out as he rode me hard, rubbing his thumb achingly fast across my clit. The water sloshed around us and I was about to lose my hold on the edge of the pool, but Tyler's grip held me firmly in place. His thrusts went deeper and deeper, until it was too much to bear.

"Fuck, beautiful," Tyler grunted. "I'm gonna come."

Hearing him say that was my undoing; it was too late to hold back. The harder he pushed, the harder I came, trembling all around him. My orgasm went on and on, getting stronger the second Tyler dug his fingers into my hips and he yelled out, cock pulsing as he came inside of me.

Breathing hard and jerking with aftershocks, Tyler kissed the back of my neck and rested his head against mine. "I love you," he murmured in my ear.

I squeezed my eyes shut and smiled, hoping the burn behind my lids would go away. Whatever happened, I wasn't going to let my brother take him away from me. "I love you too, Tyler," I whispered. "You have no idea how much."

Gently lifting me up, Tyler turned me around and held my face in his hands. "How did I get so lucky?"

"You didn't," I replied, feeling the burn come back behind my eyes. "I was the one who got lucky."

CHAPTER

24

Kacey

FOR A BRIEF moment after getting out of the pool, I thought I was starting to feel better, but I was wrong. It didn't really hit me until I got in the shower and the hot water wasn't warm enough. I had the chills and my head hurt a little too, but I blamed it on the heat and that I hadn't eaten anything.

"Baby, are you okay?" Tyler asked as he came back into the bedroom, staring at me concerned. He was so hot in his distressed jeans and a light green polo shirt, I almost forgot he just asked me a question.

I watched his reflection in the mirror as he moved closer, trying my best to put on a smile. For the past five minutes, I'd been trying to put on my mascara without jabbing myself in the eye with the wand, but I couldn't stop shaking. "Yeah, I'm fine. I'm just hungry," I assured him. If I could just get some food in my stomach, I'd be okay.

"Well, Cole just texted and said they will be at the restaurant in ten minutes. Do you need more time?"

Swallowing hard, I licked my dry lips and ran my hands through my hair. I was so nauseous. "No, I think I'm good. I'll be dressed and ready to go in three minutes."

Quickly, I closed up my makeup bag and rushed to my suitcase and pulled out my favorite white flared skirt and light blue shirt with my tan wedge sandals. "Do you always walk around in just your bra and underwear at home?" Tyler asked, a sly smile splayed across his lips.

"Maybe," I teased. "Why? Do you like it?"

Taking a seat on the bed, he gawked at my body and licked his lips. "It's hot as hell. Are you sure you don't want to stay at my house for a while?" he added, raising an eyebrow.

After sliding up my skirt, I rolled my eyes and chuckled. "I don't want you getting tired of me, Tyler. Besides, you already see me enough as it is. I work with you now, remember?"

Snatching me around the waist, he held on tight and looked up into my eyes. "I could never get tired of you, beautiful. I just want to see your face every morning when I wake up."

"Let me think about it," I laughed, pushing him away.

He got to his feet and started for the bedroom door, winking at me before leaving the room. "Fine, take your time, but I can't guarantee I won't be showing up at *your* house every night. I'm giving you fair warning."

For the most part, he'd been staying with me anyway.

Honestly, I wanted to take him up on his offer and stay with him, but I was just afraid he would kick me out once he found out about Kyle.

Shivering, I put on my sleeveless shirt and clenched my teeth together to keep them from chattering. *I wish I had a sweater.* In my purse, I knew I had some Tylenol, so I popped a couple in my hand and swallowed them down, praying they helped.

CHAPTER 25

Kacey

INSTEAD OF GOING out on the town and getting wild and crazy, we opted to stay at the hotel and eat in one of the restaurants. It was perfectly fine with me considering I felt and looked like absolute shit. Bree and Cole were waiting for us in the lobby, both laughing and talking like they didn't have a care in the world. However, when Bree saw me, she knew something was wrong. Thankfully, she didn't ask anything in front of the guys.

Once we got seated at our table, I drank some water. I guzzled it down and wanted more.

"Are you sure you're okay," Tyler asked, passing me his water and putting his arm around my shoulders. Eagerly, I took it from him and guzzled it down too, sighing when I was done.

"I don't think she is," Bree cut in. "She looks like shit."

"Gee, *thanks*," I kidded halfheartedly, using most of my energy to keep the water down. I drank it so fast, I was starting to feel sick.

"Bree's right," Tyler agreed. "Well, not about the looking like shit part, but about you being all right. Something's wrong."

"I don't know," I admitted honestly. "I started feeling bad earlier, but I worked through it, thinking it was just the heat. I thought if we kept going it would pass."

Exasperated, Tyler turned my chin so I'd have to look at him. His eyes were despondent. "Why didn't you tell me? We could have taken it easy today."

Sighing, I clasped his hand and leaned into it, exhausted. "Because you made it one of the best days of my life and I didn't want anything to ruin it."

About that time, the waiter came with our food and Tyler let my chin go as my plate was set down in front of me: filet mignon, garlic mashed potatoes, and asparagus. If I wasn't so nauseous I'd be able to eat. Swallowing hard, I closed my eyes and held my breath, hoping it would pass.

"Oh my God, Kacey . . . you're not pregnant are you?" Bree shrieked. "You look like you're about to throw up."

Leave it to Bree to make an announcement to the whole freaking restaurant. I was on the pill and I'd only had sex with Tyler twice—the first time being just yesterday. I wasn't pregnant, and even Tyler knew I wasn't by the way he rolled his eyes.

"I'm not pregnant," I hissed quietly, glaring over to Bree. "I'm just nauseated."

"What other symptoms are you having?" Tyler asked, taking my hand. "Your skin's a little dry, but that could be from the chlorine in the pool. Do you have a headache or anything?"

"Yeah, my head is killing me. That's probably why I'm nauseous, but then again, I haven't really eaten or drank anything all day."

Smelling the food only made my symptoms worse and before I could say another word, I bolted out of my seat and ran straight for the bathroom. Thank God I noticed where it was when we walked into the restaurant. Slamming open the door, I barreled into the stall and collapsed onto my knees, throwing up every ounce of water I just drank. What was my problem?

Knowing I didn't have anything else in my stomach, I flushed the toilet and slowly got to my feet. My whole body ached and all I wanted to do was go to bed and sleep for a week. Once I looked at myself in the mirror, I gasped. I looked pale and my eyes sunken and dark.

About that time, Bree rushed into the bathroom and before I knew it my knees gave out. She caught me before I could stumble onto the floor.

"Thank . . . you," I sputtered.

"Kace, what's wrong with you?" she cried. "You almost look drunk. Have you had any alcohol today?"

Once I could stand without falling over, Bree hesitantly let me go, but kept her hand on my arm. "No, no alcohol. In fact . . ."

"In fact, what?" Bree commanded.

"I haven't had *anything* to drink today. We were so busy, I didn't even eat or drink. I just kept going."

Bree huffed and held my arm tighter while leading

me toward the door. "And you wonder what's wrong with you. You're dehydrated, dumb ass. We need to get you pumped with fluids like now. Dehydration isn't something to mess around with. You should know better than that."

And I did know better, I was just too wrapped up in the day to even think about taking care of myself. Opening the bathroom door, Bree put her arm around my waist to give me support. I couldn't believe how being dehydrated really did make you feel like death, it was almost like the flu.

"Thanks, Bree. I probably need to call it a night. I feel bad ruining everyone's fun."

"Oh, whatever. You know Tyler will be more than happy to have you all to himself, even if he has to spend it nursing you back to health. I'll just take Cole back to our room and nurse him back to health too. That man is insatiable."

Bree always had a way of getting a smile on my face, even when I felt horrible. However, that smile didn't last long when I looked over at our table. "You have got to be kidding me," I hissed.

"What is it?" Bree asked, alarmed. "Do you need to throw up again?"

"No, but I think my headache just got worse." I pointed to our table and when she looked, her eyes went wide.

"Is that who I think it is?" she asked.

Clenching my teeth together, I closed my eyes and nodded, my blood boiling in my veins.

CHAPTER

26

TYLER

"WELL, LOOK WHO it is," a voice called out. "I didn't know you guys were staying at this hotel."

I froze at the voice and Cole's eyes went wide. Gabriella walked up and sat down beside me. I didn't know she was going to be there either.

As always, she looked the same with her midnight black hair and bright green eyes, wearing a pair of jeans and tight pink T-shirt. It was hard to believe that a little over a month ago we were lovers, and now our time together was just a distant memory.

"Gabriella," I greeted, turning to her with a hesitant smile. Even though we were strictly friends, I knew Kacey would get pissed if she saw Gabriella sitting beside of me. I never thought the day would come when I didn't want

Gabriella around. Kacey and I were getting closer. She trusted me, or at least I hoped she did.

"Who are you here with?" I asked, looking around the restaurant. "Is your brother here?"

"No, he's coming in first thing tomorrow. I'm here with Bradley. The Twins of Terror are also in town, but they're staying somewhere else."

"How was your visit to see Ashleigh? Have you told Ryley about her yet?"

"No, but I probably will. Something's up with her though. I don't know why she doesn't want me to tell him what happened."

"Well, whatever her reasons are, it's not just her in this anymore. She's messing with Ryley's feelings too."

Eyes wide, Gabriella sat back in the chair and laughed. "Wow, look at you being all philosophical. You seem different somehow. What's changed?"

Everything.

When I didn't answer right away, she lifted her brows curiously and smiled. "Well, whatever it is I think it suits you." She looked down at all four plates of food and whistled. "Either you boys are loading up before tomorrow's fights or you have guests. Which is it?"

Cole grinned mischievously at me, not thinking I would tell Gabriella the truth. Little did he know, I didn't care if Gabriella knew I was with someone else. Just as I was about to explain, Bree trudged forward, struggling to hold Kacey up with her arm around her waist.

"What the hell's going on?" I demanded, rushing out of my seat. Kacey looked worse than when she left the table.

Bree passed her to me and I lifted her into my arms,

cradling her to my chest. "She's dehydrated," Bree explained, grabbing her glass of water off the table. "We figured it out in the bathroom. She hasn't drank anything all day."

Looking down at Kacey, it all made sense. "What did you do with that bottle of water I gave you after we went golfing? I told you to drink it."

"And I was about to, but then I got *distracted* and never drank it," she replied weakly. Finally, she looked over at Gabriella and stiffened, then turned her glare to me, her jaw tense. She had no reason to be angry, but if the situation was turned, I'd be furious if she was talking to one of her ex's. If only she knew there was nothing to worry about.

"You know, if you can't keep any water down we're going to have to take you to the hospital." Bree passed me her glass of water and held it to Kacey's lips.

"Drink," I commanded. She did as I said, never taking her eyes off of mine, and took a few sips, then a few more until the glass was empty.

"Is there anything you need me to do?" Gabriella asked, genuine concern showing on her face. She got to her feet and came to my side. Kacey stiffened even more. "If she's dehydrated you need to make sure she drinks as much as she can, but slow so that she doesn't throw it up."

"I know," I told her, stepping to the side, holding Kacey tighter. "I'm going to take her back to the room so she can get some rest. We had a busy day, I think a little relaxation is in order."

Gabriella nodded at Bree and Cole before turning back to me, sneaking a quick glance at Kacey. By the look in her eyes, she knew Kacey was more than just one of my groupies. However, I could tell she was happy for me by the small smile splayed across her lips.

"Well, you all take care and I hope she gets to feeling better. Dehydration isn't fun. But I guess I'll see you tomorrow at the fight."

"We'll be there."

She smiled at us all and waved before taking a seat at the bar, where none other than Bradley Thompson sat glaring at me. Some things would never change. He didn't like any of Gabriella's friends, especially me because I was the one who took her away from him. But now he had her back.

"Let's go to our room, beautiful," I murmured in Kacey's ear. Her eyes were closed, but I knew she wasn't asleep from how tense she was in my arms. "She's gone, Kacey. You have nothing to worry about with her. You are the one I want to be with."

She relaxed just a little bit, but not much.

"Tyler, I'm going to have Kacey's food boxed up and we'll bring it up to you," Bree offered. "She needs to eat something."

I nodded and started out of the restaurant. When I got to the room, I carried Kacey straight to the bedroom and laid her down so I could fetch her a bottle of water. Lying beside of her, I pulled her into my arms and brushed the hair off of her face. "Are you hungry?"

"No," she whispered. "I'm just really tired."

Opening the bottle of water, I lifted her up in my arms and pressed it to her lips. "I know you're tired, but you need to drink more . . . and I also know you're pissed about Gabriella."

Sighing, she opened her lips and slowly drank half of

the bottle before lying back down on my chest and closing her eyes. "She's always going to be there," she whispered regretfully. "I can't compete with her constantly being around you."

Holding her tighter, I caressed my fingers up and down her back and kissed her forehead. "You're wrong," I murmured. "She can't compete with you."

I was hoping she would talk to me or at least acknowledge that she heard me, but once her breathing started to slow, I knew she was asleep. I needed to find a way to convince her.

By late morning, I was dressed and ready to go to the arena, but Kacey was still asleep. She had gotten up in the middle of the night to drink another bottle of water and went straight back to sleep, without saying a word. I could still feel the tension between us.

Her skin looked normal, not pale and definitely not clammy and cold like it was last night, which made me feel a little bit more comfortable. I still hated leaving for the arena without talking to her.

"Do you want me to wake her up?" Bree asked. "She's going to be pissed if we leave without her." Bree and Cole had been sitting in the living room for the past twenty minutes, while I kept watch over Kacey, hoping she'd open her eyes.

I didn't want her angry, but more importantly I didn't

want her being miserable in the stands with screaming people all around. "Yeah, but she needs her rest," I interjected. "If you've ever been dehydrated before I'm pretty sure you'd choose rest over sitting in a crowded arena. I can only hope she'll understand why we left her."

In her hands, she held a black and green MMA Pride T-shirt that matched the one she was wearing. Setting it down on the coffee table, she agreed, "I understand. If you don't want her mad at you, you can always suck up by ordering her favorite Godiva chocolates. It is the way to win any girl's heart."

Cole snorted and threw his hands in the air. "And why didn't you tell me this sooner?"

"Because," she explained, smiling wickedly up at him, "I had to make you work for it." Laughing, she kissed him on the cheek and then turned back to me, her smile waning. "I just know she'll want to see you fight, Tyler. But I understand that we need to leave her alone."

"She'll get plenty of chances to see him fight, Bree," Cole replied, putting his arm around her shoulders. "You, however, are going to get to see me kick Pax's ass tonight." By the excited gleam in his eyes, he was ready for his fight against Paxton Emerson, one of Kyle's friends.

"Let's hope so," Bree agreed. "I'm tired of seeing your ass get handed to you by Tyler every day."

"Have you seen this guy?" Cole asked, pointing at me, laughing. "He's fucking huge, just like his father. There's no way in hell I'll ever beat him." He turned his gaze toward me. "Speaking of which, is he coming tonight?"

"Yeah, he's in town. He called about thirty minutes ago to tell me he was on his way to the arena. My agent's going to meet us there too."

Both had just landed at the airport and they were going to ride over together. Instead of staying overnight, my father decided to get a flight home directly after the fight so he could get back to my mother.

"Why don't you guys head on and I'll see you at the arena in a few minutes. I need to do something first," I told them.

"All right, man," Cole replied, slapping me on the shoulder. "We'll see you there. Don't be too late because you know how your dad gets."

I knew all too well that my father wasn't a patient man. Regrettably, neither was I. "I won't be late," I promised.

Putting his hand on the small of Bree's back, Cole nodded and winked before opening the door, and shutting it silently behind them. Everything was quiet when I waltzed over to open the door to the bedroom. Kacey was buried underneath the covers and had a hand tucked underneath her cheek as she laid on her side.

Knowing she needed to eat when she woke up, I called room service and ordered an assortment of fruits and crackers with various cheeses. I even added in a special request; something I knew she would like.

Grabbing a small pad of paper and a pen, I sat down on one of the bar stools to write a note. I quietly left it on the pillow beside Kacey. This way, when she woke up she'd see it. Slowly, I bent down to kiss her cheek. Her skin felt warm as I trailed my fingers down the side of her face, hoping she'd wake up. *No such luck.*

Her food arrived just as I was ready to leave, so I tipped the young lady and put the tray in the refrigerator to keep it cool. Hopefully, the special request I ordered would soften her up from being angry at me for leaving her. Now all I had to do was handle another situation. Reaching for the phone in my pocket, I pulled it out and dialed the number I needed.

"Hey, Tyler."

Taking a deep breath, I let it out slowly and replied, "We need to talk."

The line went quiet for a few seconds. "Okay, when?"

"Tonight after my fight. Come to my room."

"I'll be there."

CHAPTER 27

Kacey

I HAD FELT his hands on my face, and wanted to wake up, but my body didn't let me. It wanted more time to rest, to rejuvenate for the past couple of years of no sleep and constant working. There always came a breaking point and I think I'd hit mine. However, now I had never felt so refreshed in my life, but I was starving, my stomach growling and cramping from lack of food.

"Tyler," I called, rubbing my eyes and feeling my mascara crumble beneath my fingertips. As I sat up in bed and pulled off the covers, I looked down to see that I was still in my white skirt and blue shirt from yesterday. What the hell? There was a note on Tyler's pillow so I snatched it up and got out of bed.

"Tyler," I called out again. Opening the letter, I sat

down on the edge of the bed and read it.

Kacey,

I'm sorry to leave you like this, but I didn't want to wake you when I knew you needed the rest. You can be pissed at me all you want. As long as you're better, that's all I care about. I ordered you some food to eat because you're going to want it when you wake up. It'll be in the refrigerator. Rest up and I'll see you tonight when I get back. I love you, beautiful.

Tyler

"You have *got* to be kidding me," I growled, looking over at the clock on the nightstand. It was closing in on seven o'clock. "Holy shit, I'm going to miss his fight!"

I had slept for almost a whole day and didn't realize it. Tyler had a lot to make up for once all of this was over. Quickly, I rushed into the kitchen and opened the refrigerator to find a tray of fresh fruits and cheeses, along with a box wrapped in silver ribbon with *Godiva* written on top.

Pulling it all out, I set the tray down on the counter beside the MMA Pride T-shirt I assumed was mine. I ate a few blocks of cheese with wheat crackers, along with some fresh ripened strawberries. Afterward, I opened the box of chocolates and ate one of my favorite truffles filled with caramel, and then another one for good measure.

"You're a smart one, Tyler Rushing. But chocolate can't get you out of everything." Once I swallowed the chocolaty goodness, I closed my eyes and moaned. "Well, maybe it can."

After eating a few more strawberries and grapes—and of course, a couple chocolates—I rushed to the bathroom and took a quick shower. Knowing I didn't have much time, I put on the black MMA Pride T-shirt with its bright green logo, a pair of jeans, and black flip flops. Sadly, there wasn't much I could do with my hair so I threw it up into a high ponytail and brushed some mineral powder on my face along with some lip gloss on my lips.

I was ready to go.

I tried to call Tyler, but got his voicemail. I also tried to call Bree and got the same result. The chance of them hearing their phones in the loud arena were slim to none. With my phone in my hand, I grabbed some money out of my purse and the hotel room key before rushing down to the front desk so they could call me a cab.

It didn't take long for the taxi to show up. It was a yellow, Chevrolet HHR with a bald man in the front seat. "Where you off to?" he asked as I got in.

"The U.S. Airways Center," I told him. "I'm going to watch the UFC fights tonight."

"Ah, yes, I love watching those on television when I get the chance. At least you'll make it in time for the last couple of fights."

"That's what I'm hoping. I have some friends fighting tonight. I don't want to miss them." Usually, the Heavyweight fights were toward the end so hopefully I'd make it in time.

"Don't worry, sweetheart, I'll get you there in no time. It's just a couple of minutes. If you need a ride back to the hotel, call this number." He passed back his business card with the name of the cab company and his number.

"Thank you. I appreciate it," I said, taking the card. About five minutes later, he pulled up as far as he could to the front and I slipped him some money for the ride and put his card in my back pocket.

"Have fun," he called as I shut the door.

I rushed up to the top of the stairs and waited in line at the ticket counter. Hopefully, I could give them my name and be let in.

When I got up to the counter, the young employee gave me her best forced smile. She had bright blonde hair just like me, but her dark roots were grown out about an inch and she was wearing way too much makeup. "Just one admission?" she asked.

"Actually, I'm wondering if my name is on a list somewhere. I'm with Tyler Rushing—he's one of the fighters. I was supposed to come with him earlier, but due to circumstances out of my control, I couldn't make it."

The girl lifted her eyebrows and then burst out laughing. "I swear you women need to come up with better lines. Do you have any idea how many people say the exact same thing?"

Mouth wide open, I stared at her in shock. First, I couldn't believe that people actually said that, and second, I was being serious and I didn't like being laughed at. "I'm being serious," I said, clenching my teeth. "I'm with Tyler."

She stared at me for a moment before looking pityingly at me. "Look, lady, I'm sorry, but it doesn't work that way. Usually, the fighter's guests go in with them. There's no way I can track down your seat."

The group of people behind me in line snickered and I knew they were laughing at me, at how pathetic I must look trying to say I was dating one of the most highly sought after MMA fighters.

Knowing Tyler wouldn't have his phone with him, I

had no choice but to suck it up and buy a ticket. I didn't care if they thought I was a liar, just as long as I got into the arena.

"Fine, I'll just buy one then," I grumbled impatiently.

Quickly, I gave her the money and got my ticket, only to find my seat was in the damn nosebleed section. Great, they would look like pissed off ants from this vantage point. I would see him on the monitors, but surely at the end, I'd be able to find him and the others.

"Ladies and gentlemen," the announcer began, his voice echoing throughout the arena. "The next fight of the evening is in the Light Heavyweight division. The winner of tonight's match will fight for the title next weekend in Las Vegas."

The crowd rumbled, hooting and hollering their excitement. Picking up my pace, I rushed through the throngs of people and found my section, stepping on a few feet as I tried to get to my seat. Cole's fight was next.

The announcer waved at the people to get them calmed down. He was older, probably in his mid-fifties, his light brown hair slicked back. Once the noise leveled off he continued, "Okay, so let's introduce our next fighter. Coming all the way from Las Vegas, Nevada, *Cole* . . . *The Bruiser . . . Beeennnnnnnneeettt!*"

Jumping to my feet, I screamed out Cole's name and whistled as loud as I could when he walked down the aisle toward the ring, strutting to his fight song, *I Will Not Bow* by Breaking Benjamin. From what I could tell, he was wearing a pair of blue and yellow shorts and a pair of blue gloves wrapped around his hands. I was hoping to recognize Bree down by the ring, but there were too many people. Once Cole got into the ring and did his rounds, the announcer called out the next fighter. My mouth dropped open when they called out . . . Paxton Emerson.

"Oh my God," I breathed, sitting down in my seat.

I didn't know Pax was fighting tonight. I hadn't seen him in so long, not since I moved away from our hometown. Dressed in his usual black shorts and black gloves, Paxton looked like a dark angel with his black hair and tattoos down both arms. One word came to mind when I looked at him . . . dangerous. Out of all of my brother's friends, he was the only one I cared about. He had been *my* friend before he joined up with my brother. Actually, we were more than friends at one time. I never understood why he chose to hang around my brother because he wasn't evil like Kyle.

My chest tightened, the guilt of my inner thoughts causing my stomach to roll. I wanted Cole to win, but I didn't want Pax to lose. Once the bell rang, I nervously sat on the edge of my seat as both attacked, jabbing and blocking each other's blows. Paxton had gotten good over time, much better than a couple of years ago. His body even proved it by how muscular and toned it was.

There were only forty-five seconds left in round one, but when the sound of the final hit echoed throughout the arena, I had a feeling it was all over. Gasping in horror, I watched as Paxton's fist connected to the side of Cole's head and he fell limp to the floor, body smacking against the mat.

Half of the crowd roared while the other half kept screaming for Cole to get up. Unfortunately, he was knocked out cold. I held my breath as the medics rushed into the ring. When they gave the thumbs up, I breathed a sigh of relief. Fighting was dangerous and many people have been seriously hurt and even killed in the ring. However, when my brother fights, I honestly don't think he cares if he accidentally kills someone. In fact, I was pretty sure he'd be proud.

Paxton, on the other hand, was genuinely concerned for Cole's well-being. Kneeling down on the mat, he waited with the medics while Cole finally became responsive. He even helped Cole to his feet. The crowd clapped and screamed their encouragements as Cole was led out of the ring, licking his wounds. He wasn't going to be happy he lost.

The announcer congratulated Paxton and lifted his arm. "Ladies and gentleman, I give you tonight's winner, *Paxton . . . The Avenger . . . Emmmeeerrrsssooonnn!*"

I clapped and whistled for Paxton as he made his rounds and left the ring, disappearing into the crowd. Out of everyone back home, I missed him the most. When I left, I changed my cell number and basically disappeared. I had to do what I needed to do in order to get away from my family and start fresh.

"All right, are you ready for the final fight of the evening?" the announcer asked, circling around in the ring.

"*Yes!*" the whole arena replied, everyone's booming voices made the stands tremble.

"Now that's what I like to hear. Again, whoever wins this match will go on to Las Vegas next weekend to fight for the Heavyweight title. So first up, let's hear it for *Joshua . . . The Tamer . . . MaaacccEnnntttiiirrreee!*"

Joshua walked out in a pair of shimmering gold shorts with his blond hair in cornrows. He used to be the Heavyweight champion, until my brother beat him and took away the title. After that, Matt Reynolds beat my brother and kept the title ever since—until now.

It was Tyler's turn to win it.

"And finally, I want to introduce you to our last fighter for the evening. Let's hear it for *Tyler . . . The Terror . . . Ruuussshhhiiinnnggg!*"

The room crackled in energy as *Bad Company* by Five Finger Death Punch, played across the loud speakers. My heart thumped wild in my chest the second he walked out of the curtains and down the aisle. I wanted to be down there with him, to have him look at me and smile when he entered the ring. Alas, he had no idea I was there. His father and his agent took up the rear, and they each took turns speaking to Tyler before he gave them a nod and jumped into the ring.

Tyler and Joshua met in the center and bumped gloves before getting into their fighting stance. As always, the arena went deathly silent as we waited on the bell to ring. When it did, the whole crowd exploded as both guys tensed and started toward each other. Tyler swung first and hit Joshua on the right cheek, and then Joshua countered quickly by connecting with Tyler's jaw. The sound was deafening and made my body hurt, yet the men didn't seem fazed by it. I had never been in a fist fight before, but I could imagine how horrible it must hurt to get hit with all of that power. They fought relentlessly and never once stopped.

Ding, ding, ding.

Joshua was tired, but Tyler had paced himself quite nicely, conserving his energy. His father seemed extremely pleased with the outcome. After a quick break and some water, it was time for round two.

"Come on, Tyler, I'll give you the ride of your life if

you win," a woman shouted behind me.

When I looked back, there were about four women, all around my age, holding up signs for Tyler, giggling. The girl who shouted was actually pretty, but she had too much makeup on her heart-shaped face, and her clothes were way too tight for her curvy body. I wanted to tell her to fuck off, but I reminded myself this was the kind of shit I'd have to deal with, dating a fighter like him. I saw it all of the time with my brother. Women were constantly throwing themselves at him.

"Sorry to disappoint you, Jenny, but he must be seriously dating someone," one of the girls responded. Immediately, I faced forward and leaned back in my seat so I could listen.

"What do you mean he's dating someone?"

"Apparently, he's not letting any more girls into his room after the fights. One of my girlfriends tried to get back there and was told to turn around and leave. The same thing happened to her when she tried to get into Matt Reynolds' room two years ago . . . and now he's married."

"Well, shit. That sucks donkey balls," Jenny sulked.

Putting a hand over my mouth, I held in my snicker. It was pathetic how some of these women were. Turning around, I sighed and nodded my head. "Yeah, it sucks a big fat one, but I think it is true," I began. "I'm staying at the same hotel as him and I saw him with another girl. They looked pretty cozy together."

"Fuck," Jenny snarled. "That's no fun."

Shrugging my shoulders, I turned back around to watch Tyler, grinning from ear to ear. He was still pumped, pummeling Joshua with everything he had. Once Joshua was on the mat and close to tapping out, the bell rang for the end of round two. He almost had him.

Looking at Joshua on the monitors, he had blood pouring down the left side of his face from a cut above his eyebrow and his left eye was almost swollen shut. Tyler, on the other hand, only had a bruise on his right jawline. His father grinned with pride and nodded in approval, which made Tyler smile in return. Steven Rushing was hard on him, but I knew it was because he loved his son and only wanted the best.

Ding, ding, ding. It was the third and final round.

"Come on, Tyler!" I shouted. If only he could hear me.

Smacking his gloves together, he smiled slyly at Joshua and went for the kill. It was as if all of his energy came out all at one time. Sweeping Joshua's feet out from under him, he fell to the mat and Tyler pounced, wrapping his arm around his neck, holding tight. About two seconds later, Joshua tapped out . . . it was over. Immediately, Tyler let Joshua go and jumped to his feet, circling around the ring with his arms in the air. The crowd went crazy, yelling and chanting his name over and over.

"Tyler! Tyler! Tyler!"

I even shouted it too; I was so happy for him. Getting to my feet, I whistled as loud as I could when the announcer lifted Tyler's arm and announced him the victor. His next fight was for the title, with my brother. Sooner or later, I had to tell him the truth. *He loves me and I love him—it has to be enough.*

It didn't take long to figure out where the dressing rooms were for the guys. All I had to do was follow the trail of skanky women. Bree was nowhere to be found because she was probably already in the room with Cole, cheering him up. I could only imagine how she planned on doing that. He had to be bummed about losing the fight to Paxton.

There were so many people walking down the hall, women and fighters alike, I couldn't figure out which room was Tyler's. There were no signs on the doors. Pulling out my phone, I texted both Bree and Tyler and told them I was at the arena and I didn't know where to go. Patiently, I waited on one of them to text me back, but then someone caught my eye. Down the hall, I saw Gabriella, dressed in a white sundress with her long, dark hair pulled high into a ponytail.

What the fuck? *Tell me she's not knocking on Tyler's door.*

My stomach coiled into knots and I held my breath as I waited on whoever was behind the door to answer. *Please* don't let it be Tyler. Slowly, the door opened just a crack and when I saw who was there I gritted my teeth tight, the pain exploding into my head. It was Tyler, wearing only a white towel around his waist. Blood boiling, I watched as he opened the door and she walked in, kissing him on the cheek as she passed.

Frozen in place, I clenched my hands into tight fists

and felt the anger boil through my veins. Before Tyler shut the door, he stopped and slowly directed his attention to me. Immediately, he glanced into his room and then back at me, wide-eyed and shaking his head. "Kacey, *no*," he shouted. "It's not what you think."

Turning on my heel, I glared at him one more time over my shoulder before taking off down the hall.

"Kacey, stop! Please, beautiful . . ."

I didn't stop, I kept going. The last thing I wanted was to be made a fool of in front of everyone—possibly people who knew my brother and who could recognize me. Instead, I kept running in hopes of getting as far away as I could, away from Tyler's voice screaming my name.

Looking back, I didn't see him behind me, but when I turned around, I ran right into a set of arms that closed tightly around my waist.

"Kacey, what the hell are you doing here?"

Immediately, I froze and glanced up into the same set of sea green eyes I used to look at almost every day of my life. "Paxton," I breathed.

Tyler shouted my name and Paxton instinctively held me tighter, protectively. "What's going on?" he demanded, glaring down at me.

He looked like he was about to leave anyway since he was dressed in a black T-shirt and jeans with his bag slung over his shoulder. Quickly, I pushed him toward one of the doors. "I can explain, but first, I need you to get me out of here."

"Is that Rushing calling after you?"

"Yes, now let's go!"

Keeping his arm around me, he rushed me toward the door and out into the heat-filled night. What the hell was I going to do now?

CHAPTER

28

TYLER

"KACEY!"

Everyone stared at me as I raced down the hallway in just a towel. At this moment, I believed I had the shittiest luck of anyone in the world. Out of all of the times Kacey could've seen me, it had to be the moment I let Gabriella walk into my room, with only a towel around my waist.

By the time I turned the corner at the end of the hall, she was gone. "Goddammit," I hissed, running my hands angrily through my wet hair. I had hoped to be out of the shower and dressed by the time Gabriella showed up, but unluckily, that didn't happen.

"Tyler, what's going on?" she asked, placing a hand on my bare shoulder.

Instead of answering, I slid away from her touch and

rushed back down the hall to my room. Quickly, I grabbed my bag and pulled out a plain gray T-shirt, my jeans, and a pair of boxers. *I have to get the hell out of here.*

"It's Kacey," I snapped impatiently, throwing on my clothes. "She saw you come in here and I can only imagine what the fuck is going through her mind." It also didn't help that Gabriella was provocatively dressed either.

"So she knows about us?" she asked.

"Yes, and seeing you come in here didn't help matters any. I've tried to tell her nothing is going on between us, but obviously I'm not giving her any reasons to believe me. I left her behind at the hotel to get better, and then I invite you into my room. How would that look to you?"

After sliding on my shoes and grabbing my bag, swinging it angrily over my shoulder, I was ready to go. Gabriella crossed her arms over her chest and stood in front of the door, her green eyes weary when she looked up at me. "Are you saying what I think you're saying?"

Sighing, I reached for the door handle and nodded. We had a history together and had been friends for a while, but sometimes good things have to come to an end—our friendship being one of them. "I'm afraid so, Gabby. I can't be around you without causing problems with her. She means too much to me. From now on, we have to keep our distance."

Sadly, she smiled and stepped out of the way so I could open the door. I rushed out, but she stopped me before I could take another step. "Do you love her?"

Over my shoulder, I looked back at her standing in the doorway. She had changed so much in the last couple of years, turning into a woman and a fighter. She was my past, and now I needed my future. "Yes," I answered in all seriousness. "I'm in love with her."

"Then stop wasting time and go find her."

"Are you going to be okay?" I asked.

Rolling her eyes, she snorted and waved me off. "Please, I'm a Reynolds. There's nothing I can't handle."

I used to think that about myself too, but now with Kacey, I couldn't help but second guess everything I did. She was angry with me and I had no clue how to handle it. I was about to find out though.

CHAPTER 29

Kacey

ONCE WE GOT into Paxton's rental car, he started it up and headed down the highway.

"I need some answers," he demanded. "What are you doing in Arizona and why was Tyler Rushing coming after you? Does your brother know you're out here?"

Leaning my head against the seat, I blew out an angry breath and closed my eyes. "No, he doesn't know, and I'd appreciate it if you didn't tell him. Tyler, on the other hand, is a different story." Paxton's loyalties always leaned toward me, but he was still my brother's friend. I had to tread carefully.

"A different story," he scoffed, staring at my profile. "Please tell me you're not fucking him." When I didn't answer, he took my chin and made me face him. As a kid,

I was never good at lying and he knew it. He could always see it in my eyes. Sighing, he let me go and gripped the steering wheel, knuckles turning white. "I can't *believe* this shit. You're actually fucking him, aren't you? I thought you were smarter than this, Kacey."

I thought I was too.

A tear escaped the corner of my eye and I hastily wiped it away, keeping my gaze on the prickly cacti rushing past as Paxton sped down the road. My heart hurt, like thorns spearing through my chest. "I tried to stay away, Pax, but I couldn't. He kept pursuing me and I gave in. When Nana died, he never left my side. I wouldn't have been able to make it through without him."

Paxton's eyes went wide. "Your grandmother died? When? You should've called me, Kace. I would've been there for you."

"She died a couple of weeks ago, and no, you wouldn't have," I snapped. "You were probably too busy getting into trouble."

"Well, if you wouldn't have changed your phone number, I would've called to fill you in. After you disappeared to Las Vegas I cut ties with your brother."

Gasping, I turned to face him, his expression serious. "What? Why?"

We stopped at a stoplight and he looked over at me, piercing me with his stare, his voice gentle. "You should already know why, Kacey. I only stayed around because of you. Yes, I got into some trouble, but I'm over that now. When you left, I put all of my concentration into training. I haven't spoken to your brother in almost a year."

"Really? Shit, I didn't know. *I've* barely spoken to my brother in the past year."

Paxton pulled the car off to the side of the road and parked. "Okay, before we go any further, where are you staying?"

"We're at the Camelback Inn," I replied, pointing down the road.

Rolling his eyes, he snorted and shook his head. "That's where I'm staying too. So you and Tyler are spending the weekend together, huh? *Great*," he added sarcastically. "I bet he'll love seeing you with me. Do you want me to take you back right now?"

My phone vibrated with an incoming call, but I ignored it. "Yes, please. It's probably best I get back and get my things before Tyler gets there."

Nodding, Paxton pulled out and started down the road. Thankfully, we were only a couple miles from the hotel. "You can stay with me if you want and I can drive you to the airport in the morning."

Before I could reply, my phone buzzed with an incoming text. Curiosity got the better of me, so I huffed and opened the message.

Tyler: Where are you? We need to talk. Nothing happened between me and Gabriella. From now on she's going to keep her distance and stay away. You have to trust me.

Paxton glanced down at my phone and his eyes hardened. "The last thing you need to do is trust him. I know there's something going on between those two, or at least there used to be."

"How do you know that?" I asked.

"Because," he growled, "when he found out I was interested in Gabriella, he made sure to tell me to stay the fuck away from her. Needless to say, I don't listen very well."

"Wait, *what*?" I hissed, anger coursing through my veins. "You actually like her?" Throwing my hands in the air, I shook my head incredulously. "Okay, this shit is starting to piss me off. First, I have to deal with her and Tyler, and now you. It was bad enough watching her go into his room with just a towel around his waist. I can only imagine what they were going to do in there."

"Is that why you left the arena?"

I hesitated for only a few seconds before nodding my head. "Yes, and now I'm wondering if he still has feelings for her."

What was it with this chick? All the guys were so hard up about her. Even my brother wanted her.

"I highly doubt they were doing anything, Kacey. Gabriella isn't that type of girl. Besides, she's too busy with her pansy-ass baseball player boyfriend to make time for anyone else."

It didn't matter if she had a boyfriend or not. It still didn't change the fact she was going to be alone with Tyler, wearing a short, skimpy dress. I wasn't stupid. "How do you know she's not like that?" I asked. "And where is her boyfriend while she's in a room with a half-naked ex?"

"I don't know about all of that, but I do know he's here at the hotel. I've seen them together. Gabriella and I work out at the same gym and when we met, I thought we got along great. Then everything went in the shitter when she found out I was friends with your brother. She didn't want to have anything to do with me afterward. I kept telling her I'm not like him, but she's hardheaded. I'll wear her down though."

I rolled my eyes. "That would be great, maybe it

would keep her away from Tyler," I mumbled, clenching my teeth.

Groaning, Paxton ran his hands through his dark hair. "Jesus Christ, Kacey, what the hell is wrong with you?" he spat, his deep voice full of concern. "You're not just fucking him, you're in love, aren't you? Do you know what Kyle would do if he found out about this? Does Tyler even know he's your brother?"

Swallowing hard, I closed my eyes and shook my head. "No. I was going to tell him this week before the title fight. I was afraid he'd think I was just like my brother. I knew he'd hate me once I told him."

"But you're *not* like your brother, Kacey. You deserve so much better than Tyler. He's just as bad as the rest of the fighters. No matter what though, you know this is going to end badly, right? Tyler fucking hates me and if he finds out we have a past, along with dumping the shit on him about your brother, it's going to be one hell of a mess."

Shrugging, I lifted my arms in the air. "I don't think it matters anyway. It's probably over. If Gabriella doesn't mess everything up, I'm pretty sure my brother will. He's already started playing his tricks on me."

"What do you mean?"

We finally arrived at the hotel, and luckily, I didn't see Tyler's truck. *Thank God for small favors.* Paxton pulled us into the parking lot, shut off the car, and we both got out. Knowing my luck, Tyler would pull up any minute and see us together.

Bumping me in the shoulder, Paxton lifted his brows when I looked up at him. "What did he do, Kacey?"

When we got inside of the hotel, I took his hand and

pulled him to a secluded corner so we wouldn't be out in the open. "What doesn't he do?" I grumbled. "Kyle's been sneaking around trying to barge into my life. I've been ignoring his calls, so he said he's going to find ways to get updates on me. Well, just the other week he did that by using someone else. I'm pretty sure you know him."

Paxton stiffened, his jaw tense. "Who?"

"Liam. Kyle had gotten him to hit on me at the bar I worked at, so he could take me on a date. That way, he could ask me questions and Kyle would know what was going on."

"And did you go on the date?" he snapped.

"Yeah, I did, but when Tyler found out, he called to warn me. If it wasn't for him, I don't know what would've happened. I bitched Liam out and then called to let Kyle have it."

Paxton put his hands on my shoulders and looked down into my eyes, his voice laced in fury. "That fucker didn't touch you, did he? I can't believe your cocksucking brother would do that. Liam's worse than him."

"Tell me about it. I heard the stories."

Sighing, Paxton pulled me into his arms and held me tight. I laid my head on his chest and wrapped my arms around his waist, wishing like hell that my life could be easier.

"I'm sorry about your grandmother, Kace," he murmured softly, releasing me from his hold. "I want you to call me if you need anything, okay? You don't have to worry about your brother with me."

"Thanks, Pax. I'll text you my new number."

He smiled down at me, but then it disappeared when his gaze lingered on something behind me.

"What?" I asked. Turning around, I saw it was none other than Gabriella walking through the door. I half expected Tyler to be with her, but he wasn't, which only meant he probably wasn't far behind. Paxton watched her until she disappeared around the corner. I'd seen that same look many years ago, when he was interested in me.

"Just to give you a heads up, I think my brother wants her too."

Instantly, his nostrils flared and he glared down at me. "You can't be fucking serious. Is he going to try anything with her?"

"I don't know," I replied truthfully. "But if you talk to her, I'd warn her. After what he did to her brother, I know she must loathe him. And when Kyle wants something, he'll go after it. I think after that whole fight with Jaden, it really got him hard up."

"Well, whatever happens I'm not going to let him anywhere near her. I'll do what I have to do, but I'm not going to let your brother fucking touch her."

About that time, I turned to look at the door and Tyler stormed in, heading straight for the hallway leading to our room. Paxton saw him too and nodded his head for me to go, but Tyler turned his head and saw us, his face full of rage.

"Fuck me," Paxton grumbled, pulling me behind him. "Here we go . . ."

"Pax, what are you doing? He's not going to hurt me."

"That may be so, Kace, but he's a fighter and you're talking to me. He doesn't know we know each other."

Shit, this isn't going to be good.

I had to admit, it was sexy as hell seeing the jealous

gleam in his eyes, but it was also scary with the way his muscles tightened, coiled for a fight.

"If you don't get your fucking hands off of her this very second, I'm going to rip your head off," Tyler hissed low as he approached.

Paxton let me go and held his arms out to the side, part way to keep me shielded and to also show he didn't want any trouble. In the past, he would rise to any occasion to fight, but now he was more responsible. I liked the new Pax.

"It's not like that, Rushing. Kacey and I were just talking. I'm not going to let her go with you until you calm down."

"Like hell you're not!"

Stepping out to the side, I rolled my eyes and put myself between them, placing my hands on both of their chests. "Guys, this is ridiculous. The last thing we need is to get kicked out of the hotel." Tyler put his hand on mine and clasped it firmly with his, carefully scrutinizing Paxton's movements.

Sighing, I turned to Pax and felt Tyler tense underneath my touch. "Pax, I'll be fine. You have nothing to worry about."

Finally, he tore his stare away from Tyler and looked down at me. "All right, I'll go. Just make sure to text me if you need me."

I nodded in reply and wished like hell I could get them separated. The tension in the room was unbearable and I wouldn't be able to stand it much longer. Thankfully, Paxton took the higher road and backed down, turning on his heel and marching off. I was afraid to look at Tyler for fear of what I'd see, because now he would know something was up between me and Paxton.

With that tension added on to the Gabriella situation, I'd say this night was going to be one hell of a fight.

Tyler's hand tightened around mine and before I could say anything he pulled me down the hall toward our room, the energy around him crackling like fire.

"Tyler, slow down," I ordered hesitantly. His grip on my hand didn't hurt, but he wasn't talking and I didn't like it.

"You said you didn't want us to get kicked out of the hotel, so I'm taking this to our room."

My heart sped out of control and my hands began to sweat. I was so nervous my stomach twisted and turned. I didn't know what was going to happen. I was still angry with him about Gabriella, but now he was angry with me about Paxton. When we got to the room, he had the key out, ready to unlock the door. My mind was set.

I refused to let him win this fight.

CHAPTER 30

Kacey

AS SOON AS the door slammed shut, I stood firm with my arms crossed over my chest and my head held high.

"What the fuck were you doing with Paxton?" he shouted.

"Don't you dare turn this around on me, Tyler. I wasn't the one inviting him into my room with only a towel wrapped around my waist. I'm sorry by the way. I didn't mean to crash your party by showing up to your fight."

Closing his eyes, he hung his head and chuckled, only it wasn't a humorous sound. "Of course, you would see it that way." Lifting his head, he took a step forward, and I countered by taking one back. "When are you going to realize that I want you, and only you?"

I shrugged. "I don't know. You kind of have a hard

time showing it when Gabriella's around. If this is the way it's going to be, I don't think I can handle it, Tyler. It's not easy seeing you with someone you used to be intimate with."

When I tried to walk off, he reached for my hand and pulled me close, holding me around the waist. "I understand that, Kacey," he murmured. "But you need to let me explain. I called Gabriella before the fight, and told her to come to my room after."

"Why?"

He brought his hand up to my face and brushed his thumb across my lips, making me tremble. "Because I knew with her being in my life, it would only cause problems between us. I told her she was my past, and that you were my future. I choose you."

He closed the distance between us and I melted against him, wrapping my arms around his neck and pulling him in tighter. His lips were warm, his tongue hot and demanding as he tasted me . . . claiming me. However, all too soon he pulled away, holding me in place with his hands on my face, his look hard.

"Now that you know about Gabriella, I think it's time you tell me about Paxton. You two know each other, don't you? The way he spoke to you isn't the way he usually is with the females."

Swallowing hard, I took a deep breath and let it out slowly. His jaw tensed and he let his hands slip away from my face and crossed them over his chest, waiting while I bit my lip nervously.

"Yes, we know each other," I confessed. "Paxton and I grew up together. We're friends."

"Friends?" Tyler scoffed. "Let me guess, he was your

high school love?" He said it sarcastically, but when all I did was stand there and not answer him, his glare turned from amused to complete stone. "You have *got* to be fucking kidding me."

Reluctantly, I slowly nodded and hung my head. "It was a long time ago, Tyler."

"Did you fuck him?" he growled.

I nodded again and kept my eyes on the floor. "Yes, I was seventeen years old at the time. He was different back then."

"So, basically you're a hypocrite. I told one of my good friends today that it would be best if we didn't speak anymore to spare your feelings, but yet I find you in the same situation."

Abruptly, I lifted my head and snarled. "I am not a hypocrite. Tonight was the first time I'd seen Pax in over a year. It's not like you and Gabriella, who had a thing just a month ago. Pax and I stopped seeing each other once he started fighting. That was *years* ago, Tyler, not just a mere few weeks."

"Whatever the situation is, I don't like him touching you. The Paxton you knew back then can't be the same guy he is now. He's bad news, Kacey. I don't want you mixed up in that," he argued.

Sighing, I walked away and leaned up against the door, peering out the glass-pained patio door that led to our private pool. "He's not like that anymore," I snapped, glaring at his reflection in the window. "You may not believe it, but I know Paxton. Of all people, you should know that it's possible to change. If not, then why am I even here? You should be out fucking your whores."

If anything I said pissed him off, it was definitely my

last retort. Angrily, he stalked toward me and turned me around, caging me in by slamming his hands on the wall. His body pressed up against mine and I could feel the hardness between his legs bulging in his jeans.

"He may be a changed man and your friend, but I honestly don't give a fuck," he growled, his lips only a breath away. "What I care about is you. I don't like him touching you and I sure as hell don't like the fact that he's been inside of you. If he so much as steps over the line, I will put his ass down. You're mine, Kacey . . . remember that."

His chest rose and fell with his angry breaths, but the second I touched his face everything calmed. Gently, I kissed his lips and smiled. "Does that mean this is mine?" I asked, running my hand over his arousal and squeezing it.

"You better fucking believe it is," he grunted, pushing into my hand.

Unbuttoning his jeans, I bit my lip and shoved my hand inside. Wrapping my hand around his bare cock, I moaned when I felt how hard he was for me. His eyes rolled back in his head and he groaned, closing his eyes when I started massaging him.

"Be prepared," he bit out through clenched teeth, "it's not going to be slow and easy tonight."

"Who said I wanted it easy?" I countered. "I'm ready to see what you got, Rushing."

Without another word, Tyler lifted me in his arms and I wrapped my legs around his waist as he carried me into the bedroom. I squealed when he slammed me down on the mattress and covered me with his body, his hands roughly massaging my breasts.

Groaning, I arched my back and he squeezed harder, pinching my nipples through my shirt. I wanted him inside of me, but when I tried to unbutton my jeans, Tyler snatched my wrists and pulled my arms up over my head, locking me in place.

He shook his head at me. "No touch. I'm going to be the one to take off your clothes."

Slowly, he pulled me up by my wrists and lifted my shirt over my head, exposing my black lace bra. The deep rumble of satisfaction in his chest vibrated all the way down to my center, driving me completely insane. He smoothed his hands down over my breasts to my stomach and then to my back where he unclasped my bra and threw it across the room. His stare was heated and dark with need, primal and raw.

I trembled.

"I'm not scaring you, am I?"

Shaking my head, I glided my hands up his chest to his face and ran my fingers through his soft, blond hair. "No," I breathed, biting my lip. "I'm just ready for that cock of yours."

A small smile splayed across his lips and it grew larger as he slowly lowered his mouth to my neck. His teeth grazed along my skin, sucking and biting, making me gasp when he bit down too hard. I was going to have marks on my body, but I didn't care. I fucking loved it. He wanted to mark me. He trailed his lips even lower and I cried out even louder when he closed his lips over my nipple and bit down, sucking as hard as he could.

"Oh, Tyler," I groaned breathlessly.

As he was sucking and kissing his way along my breasts, he unbuttoned his jeans and slid the zipper down, his cock hard and ready against my thigh. I immediately grabbed a hold of him and squeezed, starting out slow with my pumps but then doing it harder and faster, enjoying the strangled moan that escaped his lips.

"Fuck," he growled low, snatching my wrist.

He pulled my hand away and ripped my jeans apart, his eyes wild and dangerous. When he said he wasn't going to go slow, I believed him. There was nothing slow or gentle about him tonight. The adrenaline from the fight and the confrontation with Paxton left him feral, untamed, and I had to admit I looked forward to him taking control.

Savagely, he gripped the waistband of my jeans and yanked them down along with my black lace underwear, tossing them over the side of the bed. His breaths came out in deep low growls as he stared at my naked body, gliding his hands up my legs and spreading me wide when he reached my thighs.

I ran my hand over my breast, down my stomach and to the V between my legs. His eyes followed the movement like a tiger waiting to pounce. Making one swipe with my fingers, I presented the wetness to him. "I'm waiting," I taunted.

Tyler's nostrils flared. Then he lifted up on his knees with a singular focus, his pants halfway down his thighs and his hard cock jutting out, taunting me. He looked at me with half-lidded eyes and lifted my bottom off the bed. Without any warning, he plunged deep into me with one thrust. Fully seated, balls against my ass, a loud growl ripped from his lips. He wasted no time, pulling out and thrusting hard over and over again.

The pain was sweet and I'd never felt so full in all my life. I'm pretty sure I came with the first thrust, but I couldn't be bothered with that now. Locking my legs around his body, I held on for dear life.

Just when I thought it couldn't get any better, he grabbed my arms and flopped backward, bringing me to riding position in under a second. Straddling his waist, I didn't waste a single moment. Guiding his hands to my ass, I used his chest as leverage and rode him hard and fast.

His fingers dug into me and he groaned, slamming his head into the pillows. The insides of my thighs were drenched with my need for him. I slid up and down his body easily, enjoying the feel of him getting harder with each thrust.

"I'm going to come, beautiful," he growled through clenched teeth.

That's what I wanted to hear, but I wasn't expecting what he did next. He quickly wrapped his arms around my waist and flipped me onto my back, burying me into the mattress. Bringing my legs up, he held them to either side of me, pushing down behind each knee. Holding me in place, he pounded into me, slamming his hips against my thighs with untamed force.

I knew he was close when his breaths came out in deep pants as he looked down at me. "You're so tight," he groaned.

I was more than ready. Digging my nails into his back, I bit my lip as the tightness slowly began to spread inside. "Harder," I moaned.

He did as I requested and almost immediately I felt the warmth of his release filling me up as I rode wave after wave of my own climax, my body frozen until the last remnants of my orgasm subsided. Breathing hard, he let go of my legs and laid on top of me. Sweaty skin sliding against each other, he kissed me gently on the lips and then slowly pulled out of me, keeping his stormy gray eyes on mine.

The tension was gone, but I knew he wasn't done with me. The night wasn't over.

After brushing the damp hair off of my forehead, he held my face in his hands. "Thank you for coming to my fight tonight. I didn't want to leave you, but I knew you needed your rest. I was worried about you."

"It's okay," I assured him. "I'm fine now. When I woke up, I knew I had to make it there. It wasn't the easiest trip though, considering when I got to the ticket counter I told the lady I was with you and she basically laughed in my face. That wasn't fun."

Tyler chuckled, but when I glared up at him he stopped. "Okay, that wasn't funny, but I know they get that shit all of the time with people trying to get in for free. Next time, you just need to make sure you come with me."

I had a feeling next time I would be going by myself once he found out about my secret. As soon as we got home, I was going to tell him everything. I just had to pray he would forgive me.

CHAPTER

31

Kacey

HEADING BACK TO Vegas made me nervous as hell. At least until I got the text from my brother saying he was headed back home, and that he would see me next week-end when he came back for the title fight. It felt like every-thing was crashing down on me. Not only did I have to explain to Tyler about Paxton, but this morning, I had to explain him to Bree and Cole.

Unfortunately, they saw me talking to Paxton in the lobby this morning when he was saying goodbye. Tyler wasn't happy about it either, but Pax approached us as we were checking out. Thankfully, it was just a quick good-bye. Pax could see in Tyler's eyes that his patience was wearing thin.

That wasn't exactly the way I wanted my friends to

find out about Paxton, especially since Cole lost the fight to him last night. Needless to say, both Bree and Cole felt betrayed and I didn't blame them. I didn't know they saw me with him until I got a text from Bree on the way home from Phoenix asking what the fuck was going on. I was kind of glad they didn't ride with us because then I would've had to hear her bitch at me the entire time.

Now we were all back at Tyler's house, lounging on rafts in his Olympic-sized swimming pool, relaxing. Or at least I was trying to. The guys were inside getting a cooler filled up with drinks so that Bree could have her way with me.

"I can't believe you never told me," she snapped, kicking water on me. "Cole was about to kick Paxton's ass when he saw him talking to you, but then we saw Tyler right there. We had no clue what was going on."

Tyler had kept his arm around my waist the entire time, even when Gabriella happened to walk by with her boyfriend. She'd smiled at us and waved, which only made things weirder. I was in a lobby with my current boyfriend and both of our ex-lovers in the same room. It was like being trapped in a soap opera.

"Is that why you kept saying you'd never date a fighter? Because of Paxton?"

"Partly," I replied. "Paxton and I dated in high school, but when he started fighting and I left for college, things kind of changed. He was getting into trouble and I didn't like that."

"Yeah, he's made a name for himself . . . and not a good one."

"He's not like that anymore. He's a good guy, Bree. People can change."

Lowering her sunglasses to the edge of her nose, she floated closer to me and held onto my raft, looking straight into my eyes. "Or," she noted, "they could just be really good liars."

"Are you girls done arguing now?" Tyler shouted. He dove into the pool straight for me, while Cole dove in after Bree.

Before I could slide off into the water, he flipped my raft over, laughing the entire time. He was going to pay for that. When I surfaced, I coughed up the water I swallowed and opened my eyes. "It's going to be me and you arguing in just a minute," I exclaimed, splashing him in the face with water. "That was so not funny."

Wrapping his arms around my waist he pulled me over to the edge of the pool and lifted me up so I could straddle his waist. His cock growing harder the closer he got.

"I seem to remember us having some fun in the pool back in Phoenix. Want to do it again?" he asked, a mischievous smirk splayed across his face.

Wide-eyed, I glanced over at Cole and Bree who were busy talking on the other end of the pool. "With Cole and Bree out here? Are you crazy?"

Tyler chuckled and slid his hand between my legs, pulling my bathing suit to the side. "They're getting ready to leave. We just got a call a few minutes ago saying there's a party at the Labyrinth tonight. Cole's going to take Bree home so she can get ready."

I looked over his shoulder at them and they were still busy talking, not paying attention to us at all. "Then why can't we wait for them to go home?"

"Because, beautiful," he murmured, slipping his fingers inside of me, "where's the fun in that?"

I closed my eyes and moaned quietly. "Tyler, what are you doing to me?"

He slid his fingers out and replaced them with something much, much larger. I gasped and opened my eyes. His fingers tightened on my ass when he pulled me down his cock, biting his lip as I gently moved up and down. He was much taller than me so with his back to our friends they couldn't see me moving against him. I was going so slow, even the water around us was barely sloshing around.

Tyler groaned and pinched my nipple, rolling it around to make it peak. "Fuck, I wish I could suck them right now."

With a sly grin on my face, I leaned over and whispered in his ear. "You can. All we have to do is go under."

He pushed inside of me hard and bit the lobe of my ear. "I think I'm rubbing off on you, beautiful. You're not as innocent as you were when I first met you." He looked over his shoulder at Bree and Cole then back to me. "Let's do it."

We both smiled and took a deep breath, but before we could go under, Bree hollered for us. "Hey guys, Cole and I are going to head out so we can get ready for the party. We'll see you both tonight, okay?"

With Tyler still inside me, he turned us around like nothing was amiss and waved his hand in the air. "All right, we'll see you then."

As soon as they got out of the pool and headed inside, I burst out laughing. "Do you think they suspected anything?"

Tyler shook his head and pushed in deep. "No, they

were clueless. I wouldn't worry about it."

"So what do you want to do now?" I asked slyly.

Reaching behind my back, Tyler untied my top and let it float away. "I think we need to finish what we started. Are you ready?" He pushed off the side of the pool and swam toward the deep end. "On the count of three we go under. One, two . . ."

"Three," we said at the same time.

After taking a deep breath, we both went under.

"So what's the occasion tonight?" I asked as Tyler drove us to the Labyrinth. "Why is the owner throwing a party?"

Tyler shrugged and smiled over at me. "He likes to have a huge party at the beginning of each new season to bring it in formally."

"Formally? What do you mean by that?"

He looked down at my tight green and blue striped tank top and denim shorts and then back up to me. "Well, it's summer time, right? Everyone's going to be wearing summer-themed items."

Pursing my lips, I glanced down at my clothes and then over to what he was wearing. He was dressed in a pair of khaki shorts, a navy blue Oakley T-shirt with his platinum blond hair in messy spikes. Was I missing something?

"Shouldn't I be in a bathing suit then?" I inquired curiously.

Tyler's smile faded and he bit his lip. "Yeah, you could have, but I wasn't exactly thrilled with you wearing the one you wore earlier in front of a bunch of men. Besides, that's not all people will be wearing. There'll be some people in regular clothes."

He said it like he didn't believe it. It wasn't like I would want to wear a bathing suit to a club anyway. It wasn't my style. "Like who? Bree?" I asked, crossing my arms over my chest. "Did you and Cole deliberately not tell us because you thought we would argue?"

He smirked and grabbed my hand, lifting it to his lips. "You, I wasn't worried about. But Bree is a little wilder. Cole and I are just trying to avoid getting into trouble, which still might be hard considering you're hot as hell and I know everyone will be looking at you."

"You do realize you're being a little overprotective, right? Don't get me wrong, it's flattering, but you have nothing to worry about. I'll be by your side all night."

"Trust me," he said, kissing my palm, "I don't plan on letting you go. I'm only here for Jake. He's like a second father to me."

We pulled up to the Labyrinth and waiting outside the doors were people in nothing but bare skin and scraps of cloth covering their bodies. *Oh, my God.* This was his last place of employment. "Do you miss working here?"

Tyler parked his truck and sighed, "Sometimes I do, but now I'm too busy with training. I just don't have the time. I kind of like working at the gym now that we have a hot new employee."

"Yeah, I kind of like my new job too," I giggled.

"So are you ready to go in?" he asked, pointing at the

club. "The sooner we make our appearance the sooner we can go home."

He didn't have to tell me twice. I worked at a bar for so long, I was over the hype of it all. Opening my door, Tyler walked around to my side and put his arm around my waist. When we walked up to the line, I half expected us to have to wait. But of course Tyler kept going until we got to the front door and he strolled right on in.

"The VIP treatment, huh?" I teased.

"What can I say? I'm a very important person."

Rolling my eyes, he pulled me into the club and my mouth dropped wide open. Music blared over the speakers and there were people dancing everywhere. I got a little more than I bargained for when I saw a woman's breasts flop out of her bathing suit top.

Tyler shook his head. "And that is exactly why I didn't want you wearing your bikini here. I'm the only one who has the privilege of seeing your tits."

"You're such a caveman," I teased, smacking him on the arm. "I can show my tits to anyone I want."

Jokingly, he winked and took my hand. "Yeah, but they might not live long enough to enjoy them. Come on, Cole said they were going to meet us at the bar."

On the way there, a group of girls hollered out Tyler's name and waved him over, bouncing up and down in their skimpy bikinis.

"Friends of yours?" I asked, glaring up at him.

He let go of my hand and put his arm around my waist. "Do I need to shout it out to the world that I'm taken? Because I will if that'll make you happy." He waved at the girls but kept walking past, not acknowledging them any further. That earned a couple of snarls and glares sent my way, but I didn't care. I was bound to get plenty more where that came from.

"No, I just need to get used to people wanting you. I've never been with anyone that was in such high demand."

Glancing around the room there were a handful of people in regular clothes, but then I happened to get an eye full of a couple of men in Speedos. No matter how good looking a man was, there was no way in hell seeing him in a speedo was sexy. Well, maybe except for Tyler; he would look good wearing nothing but a sombrero and knee-high dress socks. I laughed picturing it in my mind.

Up ahead, Cole and Bree sat at the bar with a couple of drinks. Cole was in a pair of khaki shorts and a Hawaiian shirt, while Bree wore a little blue sundress. When Bree spotted me, she jumped out of her seat and pulled me down to the seat beside her, passing me a tequila sunrise.

"Drink up, my lady. I bet you're glad your boyfriend doesn't work here anymore, aren't you?"

Shaking his head incredulously at Bree, he sat down on the stool beside me and ordered a double shot of whiskey on the rocks. Looking around at all of the half-naked bodies, I was actually kind of glad he didn't work there anymore.

"She has nothing to worry about, Bree."

But, I did.

Bree tossed back her margarita and grabbed my hand, her eyes glassy from one too many drinks.

"How many have you had?" I asked as she pulled me out of my seat.

"Oh, just a couple. Cole and I were a little preoccupied this afternoon so I'm kind of drinking on an empty stomach."

Great, she's going to get sick.

Putting her arm around my shoulder, she glanced over at the dance floor where a slew of people were dancing. "You know what? I think we need to go out there and show those people how to dance. You up for it?"

No, not really. I knew how to dance, but I hadn't been to a dance club since I left California. I didn't want to go out there looking like an idiot. Groaning, I turned to Tyler who shrugged his shoulders, smirking.

"Don't look at me, beautiful. I'd be happy to watch you two dance."

"So would I," Cole agreed, coming up behind Bree, wrapping his arms around her waist. "Show us what you got, mama."

Tilting her head to the side, she kissed his lips and winked. "With pleasure."

Here we go.

I looked back at Tyler, hoping he would save me, but all he and Cole did was laugh and turn their stools toward the dance floor so they could watch us. *Typical men.* If he wasn't going to dance with me, I was going to make sure he regretted it. Smiling wickedly, I got behind Bree, putting my hands on her waist, and danced provocatively behind her, keeping my attention on Tyler.

Slowly, he brought the glass of whiskey to his lips and watched me over the rim.

"I think they like this," Bree shouted, giggling.

"Yeah, but they're not the only ones," I replied, looking around the room at a few other men who had eyeballs fixed on us . . . one of whom I recognized. Especially since his chest was bare and I could see the skull tattoo that took up his whole left bicep.

Underneath the baseball cap he had sitting low on his forehead, I knew there would be dark brown hair and a set of hazel eyes peeking from underneath. And by the mischievous leer on his face, he recognized me, which wasn't a good thing. His name was Jordan Graham, and he was a friend of my brother's. If he was at the club, my brother was close by.

Quickly, I glanced over at Tyler, but his attention was set on a middle-aged man with salt and pepper hair, dressed in black slacks and a blue button down shirt. If I had to make a guess, I'd say it was probably Jake, the owner.

"Bree, I need to get out of here," I shouted in her ear. I turned to look for Jordan, but he wasn't there anymore. *Shit!*

Bree turned around and cupped her ear, still dancing to the song with a goofy grin on her face. "What did you say?"

About that time, a set of arms wrapped around my waist and I immediately stiffened when I noticed the skull tattoo out of the corner of my eye.

I elbowed him in the arm, but it didn't faze him. The prick laughed and held me tighter. Bree's eyes went wide and she rushed off toward the bar, no doubt to get Tyler. "You need to get off of me," I warned him, clenching my teeth.

"Or what? You're going to get your boyfriend to kick my ass? I'd like to see him try. Ooh . . . maybe we could even get him suspended from the fight?"

I gasped. It was a trap. Jordan wasn't a fighter, so no one would recognize him. My brother set it up perfectly.

When Jordan's hand lifted to my breast I saw nothing but red, an insurmountable rage boiling through my veins. I was going to kill my brother for this.

Thankful I was wearing a shoe with a heel, I lifted my foot and slammed it down on Jordan's as hard as I could. He growled and let me go, but when I tried to run through the crowd, he caught my arm and pulled me back, his grip brutally tight.

"You're not going anywhere, Kacey. I haven't had my fun yet. Don't you want to stay and watch? Your boy-friend's almost here."

He swung me around so that I faced him. Over his shoulder Tyler's gaze finally landed on us once Bree rushed up to him. I tried to push Jordan away, but he held me too damn tight. My struggles only infuriated Tyler even more when he realized what was happening. The room crackled like fire as he stormed his way through the crowd, everyone giving him a wide berth.

Jordan cackled in my ear. "Show time."

Once Tyler made it to us, Jordan pretended to be oblivious and grinded against me.

"You need to let her go, *now!*" Tyler demanded.

Jordan smiled down at me and winked before turning to acknowledge Tyler. "Oh, hey man, what's up? Is this your chick?"

He let me go and I rushed over to Tyler's side, grab-bing a hold of his arm. I couldn't let him fight. "Tyler, let's go. He's just a drunk asshole. The last thing you need is to get into a fight."

Nostrils flaring, he glared at Jordan and clenched his hands into tight fists. "Easier said than done when you watch a piece of shit putting their hands on what's mine."

Desperately, I looked up at Cole who was on Tyler's other side and silently demanded his help.

Cole nodded and slapped Tyler on the shoulder. "Come on, Rushing. This cocksucker isn't worth fucking up your title fight this weekend. Let's get out of here."

"Please, Tyler, let's go," I pleaded, pulling on his arm.

He snarled at Jordan and thankfully turned on his heel, placing his arm protectively over my shoulders. The front door felt like it was miles away, but we got there quickly and started for his truck. As fast as we went, we didn't get out of there before Jordan started in on round two, following us.

"You know, I have to say your chick can really move on the dance floor. My dick got so fucking hard rubbing it against her ass," he said. Then he pointed to Bree. "Actually, I was hoping to get a little double action, if you know what I mean."

Abruptly, Tyler stopped and I knew it was over. Even when I looked over at Cole he knew it too.

"Tyler, please," I begged. "Keep walking. He's trying to get you in trouble. Don't let him win." He wouldn't look down at me—it was like he wasn't even there.

Jordan, however, didn't stop. He kept adding fuel to the fire. "When you get tired of her, make sure to pass her my way. I know guys like you can go through several in a week."

Tyler moved so fast, all I felt was the rush of wind as he took off and tackled Jordan to the ground. Jordan might not be an MMA fighter, but he learned how to fight from my brother. And my brother was dirty. Tyler pounded on Jordan's face, but then Jordan got free and rolled away, getting to his feet quickly.

Laughing, Jordan wiped the blood off of his lip with the back of his hand. "So . . . the elusive Tyler Rushing is hard up over a female. Since you're not going to share, can I at least compliment her nice rack? I got a pretty good handful of them earlier."

Tyler lunged again, but this time he hit Jordan so hard on the side of the face, he fell limp to the ground, smacking his head on the concrete. Gasping, I closed my eyes and covered my face with my hands, tears streaming down my cheeks. It was one thing to see a fight in the ring, but it was another seeing it for real, with real emotions.

With his back to me, Tyler hung his head as Cole knelt down by Jordan's limp body to check on him. Bree rushed to my side and put her arms around me, crying hysterically.

"Oh my God, Kace, what are we going to do?"

About that time, two sets of blue lights pulled into the parking lot and came straight toward us. Two officers jumped out of the car, one heading straight for Tyler and the other toward Cole and Jordan. The one who approached Tyler shook his head and sighed. Apparently, they knew each other.

"When I got the call, I didn't expect it to be you, son," he announced regretfully. "You know I'm going to have to take you both in for questioning."

With his hands bloody and torn up at his sides, Tyler looked over at Jordan; who finally rolled over onto his back and slowly got to his feet, blood dripping down the side of his face. Since he was shirtless, the skin on his back was torn up from sliding across the pavement.

"That's fine, detective," Tyler replied. "The cocksucker deserved it after physically harassing my girl-friend."

The detective turned his attention to me and Bree and lifted his brows. I raised my hand so he'd know it was me Tyler was referring to. When the detective approached, Tyler finally turned around and looked at me, he looked regretful.

"I'm Detective Ryan Griffin," he announced, extending his hand.

I took his hand and shook it. "I'm Kacey Andrews."

The detective pointed to Jordan who was talking to the other officer. "Is that the guy who harassed you, Miss?"

"Yes," I answered.

"What did he do?"

Tyler turned his head, clenching his jaw. He didn't want to hear it. As quietly as I could, I leaned forward and replied, "He grabbed my chest while we were in the club, detective. And then he followed us out here to the parking lot and instigated the fight. He also mentioned something about seeing if he could get Tyler suspended from the next fight."

He glanced at Cole and Bree and they both nodded in agreement. "All right, Miss Andrews, if you don't mind, I'd like you to follow us to the station. It might be a little while before Tyler gets out, but I'm sure he'd rather have you there waiting for him instead of his father." Turning to Tyler, he pointed to his car. "Let's go, son."

Instead of going to the police car, he came to me and reached for my hand, giving me the keys to his truck. "I'm sorry, Kacey. I should've walked away, but I just couldn't knowing that he touched you. Please say you forgive me.

You don't have to wait for me at the station."

I leaned up on my tip toes and gently kissed his lips. "I'm coming, Tyler. I'm not going to leave you there. I'll wait for however long it takes."

Folding me in his arms, he kissed the side of my neck. "I love you."

"I love you too."

All too soon he was out of my arms and in the back of the police car, being driven away. I had no clue what was going to happen or what his future held. If he got disqualified from the fight this weekend, then my brother had won. However, if Tyler didn't get disqualified, then my brother was going to strike again. I had to tell Tyler the truth, now.

CHAPTER 32

Kacey

ABOUT FIVE HOURS later, it was closing in on four o'clock in the morning and I was still at the police station. I watched as a couple of drunk men were brought in and taken away, along with a couple of prostitutes who were dressed in strips of cloth. It was an interesting night. It brought back memories of the times I had to pick my brother up from the local jailhouse.

"Kacey?" a voice called out.

Standing, I turned around to see the middle-aged guy, who was talking to Tyler in the club, head my way. "Jake?" I asked.

He nodded. "Yes, ma'am. I wanted to get here sooner, but I had to close up the club. I'm sorry about what happened." He held out his hand toward the seats, so I sat down with him joining me.

"It's just a huge mess," I complained. "What if Tyler can't fight this weekend? What if he gets in trouble?"

"That's not going to happen. I know the people here and so does Tyler. He was just defending you."

"You think so?" I asked, hopeful.

He turned to me and smiled. "I know so."

About two hours and several cups of stale coffee later, Jake had already told me about his wife who passed away from cancer, how he started the club, and how Tyler was like a son to him. He even told me about the time he made Tyler wear a toga one night for work. I would've loved to have seen that. I was sitting there laughing about it when Tyler strolled around the corner with the detective by his side. Jake and I both got to our feet, waiting on the verdict.

Curiously, Tyler lifted his brows. "Do I want to know what you're laughing at?"

I snickered again. "Jake was just telling me stories about you and your toga wearing days. I needed to hear something funny to take away the edge."

Detective Griffin smiled and patted Tyler on the back before nodding at me and Jake. "It's all good. Tyler can go now." Turning on his heel, he waltzed off and passed Tyler's file to the guy at the desk.

"So, what's going on?" I asked, glancing down at Tyler's hands. They were clean, with no traces of blood, and only minor scratches.

Tyler followed my gaze and looked down at his hands, sighing. "I'm in the clear. I can fight this weekend. However, I was told that I might need anger management classes."

Jake sniggered and slapped him on the shoulder. "No, you don't. Any full-blooded male would've beaten the shit out of that guy for doing what he did. Just go home and get some rest. Your father isn't going to lighten up your training just because you spent the whole night in jail."

"Isn't that the fucking truth," he grumbled.

Once Jake said his goodbyes, I walked with Tyler out to the parking lot and to his truck. I still had his keys, so I unlocked the doors and hopped in the driver's seat.

"Have you been here the whole time?" he asked.

Nodding, I started the truck and slowly crept out of the parking lot. "Yep," I replied. "I wasn't going to just leave you there. Jake kept me company after a while, so it wasn't that bad."

"Well, I'm glad he could entertain you. Once everything is said and done, I'm going to need a good laugh as well. I came so damn close to not being able to compete."

Licking my dry lips, my heart pounded so hard it hurt and my hands started to sweat. "Tyler, there's something I want to talk to you about."

He leaned his head against the seat and turned his attention to me. "What is it, beautiful?"

We pulled into his driveway and parked. I swallowed hard and turned off the ignition. My Toyota Camry sat vacant beside us and I knew that after I told him the truth, I would be getting in my car and driving away. The thought terrified me, but he had to know that my brother was going to come after him again.

"Tyler, I . . ."

That was as far as I'd gotten before his phone rang. When he looked down at it, he groaned and ran his hands down his face. "It's my father," he said, "I'm sure he just found out. I'm sorry, beautiful." He got out of the truck and I followed suit, losing my nerve with each second that passed. I grabbed my purse out of his truck and pulled out the keys to my car, leaning against it as I waited on Tyler to get off of the phone.

When he did, he came over to me and wrapped his arms around my waist, holding me tight.

"Is he angry?" I asked.

"A little, but he needs me at the gym, so I have to go. He's going to run my ass hard today."

"But I need to talk to you. It's kind of important."

Pulling away, Tyler tilted my chin up with his fingers. "Are you okay? Are you mad about what happened?"

Gently, I shook my head and leaned into his touch. "No, I'm not mad."

Visibly, he relaxed and kissed me, murmuring against my lips, "I tell you what. Why don't you get some sleep and once you've rested up, come to the gym and you can talk to me all you want. Can you do that?"

I didn't want to wait, but it was looking like I had no choice—he had to go. "Okay," I agreed reluctantly. "I'm going to go home for a while and then I'll see you as soon as I can."

Before getting into my car, I kissed him quickly and watched him rush off inside his house. On the way home, I rode in silence trying to envision how I was going to tell Tyler the truth. Should I just come right out and say it? Or should I try to soften it up? Either way, it was going to be a messy disaster.

Ring, ring, ring.

Looking down at my phone, I figured it would be Tyler or Bree, but I couldn't have been more wrong.

"What the hell do you want?" I snapped into the phone.

"We need to talk. It appears you've been a little busy behind my back. Care to tell me what that's all about?"

"I don't think it's any of your business what I do now is it? Besides, you already know what's going on. Or at least, I assume so, judging by what happened last night."

He snorted. "Yeah, but it appears my plan didn't exactly work. I must say, I don't know whether to be disappointed or proud of you. I never thought the day would come when I'd see you fucking one of my enemies."

"Whatever, Kyle, it's over. Why don't you leave me the hell alone?"

"That's not how this is going to work. Either you talk to me now, or I go straight to Tyler and tell him who you are. I'm waiting for you at the house."

Could I not catch a break? After seeing Jordan last night, I knew Kyle had lied when he texted me saying he went home. But then again it made me wonder . . . "How long have you known about me and Tyler?" I asked.

Kyle chuckled. "Long enough to figure out my next move. Now hurry, sis. We have lots to talk about."

CHAPTER 33

TYLER

ON THE WAY to the gym, I didn't know what to expect. My father didn't necessarily sound angry on the phone, but he didn't sound happy either. I wasn't sorry for kicking that guy's ass, but I was sorry for doing it in front of Kacey. I didn't want her ever looking at me with fear in her eyes ever again. When she said she needed to talk to me, the first thing that came to mind was that she was done; she'd made a mistake being with me.

I pushed her off for that reason alone. I didn't want to hear it just yet.

Walking through the front doors of the gym, I found my father down by the ring, punching the bag as hard as he could. He was dressed in his black and gold fighting shorts, the same ones he wore when he competed. There was no one around . . . just me and him. I hadn't seen him hit the bag in years.

"I hope you're ready to work. We have lots to do before Saturday," he called out.

Opening my bag, I pulled out my hand wraps and gloves and taped up my hands. "So you're not going to bitch at me for getting arrested?"

Breathing hard, my father steadied the punching bag and turned to face me. "No, son, I'm not. Jake called and told me what happened. I'm actually proud of you. I probably would've killed the guy if he did the same thing to your mother."

"Trust me, it was hard to control myself." I'd wanted to keep going.

Tightening his gloves, my father hopped up into the ring and beckoned me to join him. "Your mother and I have been talking. How would you feel about taking full responsibility of the business?"

Wide-eyed, I joined him in the ring. "You mean, take over the gym? I didn't think you were going to retire so soon. What changed your mind?"

Getting into stance, my father attacked with a jab and left cross. I ducked and roundhouse kicked him in the back of his head. I didn't hit him hard, but it still threw him off balance.

Righting himself, he nodded his head with a huge smile on his face. "Good one, son. You've gotten much better at anticipating. But to answer your question, your mother and I feel you're ready to take over. At the end of the year, we're stepping down and you'll be the one in charge. Do you think you can handle it?"

For so long, my father had made comments about

how I wasn't ready and how I was never good enough. My time had finally come and I knew it was all because of Kacey. She was the one who made me want to be better, to rise above everyone else and show them I was worthy. I was more than ready to take that final step. And I sure as hell wasn't going to let my family down.

"Yes," I answered wholeheartedly. "I'm more than ready."

My father and I trained for another hour before the doors opened up and a swarm of people came in for their early morning workouts. I wanted to call Kacey and tell her the good news, but I knew she had to be exhausted. I was on air and happier than I ever thought I could be.

After running on the treadmill, I started toward the break room to grab an energy bar before I began my next workout routine. However, I stopped when none other than Jaden Eller stepped in my path.

"What are you doing here?" I grumbled. "Aren't you in the wrong city?"

Jaden Eller was one of the UFC's female MMA fighters and Kyle Andrews' whore. She and Gabriella fought here in my gym just a couple of months ago when Gabriella kicked her ass. Her long dark hair was pulled tight into a ponytail and her blue eyes stared at me in full blown lust. Usually I got off on that shit, but now things had changed. I wanted her to get the fuck away from me.

"I'm in town for the time being, at least until Kyle wants to head back home. He wanted to visit his family," she informed me.

"That's great," I commented sarcastically. "Enjoy your time in town." Quickly, I walked around her in hopes of getting away. Unluckily, she wasn't done with me.

"Oh, I'll definitely enjoy my time. But there's something I thought I should tell you. You seem like the type of guy who likes honesty."

"What the fuck are you talking about?" I snapped impatiently. "You better start making some sense before I get pissed off."

Smiling, she lifted her hands and nonchalantly inspected her short, pink fingernails. "Oh, I just wanted to let you know your girlfriend has a secret. I'm pretty sure she hasn't told you yet. 'Cause if she had, I highly doubt you'd have anything to do with her."

"Like I'd believe anything that came out of your mouth," I hissed. "You need to get the fuck away from me." I was done. Turning on my heel, I marched off to the back room, hearing her obnoxious laugh behind me. Before I could turn the handle and be done with her for good, she stopped me with her next words.

"Kacey is Kyle's sister, Rushing," she blurted out.

I froze and the whole gym grew silent. *No, there's no fucking way that's true.* Her last name is Andrews, but she couldn't be related to that fucker.

"If you don't believe me, call her and ask. Kyle's over at her house right now—I just came from there. I must say out of all of the things he's done, this one takes the cake. He got you to fall in love with the enemy. I didn't think it would be possible."

Hearing her cackle and the whispers in the room set me off. My body was on fire, anger and rage surging through my veins. All I could see was red, as I stormed through the gym. I had to get out of there. Clenching my teeth, I grabbed my keys and headed for the door.

"Son," my father called out.

I didn't turn around, but I did stop.

"I'm not going to try and stop you because that would be foolish, but I want you to keep your wits about you. You can't always believe what you hear. Don't let your anger cloud your judgment."

Easier said than done. Without another word, I slammed open the door and charged toward my truck. The pieces were sliding into place and it all made perfect sense now. She knew Paxton and he was one of Kyle's best friends, she grew up in California where Kyle was from, and I bet she knew the guy from last night that messed with her. Was it all a ploy from the very beginning? Whatever was going on, I was about to find out.

Either way, Kyle Andrews was fucking dead.

CHAPTER 34

Kacey

KYLE WAS WAITING for me on the front steps with an evil smirk. I couldn't wait to see Tyler punch that look off of his face.

"It's good to see you again, sis," he called out.

Shutting my car door, I stormed up to him and slapped him across the cheek. His head snapped to the side, but his leer grew even bigger. I hated him. "How dare you do this to me. Why do you always have to tear people down to get ahead? Why can't you do what normal people do and just work hard to be the best?"

He rubbed his cheek and sat down on the steps. There was no way in hell I was going to let him inside of my house. "There's no fun in that," he admitted slyly. "Besides, it was kind of interesting to see how protective Captain Fuckface was over you. The fool actually fell in love. I couldn't have planned it more perfectly."

"Planned what?" I snapped. "I love Tyler. I'm not going to let you come between us."

Snickering, he leaned back on the steps and shook his head. "Do you honestly think Tyler's going to want anything to do with you now? Obviously he doesn't know who you are. If he did, he wouldn't touch you with a ten foot pole."

"He loves me, Kyle," I spat. "He can't blame me for wanting to keep my ties with you a secret. Anyone in their right mind would be ashamed of you." *Don't let him see your fear.*

Kyle got to his feet, his smile gone as he approached me. "You're ashamed of me?"

I stood my ground and lifted my head defiantly. "Ashamed doesn't begin to cover it. I'm mortified. I know about the things you've done and it makes me sick."

"Well, you want to know what makes me sick? You and Tyler. You're my family, my *blood*. You're supposed to be on my side. You're going to pay for disappointing me."

I stepped back to my car and opened the door. "Believe me, Kyle, I've been paying for years. Tyler may get angry at me for keeping the truth from him, but he loves me. I'm not going to let you win." I got in my car and shut the door.

"Where do you think you're going?" he shouted.

Flipping him off, I started my car and fastened my seat belt. "It's about time I tell Tyler the truth!"

Kyle put his hands on the hood of my car and smirked. "I think it might be a little late for that, sis. He already knows." He nodded toward the end of the street and that was when I heard the tires squeal. In my rearview mirror, I watched in dread as Tyler sped down my road and locked his brakes in my driveway.

"What did you do?" I shouted, getting out of my car. Immediately, the tears started to fall, especially when Tyler glared at me with utter disdain.

Kyle, on the other hand, smiled wide. "Oh, I just had Jaden pay him a little visit. I must say, he doesn't look too happy."

Tyler got out of his truck and slammed the door.

"Babe, you have to let me explain," I pleaded.

"What, that you fucking lied to me?" he shouted, veins bulging from his forehead.

I rushed over to him, but when I tried to touch him he stepped back. It broke my heart. Lips trembling, I shook my head and cried, "No, I didn't lie. I knew if you found out Kyle was my brother, you would think I was just like him. But I'm not! I need you to trust me."

"Oh sis, you don't have to keep pretending," Kyle chided, coming to my side. "He already knows the truth. You succeeded. Now he's just a played *bitch*. Let him go lick his wounds."

Frantic and wide-eyed, I pushed him away. "Stop lying!" Then to Tyler, I clasped my hands in front of my heart, begging with tears streaming down my face. In his eyes, I could see he was letting his anger get the best of him. Yes, he was furious at me for lying, but he couldn't see the truth. He couldn't see my love for him, or that it was real. How could I get him to see it? "Tyler, please, don't listen to him. I don't know what Jaden told you, but you have to know I would never do anything to hurt you. I love you!"

Tyler snarled, "And you expect me to believe that?" He glared at my brother over my shoulder, completely dismissing me.

I was so close to him, yet so far away. He wouldn't let me touch him, and the thought of never being able to touch him again, ripped my soul apart. I needed him.

Backing away, he pointed at my brother and growled, "If you think this got me down, Andrews, you're wrong. I'll be ready for you Saturday. You can count on that." Opening the door to his truck, he got in and started it up.

Before I could rush to him, my brother grabbed a hold of my arm and held me back. "Let me go!" I screamed, trying to yank my arm out of Kyle's grasp.

"Sorry, Kacey, but it's for the best. He wants nothing to do with you now. I'm just trying to protect you from making a fool of yourself."

I tried to fight him off, but his grip was too tight. Tyler backed out of the driveway and never once did he look at me. "Tyler! Tyler, please, you have to trust me!"

He kept going . . . and the farther away he went, the bigger the hole in my chest grew. I was alone for the longest time before he came along, and now I was alone again. I had nothing if I didn't have him.

"Trust me, Kacey, it's for the best. You deserve much better."

Actually, I deserved what I got for not telling the truth, but I sure as hell was going to redeem myself. I refused to let my brother dictate my life and drag me down with him. I had to fight for what I wanted.

Pushing my brother away, I marched up the front porch stairs and unlocked the door, slamming it in Kyle's face when he tried to follow me in. If there was anyone who was a master at persuasion, it was Bree. I needed her help, but in getting it, I had to be honest with her too. All of my secrets had to come out.

Reaching for my phone, I dialed her number and waited. She would just have to understand why I did what I did. Hopefully, she could convince Tyler.

CHAPTER

35

TYLER

MY PHONE WENT off non-stop after I left Kacey's. I refused to listen to any more lies, so I threw my phone across the seat and sped down the road. I had to get away. Once I got home, I rushed inside straight to my room and packed as many things as I could fit in my duffle bag. There was no way in hell I could stay in town knowing Kacey would be everywhere I went. She even worked at the gym now. What was I going to do?

Her betrayal hit deep and I wasn't going to give Kyle the satisfaction of knowing it broke me. Once I had my bags loaded in my truck, I started out of my driveway, but was blocked in when a little silver Honda pulled in.

Fuck my life. It was Bree.

I rolled my window down when she approached looking all pissed with her lip curled, and wearing a pair of Bugs Bunny pajama pants with a white tank top. "Let me guess . . . you were in on it too?" I snapped.

Crossing her arms over her chest, she glared up at me, tapping her foot. "Don't give me that bullshit, Tyler. I didn't know any more than you did. You need to stop running, and talk to Kacey."

"Why? So she can feed me more lies?"

"Really? So that's how this is going to go?" she scoffed, narrowing her gaze. "How is it that I can find out the truth just a few minutes ago and understand where she's coming from? Can you blame her for wanting to keep her life a secret? Look where she comes from, Tyler. You may not believe her, but I sure as hell do. She's been my best friend for the past year and never *once* did she tell me about her brother.

"Kacey just wanted to escape from the hell he put her through. Whatever Kyle said, it's a bunch of horse shit. If you remember correctly, she tried to stay away from you . . . *you* were the one who pursued her. You know what else? I'm the one who dragged her to your gym that day. Why don't you let that sink in for a while before you start acting like an ass?"

Turning on her heel, she stalked off, got in her car and sped out of my driveway.

I couldn't listen to anymore bullshit. Reaching for my phone, I dialed my father's number and waited on him to pick up. "Son, where are you?" he asked, answering the phone.

"I'm at the house, but I'm going to take off for a while." I put my truck in gear and started out of the driveway. I had a long drive ahead of me.

"Running away from your problems isn't the answer, Tyler, but if you feel it's what you need to do, then go. I trust you'll work hard this week to get ready for your fight."

Gripping the steering wheel tight, I imagined it was Kyle's neck in my grasp. "You have nothing to worry about. I'll make sure I'm more than ready."

I hung up the phone and sped down the highway, the start of my nine hour drive to Santa Rosa. I had friends there who could help me and I was going to need it.

CHAPTER 36

Kacey

SINCE TYLER WOULDN'T answer my calls, I grew desperate and sought him out, stopping first at his house and then at the gym. When I walked in, everything was normal, people were working out and enjoying their day just like usual. My life, however, was crashing all around me. I didn't know whether to come or go.

"Are you going to work, or are you just going to stand there?"

I turned around and there, leaning against the wall with his arms crossed, was Tyler's father. He was dressed in a pair of black and gold fighting shorts with a plain white T-shirt drenched in sweat. He and Tyler looked so much alike, I wanted to burst into tears where I stood. They had the same blond hair and cut, even though Steven's was showing some gray. They also had the same body type, tall and muscular. Luckily, I held the tears back and peered over at the empty desk . . . my desk.

"I didn't know if I was going to be allowed back." I whispered. "I need to find Tyler."

Sighing, Steven reached for one of the clean hand towels we always had stacked neatly on the desk. "He's not here, Kacey. I don't think he'll be back for a while."

"What do you mean he won't be back for a while?" I gasped.

Steven shrugged his shoulders. "He called and said he wanted to get away. I trust that he's making the right decision. He knows what he needs."

"So I guess you know what happened?" I asked nervously, hanging my head. I didn't want to see the accusation in his gray eyes. I saw enough of it already in Tyler's.

"Yes, I was here when Tyler found out. I don't know the whole story, but I do know that you're not a bad person, Kacey. Anyone who talks to you can see that."

"Tyler can't," I noted sadly. "He let me go without letting me explain."

"Listen," he murmured softly. "Tyler is just like me when it comes to his temper. He's quick to act before thinking. Sometimes I don't know how Mary puts up with me. However, my son is smart. He needs his space right now to sort everything out. You're just going to have to let him go and hope he comes back to you."

That's what I'm afraid of— he won't come back.

Two Days Later

I HAD JUST gotten done with my morning run when I noticed Kyle's red and black sport bike sitting in the driveway. It was Wednesday morning and I still hadn't seen or heard from Tyler. I tried his phone twice and it went straight to voicemail both times. Even Bree seemed to be acting weird every time I talked to her, which made no sense. I felt like I was losing everyone, except my damn brother, who's incessant badgering was about to drive me insane.

"What, are you stalking me now?" I grumbled, glaring at him as he took off his motorcycle helmet.

Smiling, he ran his hands through his tousled blond hair and set his helmet down on his bike. He always rode with no protection on his skin, which was kind of stupid given how wild he was on the bike. If he wrecked, I was sure his shorts and tank top wouldn't protect him much. He felt like he was invincible and I just waited for the moment when he could be proven wrong. Sometimes, it felt like that time would never come.

"Nope, I'm actually staying in Vegas until the fight this weekend. I got word your ex is having a hell of a time during training. I guess I really fucked him up. I thought you should know. However, it appears he doesn't want you back from the shit he's been saying. I guess it's better you found out now, so you can stop moping around."

"How do you know that?" I snapped. "Where is he?"

Pulling out his phone, Kyle scrolled through his videos until he found the one he wanted. "This one was sent to me last night. Tyler's in California, training with Matt Reynolds." He handed me the phone.

"But isn't Matt training Gabriella?"

Huffing, he nodded and pressed the play button on his phone. "Yes, which means your loverboy is there with her."

And given the situation, it also meant he was probably bound to do something stupid. "You know she hates you, right Kyle? You fucked over her brother. Why do you have this fascination with her?"

He shrugged his shoulders. "I don't know. She's hot and she can kick ass. Guys like that kind of shit. Now watch, and listen to what he says," he commanded, pointing to the phone and turning up the volume.

It was Tyler in a practice ring with Matt Reynolds, his moves sloppy and poorly executed—he was fighting terrible.

"What the fuck is wrong with you?" Matt snapped, throwing his hands in the air. "If you think you're going to win the title like this, you're wrong. You might as well throw in the towel now."

"Or you could always get laid," another guy added.

What the hell? I wanted to jump through the phone and tell him to mind his own business. I recognized him though, he was one of the Twins of Terror. It was either Ryley or Camden Jameson—I could never tell them apart—but this one had changed his hair from blond to dark.

Breathing hard, Tyler put his hands on his bare hips

and I felt bile rise up my throat as I watched him nod. "You're absolutely right, Ryley. Fuck 'em both. I'm sick of this shit. Let's go out and have us some fun."

Ryley hopped into the ring and fist bumped him. "Now that's what I'm talking about. I know a couple of women who'll make you forget about everything."

"Fuck yeah."

Handing Kyle back his phone, I closed my eyes and collapsed onto the front porch steps. I couldn't watch anymore.

"You know what'll make all this just perfect?" Kyle mentioned excitedly.

Gritting my teeth, I rested my elbows on my knees and hung my head. The thought of Tyler going out and fucking other women made me sick. Did I mean so little to him? "What are you talking about?" I whispered, swallowing hard to keep from throwing up.

Kyle sat down beside me and bumped me in the shoulder. "You should come to the fight on Saturday and sit in my corner. Show the bastard that you're not moping around. This crying bullshit is pathetic. He's not crying over you, now is he?"

Obviously not.

"Fine," I snapped, getting to my feet. "You win. I'll sit in your corner. Just do me a favor and leave me the hell alone about Tyler. I don't want to see or hear anything about him again." I stormed to the door and opened it wide, looking in at what used to be the only place that felt like home. If my grandmother was alive, she'd tell me to go after what I wanted.

I knew what I had to do.

CHAPTER 37

Kacey

ONCE MY BROTHER left, I booked the first available flight to Santa Rosa. Unfortunately, it was later in the afternoon, which had me arriving around seven o'clock. I had no clue if Tyler would be at the gym, but I was determined to find him, even if I had to drive around all night in my little rental.

The gym was vacant when I drove by so I decided to get something to eat at Panera Bread to kill some time. The only problem was that I wasn't hungry for the soup and salad. I ate it anyway, knowing I'd get sick if I didn't.

Chirp.

Startled, I jumped in my seat and fumbled for my phone which was in my back pocket. It was the first text message I'd gotten in days. Of course, it was wishful thinking to believe it would be Tyler, and when I looked at my phone it happened to be from Paxton.

Paxton: Am I seeing things or are you in California?

What? Hastily, I searched around the restaurant . . . nothing. It wasn't until a knock on the glass made me turn around. There he was. Smiling, I quickly grabbed my tray, dumped my food into the trash, and hurried outside. I was relieved to see a familiar face. California felt so foreign to me now; it wasn't my home anymore.

"What are you doing here?" he asked, lifting me up in a huge hug. His arms were sweaty and he was dressed in a gray tank top, black running shorts, and wearing an Oakland Raiders baseball cap. When I didn't answer, he set me down and his smile disappeared. He already knew.

"I'm here to see Tyler. He's not speaking to me right now."

"Yeah, I know. News travels fast in the UFC world, especially, when it involves someone like Tyler and your brother. Are you okay?"

I shook my head, closing my eyes to hold back the tears. "Not really, Pax. Kyle made Tyler believe that it was all a setup, that I made him fall for me so we could mess him up before the fight. I know he's out here somewhere and I don't know how to find him."

Sighing, Paxton bit his lip, his eyes guarded. "I know where he's at, but I don't think it's a good idea for you to see him right now."

"Why not?" I exclaimed. "Is he with Gabriella? I'm not leaving here until I see him." I didn't want to imagine him with her, but he had to hear me out, even if he ended up slamming the door in my face.

Starting toward the car, Paxton followed and grabbed

my arm. "What are you doing, Kacey? I'm not going to let you drive around all night."

With my other hand, I flung open the door and snapped, "Watch me."

"Dammit," he snarled. "Fine, I'll tell you where he is, but you're making a mistake. It's not the right time."

"It'll never be the right time, Pax. I need to get everything out in the open."

Hanging his head, Paxton groaned and took off his hat, running his hands through his dark hair. "Fine. He's at the gym."

"No, he's not. I just drove by there an hour and a half ago and it was vacant."

"Trust me, he's there, Kace. I'm going to follow you over there and wait for you in the parking lot. You're going to need me."

Furrowing my brows, I gazed up at him nervously. "Why do you say that?"

"Because," he murmured, tucking a strand of my hair behind my ear, "you're going to get hurt and I don't want you running off by yourself." Sadly, he smiled and turned on his heel. "I'll meet you there."

I was already hurt, so it didn't matter if I got hurt even more. My nerves, however, were shot by the time I pulled into the parking lot at the gym. Paxton was right—Tyler's truck was there. Pulling into the space beside me in his yellow Hummer, Paxton nodded toward the door and waved me on.

Swallowing hard, I took a deep breath and opened the door, clenching my hands into tight fists to keep them from shaking. Before reaching the front door to the gym, I looked back at Paxton one more time for any hope of reassurance, but all he provided was a sad smile.

I can't be a coward. Be strong.

Stopping at the door, I repeated those words over and over, until I saw Tyler in the ring with Matt Reynolds. He was fighting perfectly, like nothing was wrong. He didn't even look like the same guy I saw in the video. In fact, he was doing amazing. Licking my lips, I held onto the handle and slowly opened the door as to not draw any attention to myself—it didn't work.

Tyler stiffened at the noise, his tattooed muscles clenching tight as he slowly turned his head, his eyes going wide in surprise when he saw me. He wore his signature green and black fighting shorts and his platinum blond hair was spiky from being drenched in sweat. My God, I missed him, but I was furious with him too. We stared at each other for only a fraction of a moment before it all changed and he got back into position, turning his attention to Matt.

Matt, on the other hand, acknowledged me with a nod and took off his gloves. "Take a break," he announced, "I'll be back in five."

He disappeared to the back, leaving me alone with Tyler. The tension in the room was so palpable I could cut it with a knife. I was afraid my voice wouldn't work, so I took a deep breath and shouted, "Are you not going to say anything?"

Not looking at me, Tyler hopped out of the ring and went straight for the punching bag. "What do you want me to say, Kacey?"

Circling around the ring, I came up behind him and stopped while he pounded on the bag. "I want you to listen to what I have to say. Stop running from me."

"I'm not running. I just choose to be here, away from you and your jackass brother."

"So that's it, huh? You automatically assume I'm like him, so you run off and start fucking the first girl you can find." Immediately, he stopped, his chest rising and falling with his ragged breaths. "Yeah, my brother was all too happy to show me a video of you talking shit."

Tired of looking at his back, I grabbed his arm and pulled as hard as I could, but he turned around willingly. My lips trembled and I dug my nails into my palms to block out the pain in my chest. For a split second he looked sad. Then, I blinked and it was back to stone.

"Tyler, I accept the fact you don't understand why I kept my family history a secret, and why would you? You come from a perfect home, where your parents love you. I come from one of greed and malice. I've never had the pleasure of meeting a functional family until yours. It made me realize happiness is possible. I even started believing I could have that someday.

"My brother is a dick and when I had the chance to move away from home, I did. I left and never looked back. I never anticipated falling in love with you. Hell, I wanted to stay away from you and the fighting world."

I paused and closed my eyes, the burn welling up behind my lids. "My one regret," I began, my breath hitching, "is that I was selfish. I didn't want to let you go, but I can promise you . . . I was myself the entire time we were together. I need someone who can love me for who I am, not hate me because of where I come from."

Jaw clenching, he looked away and stayed silent. I jumped when Matt slammed open the back door and started sliding on his gloves. He busied himself with other

245

things, pretending not to notice us, but the awkward silence was deafening.

"Say something," I whispered.

Tyler glanced over at Matt and never once looked down at me. "I have nothing to say."

The tears flowed freely now that my heart had shattered into a million pieces. I wanted Tyler to look at me, to touch me, but he didn't. He turned away from me and started punching the bag again, harder with each jab. I was too embarrassed to look at Matt, so I kept my head held high until I got to the door. I could see Tyler's reflection in the windows, and he never wavered. He was done with me. As soon as I opened the door and the fresh air blew across my face, I broke down and ran, hoping I could get as far away as fast as I could.

However, when I turned the corner, I ran straight into Paxton's arms, burying my head in his chest. "Get me out of here, Pax," I cried.

Keeping his arm around my waist, he led me over to his Hummer and opened the door. I slid in while he grabbed my suitcase and purse out of my rental and set them in the back seat. "We'll come get the car tomorrow. You can stay at my place tonight."

I laid my head against the window and closed my eyes. There were too many tears, I couldn't see anything. "I thought he loved me, Pax. Instead, he was cold . . . detached. I've never seen him like that."

Pulling out, Pax huffed and squealed his tires as he sped out of the parking lot. "I told you it wouldn't be good, but you didn't listen, Kacey. Things are really screwed up right now. You picked a bad time to come out here."

When I looked in the side view mirror, Tyler burst out of the gym, and slammed his arms into the brick wall when he saw Pax's vehicle speeding away. More tears flowed from my eyes, obscuring my view of him as we slipped further and further away. I couldn't breathe, my chest ached, and the harder I tried to breathe the more lightheaded I got. "From the way he looked at me, I don't think there was ever a good time, Pax. I just want to go home and forget all of this ever happened."

Closing my eyes, I could feel my lungs tightening up with each breath. In my lifetime, I'd only had a handful of panic attacks, my worst one being when my father died. This one, however, felt like I was going to die.

"Kacey! What the fuck? Hold on, we're almost there."

The whole world felt like it was closing in on me, strangling me, taking away every precious breath. I had lost everything. Before passing out to my sweet surrender, I saw Paxton's face above my own, his green eyes terrified.

"Breathe," he commanded, his voice sounding so far away.

Closing my eyes, I heard frantic voices all around me, and hands touching my skin.

"Breathe, beautiful. I need you to come back to me."

Tyler.

His voice echoed in my ear and I knew it was my own hallucinations imagining he was with me. It was most likely the last time I would ever hear his voice. "I want to hear it again," I rasped. "Say it one more time."

My vision was cloudy, but I felt something warm close over my lips, calming me. "I need you to come back to me, beautiful."

Too exhausted, I closed my eyes and slowly fell into the darkness. "No," I replied. "It's too late."

Head throbbing, I scrunched my eyes and could already tell they were swollen, and most likely red. When I tried to stretch, I couldn't move my body because a set of arms held me tight and I was wrapped up in a gazillion blankets. "What the hell, Pax? I'm not a burrito."

"Sorry to disappoint, but I'm not Paxton. If it were him, he'd be losing his limbs right about now."

Wide-eyed, I rolled out of his arms and fell onto the floor, groaning when I knocked my knee on the bed frame. "What are you doing here?" I snapped angrily, glaring up at Tyler. "You have no right to touch me."

He held his hands up in defeat. "I know, but you need to let me explain."

Stalking around the bed, I flipped him off and slammed open the door to find Paxton waiting just outside. "I don't need to let you explain shit," I challenged, glaring back at Tyler. Then to Paxton, I crossed my arms over my chest defiantly. "Tell me what's going on, Pax."

Tyler slipped out of bed and slid on his jeans and a wrinkled white T-shirt. "You had a panic attack last night, Kacey. After you left, I couldn't let you go, so I got in my car and followed you guys. Paxton pulled over when you started struggling for air."

"Like you care," I hissed, glaring at him.

"I *do* care and I'm so, so sorry. You have no idea how hard it's been."

What was he talking about? Glaring at both guys, they both looked sheepish. "Okay, what in the holy fuck is going on here? What are you talking about? And since when did you two become friends?"

They both glanced at each other and then Tyler grumbled, "We're not friends. We have a mutual understanding. When he saw I was in town, he warned me your brother was keeping tabs on us. I kind of figured he would." He wrapped his arms around my waist and pulled me in tight to his chest. His scent engulfed me and I breathed him in, relaxing in his hold without thinking about it. "I'm sorry for doing what I did, but I had no choice. This whole week has been a ploy to keep your brother in the dark."

Stepping away, I turned around and faced him. "A ploy? What are you talking about?"

This time it was Paxton who stepped forward and spoke, "Like we said . . . your brother's been keeping tabs on him. I'm sure you found that out when you saw the video."

How could I forget? But was it really just a hoax? "Yes, I saw it," I snapped, turning my glare to Tyler. "So are you saying it was fake? That you didn't go out and sleep with the nearest whores you could find?"

When I tried to walk away, Tyler grabbed my arms and held me firm. "Goddammit, Kacey, *no*. It was a scam . . . all of it. That video was intended for you and Kyle both to see it. I didn't go out that night and fuck a bunch of women. Kyle needed to see me fighting like shit and he needed to see you upset. I wanted it to be believable."

Paxton nodded his head when I looked over at him. "It's true, Kacey. I'm the one who took the video and sent it to your brother."

"What? But I thought you weren't speaking to him anymore?" I asked skeptically.

"I wasn't, until he called me. When word got back to him that we were seen together in Phoenix, he called and told me about what happened between you and Tyler. I played along and told him I wanted you back and would help him. That's why I sent him the video and told him to show it to you."

"So what happens now? Did you tell him I'm here in California?"

Tyler's jaw clenched and Paxton sighed. "Yes, he knows you're here. Thankfully, none of his friends saw you go to the gym last night and break down. Your brother thinks you're here with me . . . and that we're back together."

"Oh my God," I grumbled. Paxton bit his lip and stared at me, his expression troubled. Tyler, on the other hand, was tense and angry. "Why do you both look like that? Is there something else going on I should know about?"

Tyler took my hands and pulled me to him. "Your brother wants Paxton to show you off at the fight in hopes of distracting me."

That didn't surprise me. "Yeah, he mentioned something about me sitting in his corner. What's so bad about that? You know it's not like that anymore between me and him."

"That's not the point, Kacey. To be convincing, you

can't just sit beside each other and everything be good. He's going to need to touch you and make it look real. I can't stomach the thought of his hands on you, or worse . . . seeing you enjoy it."

"Also," Paxton said, cutting in, "I'm fighting for my own title Saturday night, so I'll need you with me. I'll be in Vegas on Friday and I know Kyle expects us to be together. I figured you could either stay with me in a hotel room, or I could stay at your house. Which do you prefer?"

"Neither," Tyler mumbled.

"You can stay at my house," I told him. "I have a spare bedroom you can sleep in."

Tyler's jaw tensed. "And so help me God, you better stay in that room, Emerson."

Paxton chuckled and picked up my suitcase and purse. "I'll think about it," he taunted wickedly. "Now get out of here. I told Kyle that Kacey would be heading back to Vegas later tonight. So you have the day to yourselves." He handed Tyler my things.

Before walking into the hallway, I lifted up on my tiptoes and hugged him tightly around the neck. "Thank you, Pax," I whispered. "I'm sorry you're getting drug back into my brother's mess."

Rubbing his hands down my back I could hear the smile in his voice. "I'm not worried about it, Kace. I'd do anything for you, you know that."

"I know."

For once, I actually felt whole again. It almost seemed surreal. Tyler was mine, but it was only for the day. If there was a way to freeze time, this would be the day.

CHAPTER 38

Kacey

BEFORE LEAVING PAXTON'S house, I washed up in the bathroom, changed into an olive green tank top and jeans, and brushed my teeth. While waiting, Tyler called Matt and told him what happened and that he wouldn't be at the gym. I didn't want him to lose valuable training time, but I also wanted to be selfish and have him all to myself.

"Are you sure you don't need to train today?" I asked, tying my hair up into a ponytail. Tyler reached for my hand and brought it to his lips. "No, I'll train tonight. All I want to do is spend today with you. I know we have a lot to talk about." That was an understatement.

"Where have you been staying since you've been here?"

"At a hotel. I'm going to take us to another one just in case he has someone watching." He looked over at me, lifting his brows. "Why?"

"I don't know," I mumbled, shrugging my shoulders. I turned my head and looked out the window. "I guess I figured you'd go running back to Gabriella after what happened."

"Kacey, no," he thundered. "I haven't even spoken to her since I've been in town. I've stayed true to my word and kept my distance because I love you."

"Then why were you so cold to me last night? Why would you do that to me?"

His expression darkening, he looked weary. "Because, I never know when one of your brother's friends are watching. I took a gamble coming after you last night, but I couldn't let you go. My plan was to find you after the fight on Saturday and tell you everything. And then, when you came in and I saw you in pain, it was the worst feeling I'd ever felt in my life. In that moment, I didn't care about anything other than finding you."

"So it *was* you talking to me last night," I whispered. "I thought I imagined it all. When I started to black out I heard your voice and held onto it. I didn't want to wake up."

Tyler pulled into the hotel parking lot and turned to face me. "Yes, it was me. When I got to Paxton's and watched him pull you from the car, I rushed over and saw you gasping for air. It was the most terrifying thing I'd ever seen, and what's worse—I was the cause of it. You never told me you had panic attacks."

I never liked talking about my attacks. They made me feel weak, like I couldn't handle the stress. "I've only had a couple that grand-scale. The last one happened when my father died. Paxton was who helped calm me down then."

He shook his head. "I'll admit, I saw a side to him I never would've thought possible. He was terrified when he couldn't help you."

I smiled. The times I had with Paxton were some of my best childhood memories. "He's a good friend, Tyler. The only reason he hung around my brother was so he could stay close to me. He was my friend before he became Kyle's. I would have been lost without him."

Tyler groaned and opened his door. "And now I have to watch you and him together this weekend. Are you sure he doesn't want you back?"

"I'm sure," I replied, getting out of his truck. "He still has a thing for Gabriella." I watched him intently to see if I could find any shred of jealousy, but he didn't tense at all.

"I wish him luck on that one. She's protective over her brother, so anyone who's had any ties with Kyle is on her shit list."

And I guess that includes me, I thought.

"Well, then I should let you know that Paxton isn't the only one interested in her. My brother is too, and you know how he is when he wants something."

Tyler slammed his truck door. "You can't be serious?"

"I wish I wasn't. I told Paxton already, so he's going to make sure Kyle stays away from her."

Tyler sighed and grabbed my suitcase out of the back seat. "I sure hope so. But I've seen Gabriella take on your brother. If there's any female who could put him in his place, it'd be her."

Once inside the hotel, I followed Tyler to the check in

desk so he could get us a room for the day. After that was all said and done we sauntered to the elevators and as soon as the doors closed, my heart started to race. Tyler set my suitcase down and brought his hands to my face, his lips firm and warm as he closed them over mine. "I've missed you so much, beautiful. I have three days to make up for in only one afternoon."

"So do you understand now why it was so hard to tell you the truth? Actually, I was going to tell you on two different occasions. The first time, we were sitting on my front steps and were interrupted by Cindy telling me Nana had passed. And then again, after our night at the police station, when I told you the other day that we needed to talk and you wanted me to wait until later."

He kissed me again, except this time it was deeper, his tongue caressing mine. "Yes, I understand, Kacey. I realized it a little too late. I let my anger control me, and I couldn't see what was really there. All I could see was that you lied to me. I didn't take the time to think of why."

The elevator doors opened and reluctantly Tyler let me go so I could follow him to the room. Once he slipped the key in the door, we walked inside and he immediately grabbed me around the waist and pulled me to him. "We only have this afternoon. I want to make love to you. I've missed the way you feel in my arms, and the way your skin tastes. I never thought I'd get the chance to be with you again."

Tilting my chin up, I closed the distance between us and slid my fingers through his hair. "We're together now, and after Saturday we don't have to worry about anything coming between us again. I don't care what my brother does, I know I'm not going to let him win."

Slowly, Tyler trailed his fingers around the waistband of my jeans and gently unbuttoned them, sliding the zipper down. "Neither am I, beautiful. His end will come."

Picking me up in his arms, he carried me over to the bed and laid me down, the sheets white and crisp beneath me. The hotel room was small, with a king-size bed, a desk, and bathroom with light green walls. It wasn't the same as being home, but anywhere with Tyler was home for me.

Tyler stood and lifted his T-shirt over his head, as I did the same—along with discarding my bra. Unbuttoning his jeans, he let them and his boxers fall to the floor. He was already hard between his legs and it made my insides throb.

Crawling across the bed, he gripped the waist band of my jeans and pulled them down my body, keeping his eyes locked on mine.

"Shouldn't you be refraining from any sexual activities before a big fight? I mean, I know you haven't the past couple of times, but shouldn't this one be more important?"

Spreading my legs with his knee, he trailed his tongue up my body, from my clit on up to my breasts, and circled them both before biting down on one of my nipples. "You have nothing to worry about," he growled. "I hate your brother enough to get the testosterone flowing. Not to mention, I'm still going to be watching you and Paxton together."

Taking his face in my hands, I kissed his lips, tasting my desire. "And you have nothing to worry about. I'm all yours . . . now make love to me already."

He grabbed his cock and we both watched as he gently circled his tip around my opening, getting it wet before pushing in slightly, inch by inch. I missed the fullness of having him inside me; there was no greater pleasure. Closing my eyes, I trailed my fingers up his back and down his arms, loving the way his muscles flexed and tightened under my touch. I felt safe in his arms, protected. "I love it when you touch me," he murmured heatedly.

His warm breath tickled my skin as he kissed his way up my neck and over my cheek to my lips. With his hands on both sides of my face, he held me firm as he kissed me, harder and deeper with each thrust between my legs. My orgasm slowly began to build and even more so when Tyler lowered a hand to my breast and squeezed, massaging it hard. It felt good when he pinched my nipples—the pleasure and pain of it always sent shock waves down below.

Tyler pushed deeper inside of me, holding me tight. He was making love to me, slow and gentle, and I didn't want it to end. I didn't want to leave him in California and go back to Vegas without him . . . but I had to.

"Do you promise you'll come back to me?" I asked, tears welling in my eyes.

Still pushing deep inside of me, Tyler lifted his head and gently kissed my lips. "I promise, beautiful. I'm never going to leave you again."

He wiped away my tears and picked up his pace, thrusting harder. In his eyes, I could see the pain, and he wanted me to see it. He needed me to know that none of what happened was easy on him either.

Listening to the deep groans in his chest, I knew he was close. Wrapping my legs around his waist, I thrust my hips against him and arched my back when he lowered his lips to my breasts, suckling each one. The harder he sucked, the closer I got.

"Tyler," I moaned, fisting my hands in his hair.

He fisted his own hands in my hair, pulling tight as his pace picked up. After a couple more thrusts, my body exploded. Digging my nails in his back, I screamed out my pleasure as Tyler growled in my ear, pulsating as he released inside of me. Breathing hard, he kissed me softly and turned over on his back, taking me with him, so I was straddling him. He was still hard inside of me and by the smile on his face he was ready for more.

"That was one day down, beautiful. We still have a few more to make up for. Are you sure you're ready for this?"

"Oh, I'm ready," I vowed, reaching behind my ass so I could cup his balls as I rode him. "I'm just getting warmed up."

CHAPTER 39

Kacey

SAYING GOODBYE TO Tyler wasn't easy, considering we had just one afternoon together after the fall out. Thankfully, Bree was waiting for me when I got home. I got her text saying she knew what happened and she wanted to see me.

"You knew the whole time, didn't you?" I announced, getting out of the car. I grabbed my suitcase from the backseat and set it on the ground.

Biting her lip, Bree slowly trudged toward me and hung her head. "Are you mad? Tyler called me the day he left and told me what he had planned. I'd given it to him hard and it finally sank in."

"You did, did you?" I teased. "What did you do, threaten to kick his ass? I'm sure you really scared him with that."

Lifting her head, she laughed and gave me a hug. "Hey, don't underestimate me. I could've sworn I saw him tremble in fear."

Both of us laughing, I grabbed my suitcase and we headed up the front porch stairs to the door. Once inside, I turned on the lights and rolled my suitcase into my room before joining her in the kitchen. She already had the refrigerator open and was pulling out one of my bottles of white wine. *Mmm . . . Riesling, my favorite.*

"After everything you've been through, I'd say you need a glass of wine. I hope that's okay," she said, setting the bottle down.

I pulled my cell phone out of my back pocket and hopped up on the kitchen counter. "Nope, it's perfectly fine. I think you read my mind."

After she opened the bottle of wine, she poured me a glass and handed it to me before pouring her own. I missed my grandmother's kitchen, the way it smelled as she cooked dinner when I was a kid, and the way her imagination would come up with unique dishes at each holiday. She taught me so much when it came to coming up with new ideas. My desire to open my own restaurant was all because of her.

Hopping up beside me, Bree held her glass out and tapped it against mine. "I'm toasting because I'm thankful I don't have to keep anything from you anymore. It killed me not telling you the truth, Kace. I saw how upset you were and there were times when I almost buckled.

"I kept telling myself how it was just one week of keeping you in the dark, but then it started to be the longest week of my life. Hearing you cry and knowing you were alone here didn't help."

"Tell me about it," I replied. "I had never felt so lost in my life. But now it doesn't matter. I know he loves me and he understands."

Bree nodded. "Yes, he does. He may be a temperamental ass sometimes, and speak before he thinks, but he's a good guy. I think we both have great men."

"That we do."

"I'll admit though, it hurt you didn't tell me the truth. We're friends and you can tell me anything. You don't ever have to be ashamed. I love you no matter what."

I bumped her in the shoulder and took a huge sip of my wine. "Thanks, Bree. Just to give you a heads up, I'm not going to be sitting with you and Cole during the fight. I'll be with Paxton and Kyle's friends. Apparently, Pax told my brother he and I were together again."

Bree choked on her wine and coughed, glaring at me with wide eyes. "Does Tyler know you're doing this?"

Tilting my glass, I drank the rest of my wine and sighed. "Yes, he knows. He's not happy about it, but until Saturday night, I have to do what I have to do."

Bree shook her head and poured me another glass of wine. "I swear, your life is never boring."

Before I could lift my glass to my lips, a text came through on my phone.

"Please tell me that's not your brother," Bree groaned.

When I opened it up, I smiled.

Tyler: I left a surprise in your suitcase. I figured it was time for you to start thinking about your future. I was planning on giving it to you on Saturday as kind of a peace offering. Don't worry though, I'll make you work for it.

See you in two days, beautiful. I love you.

"It must be something good for you to be smiling like that," Bree chimed.

Jumping off the counter, I rushed to my bedroom and turned on the light. Immediately, I grabbed my suitcase and dropped it onto my bed. I fumbled with the zipper and hastily opened the suitcase, my heart beating rapidly.

Inside, there was a large envelope with my name on it in Tyler's hand writing.

"What's in it?" Bree asked curiously, taking a seat on my bed.

I opened up the envelope and pulled out the stack of papers enclosed. On top, there was a letter with a check attached to it . . . a ten thousand dollar check. *Holy shit!*

Bree's eyes went wide and she screamed, "Oh my God, that's ten thousand dollars! What the hell did you do, go all *Pretty Woman* on his ass?"

"No," I shrieked. "Let me read the letter and see what's going on."

Kacey,

Let me start off by saying, you better not rip up the fucking check. I know how stubborn you are and I know you want to work for your money, but I'm ready to see you achieve your goals. I'm impatient and I know you've worked hard for what you have. With that being said, I AM going to make you work off the money, but at least now I know you have enough to get your restaurant opened and running. I have faith in you and in your abilities to do this.

Attached, you'll find vacant properties in the Vegas area, all in good locations. Bree should be there with you, so I want you to look at the different places and decide which ones would be best. By this time next week I want to see you achieving your dreams. I'm going to be there with you every step of the way, for as long as you can put up with me. I love you.

    Tyler

Speechless, I passed the letter to Bree and rummaged through the papers.

"Holy shit, is he for real? This is insane," she exclaimed. I handed her some of the ads and we both curled up on the bed and inspected every single one.

"I think it's time, Bree. I know we're still young and we didn't expect this to happen so soon, but I think we can do it. Are you ready to take the leap?"

"You better fucking believe it."

Kacey

Fight Night

INSTEAD OF COMING on Friday, Paxton missed his flight and decided to head up early Saturday morning, instead of waiting at the airport for a later flight. It made Tyler happy that I didn't have Paxton sleeping in the same house as me.

I couldn't wait to see Tyler and tell him the good news—Bree and I were ready to put in a bid for the restaurant. As soon as he won the fight tonight and I had him home, I was going to show him the place.

Paxton: I just got my luggage. I'll be out in five.

I hadn't been waiting for long before the text came

through. It was closing in on three o'clock in the afternoon, so we didn't have much time before he needed to be at the arena. Once the five minutes was up, I drove around to the pickup lane and there he was in a pair of jeans and gray T-shirt, his black hair covered by a navy blue baseball cap.

I pulled up beside him and unlocked the doors.

"Thanks for picking me up," he said, putting his bags in the back and getting in, reaching over to give me a hug.

"You're welcome. I am your girlfriend for the evening, remember? It wouldn't be very loving of me to leave you at the airport, now would it?" I teased.

"No, it wouldn't. Have you talked to your brother today?"

As soon as the driving lane cleared up, I slid out and started on our way to the arena. Shaking my head, I turned to him and replied, "No, why? Have you?"

Pursing his lips, he sat back in the seat and furrowed his brows, looking worried. "No, I haven't. I'm surprised he hasn't tried calling one of us."

"You don't think he suspects something, do you?"

"How can he? We've been super careful." Pax's words were confident, but his face looked worried.

Have we been careful enough? My brother was an expert on finding things out. He always had a way of being in the right place at the right time. It's like he had his own private camera in every place imaginable. Maybe he should've been a private detective.

"If I call him, it'll definitely look weird. I never do unless I'm pissed at him. I'm assuming we should just continue on with our plan. What time do we absolutely have to be at the MGM?"

Sighing, Paxton shrugged his shoulders. "I would say in another hour and a half at the latest."

Looking at the clock, we had about ten more minutes before we reached my house. I had just enough time to take a shower and get ready before we had to be at the arena. Unfortunately, I had a feeling something wasn't right, and Pax felt it too. Maybe it was just nerves? Somehow I didn't believe that.

I had just gotten out of the shower when I heard several voices in the living room. "Pax?" I called out. Tightening up my robe, I stuck my head into the hallway and gasped. My brother, along with three of his friends, including Jordan, were out there, and they all turned my way. I glared at Jordan who in return smiled and winked at me. Disgusted, I flipped him off.

Paxton kept his face blank when he looked at me and I had no clue what was going on. "Kyle, what are you doing here?" I asked, crossing my arms over my chest. The devilish look in his mismatched eyes was scary, almost malicious.

"I came here to see you and Paxton before the fight. Is there something wrong with that?" he countered.

When I looked over at Paxton, he shrugged his shoulders and rolled his eyes.

"No, I guess not," I replied. "But I need to finish getting ready, so I'll be out in just a few."

"Kacey, wait," Kyle commanded as his phone started to ring. He held up his finger. "Give me one second."

Sighing, I leaned against the door frame and waited for him to get off of the phone. *I really can't wait for this day to be over with.*

Hanging up his phone, he took another step closer to me. "All right, it looks as if there's been a change in plans. Judging by the way you look right now, I don't think you'll make it in time," he said to me.

I was in my robe, my wet hair tied up in a towel. I still had an hour before we were supposed to be at the arena. "What's going on?"

Kyle put his phone back in his pocket and shrugged his shoulders. "It looks like we need to get there early. We all have to be ready for the photo shoot in twenty minutes."

There was no way in hell I'd be ready and at the arena in twenty minutes. "So what are you saying?" I asked impatiently.

He looked at his friends and nodded toward the door. "I'm saying, we need to leave *now*. Paxton can come with me and you can meet us out there." He reached in his back pocket and handed me an envelope. "It has your ticket in it if you run late."

Paxton got to his feet and grabbed his bag and walked over to me, his gaze guarded.

Kyle smiled at me and then fist bumped Paxton.

"I'll see you outside," Pax said to him.

Once Kyle and his friends were out of the house, Paxton turned toward the door and stared at them through the window. "I don't know what's going on, but I want you to be careful, okay? Something's not right."

Yeah, I felt it too. I knew something was off all day.

"Same to you," I whispered. "I'll see you in a little bit okay?"

He nodded and leaned down to kiss my cheek. "Make sure you call me if you need me. I'll find a way back to you."

"I will. Now go." I shoved him toward the door.

Paxton looked back at me once before heading out the door and down to Kyle's car.

What was going on?

I had just put my ticket in my purse and was ready to leave, when a knock sounded on my front door.

"What the hell do you want?" I snapped when I was confronted with my guests.

Smiling wolfishly with his devilish green eyes, Liam opened the screen door and leaned against the frame, Jordan loitering around behind him. I wanted to slam the door in Liam's face, but I didn't want him to know I was scared—he fed off of that shit.

"We're here to keep you company, sweet thing." He pushed off the frame and barged into my house, grabbing a hold of my arm and pulling me inside.

"Hey, what are you doing?" I asked frantically. I looked back and Jordan shut the door, locking it, along with closing the blinds in the surrounding windows. Terrified couldn't begin to describe the way I was feeling inside.

Liam stopped me in the middle of the living room and leered up and down my body. "You look really cute in your dress, sunshine. Where's your cell phone?"

It was in my purse, but I wasn't going to tell him that. Liam let my arm go and I instantly crossed my arms over my chest, defiantly. "I don't know," I snapped. "Where's Kyle?"

Jordan stopped in front of me with a malevolent sneer, his hazel eyes amused. "Don't worry, Kyle knows we're here. Now, answer the question . . . where's your cell phone?"

"I'm not telling you shit," I spat. "I have to get to the arena. Everyone's waiting on me."

Coming up behind me, Liam brushed the hair off my neck and lowered his nose to my skin, breathing me in. Instantly, I jumped and tried to move away, but he and Jordan had me sandwiched in. "Sorry, sunshine, but you're not going anywhere. Before I say anymore, I need your cell phone."

When I didn't answer, they both chuckled. "Okay, I see how it is," Liam said. "I'm just going to have to go looking for it." His arms wrapped around my waist and he frisked me, even though it was clear I didn't have it on my body with the dress I was wearing. "I wonder if it's up here?" he moaned in my ear, sliding his hands up to my breasts.

It's a strange feeling to be touched by someone you absolutely hate. It's like all of your fighting instincts appear. As hard as I could, I elbowed him in the side and he doubled over. My car keys were on the kitchen counter, so I raced toward them. I didn't get very far, as I was tackled to the floor by Jordan, his body heavy on top of mine. He flipped me over and straddled my waist, holding my arms above my head.

"Now that wasn't very nice," he taunted. "We can't have that." His breath smelled like cigarette smoke, so I turned my head and tried to keep from gagging. However, I knew I was in trouble when Liam stood above me.

Licking his lips, he smiled down at me with a set of cable ties in his hands. "No, we can't, and I have just the right solution. Let's get her to her room."

Grasping my wrists tight, Jordan roughly pulled me to my feet and slung me over his shoulder, rough hands sliding up my bare thighs.

"So help me God, if you don't get your hands off me . . ."

"Oh, stop being so dramatic," he griped, smacking me on the ass. "I'm just having a little bit of fun. Once the fights are over, we'll let you go."

Jordan slammed me down on my bed and before I could move, Liam straddled my waist. Pulling my arms up to the headboard, Jordan held them tight while Liam wrapped the cable ties around each wrist. I tried to move, but the plastic bit into my skin. The searing pain, along with fear of being tied down, brought tears to my eyes.

"Guys, this really hurts. Please let me go."

"Sorry, sunshine," Liam replied, sliding off my body, "but no can do." He opened my closet door and rummaged through my things, until he found a couple of my silk scarves—one cream colored and the other black.

Taking them out, he smoothed them through his fingers and moaned when he peered down at me, helpless and completely at his mercy. *Kyle won't let him do anything to me, will he?* That was the million dollar question. Obviously, he was so wrapped up in his desire to win he would put me at the mercy of someone as sadistic as Liam.

As Liam spread my legs and tied me to the posts on my bed, all I could think about was Tyler. If I didn't show up to the arena, he would know something was wrong and he wouldn't be able to concentrate. This was a much surer way to fuck with his head, instead of him only seeing me with Paxton.

Looking at the clock, I had two hours until Tyler's fight with my brother. Until then, I was in hell. *Please God, let Tyler win.*

Paxton

IT WAS TEN minutes before my fight and Kacey was nowhere to be seen. I texted her and called her, but she never answered. Something was wrong. If Kyle was up to something, I would kill him. My coach, Darren Blake, watched me pace along the floor of my room, staring curiously at me. He didn't know what was going on.

Darren was in his mid-thirties with light brown hair he kept shaved close to his scalp, and arm muscles that were as big around as my thighs. He always wore form fitting clothes, so the ladies could see how big he actually was. The guy was a monster and it was because of him and Kacey that I decided to turn my life around—to be the type of fighter I knew I could be.

"Do you want to tell me what's got you all pissed off?" he asked casually. "Is it because Kacey's not here?"

He made it sound like she stood me up, but I knew that wasn't the case.

"Yes, but it's not in the way you think. Something's wrong."

Storming out of my room, I saw Tyler standing in the doorway of his own room, talking to his father. He tensed when I walked by, but I didn't acknowledge him because there were too many people around. I was pretty sure he knew something was wrong when he saw Kacey wasn't with me.

When I got to Kyle's room, I pounded my fist angrily on the door. The door opened and his brows lifted amusingly when he saw me standing there, fuming. "Can I help you? Shouldn't you be about ready to fight?"

"Where's Kacey?" I thundered. "She's not here." Glancing into his room, there were two people missing . . . Liam and Jordan. *You have got to be fucking kidding me.* And Kyle had the gall to look at me like nothing was wrong.

"Oh, I know," he replied. "Did she not call you?"

"No," I snapped. "What the fuck's going on, Kyle? If you have some sort of plan involving Kacey you better rethink it, now."

Kyle chuckled and slapped me on the shoulder. "Calm down, my friend. She wasn't feeling good, so she decided to stay at home. I guess I don't get to see the torment on Tyler's face when he sees you two together. Oh well, I'll kick his ass without her here. Now go and finish getting ready. We're going to get our seats so we can watch you win your title."

He held out his hand and reluctantly I shook it, wishing deep down I could break his fucking face. "All right,

I'll see you out there." *Fucking liar.*

Turning on my heel, I headed back to my room and watched him and his friends walk down the hall toward the arena. Out of the corner of my eye, Tyler noticed them leave too. I opened my door and stepped inside, leaving it cracked because at any moment Tyler would be storming in. It took all of three seconds. He was already dressed in his black and neon green fighting shorts and black robe, his body tense.

"Where is she?" he growled, shutting the door.

Darren got to his feet. "Dude, what the fuck?"

"Darren, it's okay," I said, stepping in his path. "Tyler and I are on the same side here." Turning to Tyler, I picked up my phone and checked to see if Kacey had called . . . nothing. "I don't know what's going on. I've tried calling and texting her, but she's not responding. Kyle said she was sick and told him she wasn't coming. You and I both know that's a load of horse shit."

"Goddammit," Tyler hissed, angrily fisting his hands in his hair. "Where do you think she is?"

"Pax, man, we need to get going. Your fight starts in five minutes. You need to get into position, or you forfeit," Darren warned regretfully.

As dread settled in the pit of my stomach, I could see the anguish in Tyler's eyes. "I don't think the problem is where she's at, more so than who she's *with*."

Tyler's eyes went wide. "What do you mean?"

"Did you notice Liam and Jordan weren't with Kyle just a few minutes ago?"

"Holy fuck," he growled as realization set in. Turning on his heel, he started for the door and angrily slammed it open. "I'm going to find her."

"I'm going too," I announced. "If those cocksuckers are with her, you're going to need my help."

Impatiently, Tyler slammed the door and turned around. "No, you have to stay here. If you forfeit your fight, Kyle will know something's wrong. Kacey wouldn't want you missing this chance to win a title."

"What about you? She would say the same thing to you. If you go and don't get back in time, you'll basically be letting Kyle win," I exclaimed. "You can't let that happen."

"It doesn't matter. Making sure Kacey is safe is the only thing on my mind right now. She's worth more than any fucking title." With those last words, he disappeared out the door.

For the first time in my life, I felt helpless. I was worried about Kacey and I didn't know what to do.

Darren stopped at my side and put his hand on my shoulder. "I know you want to help, but he's right, you need to go out there and fight. You going out there will help Tyler more than you think."

"How is that?" I asked blandly.

He turned and looked me in the eyes. "By you going out there, you will give him the time he needs to find Kacey and get back. Stretch the fight out for as long as possible, to the third round if you can. I know you can do this."

Sighing, I nodded my head and opened the door. "Let's do this."

I'll do it for Kacey.

CHAPTER 42

TYLER

"SON, WHAT ARE you doing?" my father shouted as I stormed past him into my room. He had everything ready on the table for me to tape up my hands, and he even had on his black and green T-shirt with *Coach* printed on the back.

"I'm going to get Kacey. She's in trouble." I grabbed my keys and started for the door, but my father stepped in my way.

"You can't leave, Tyler. What about the fight . . . your title?"

Breathing hard, I closed my eyes and tried not to picture Kacey screaming for help with Liam's hands all over her. I could feel the anger boiling in my veins.

"If I don't get her, I'll lose more than just the title,

dad. She needs me right now."

I expected my father to argue with me, but I was surprised when he nodded his head and opened the door. "Then I'm coming with you. You're not going to do this alone. Now come on, let's go. There's still time."

We started down the hall, pretending everything was okay, but as soon as we got outside of the arena, we both ran as fast as we could. I hadn't seen my father run like that in years.

"Let's take my truck. If anyone sees yours, it'll blow our cover. Are Kyle's goons with her?" he asked.

"I think his agent is. You know who Liam is, right?"

My father snarled, "How could I forget?"

"And I think the guy I beat up at the club is with her too. He's one of Kyle's friends."

"Well, doesn't this just keep getting better? Whatever happens, I want you to concentrate on getting Kacey. Let me handle the dirty work. You need to conserve your energy for the fight."

Speeding down the road, I didn't care if I got pulled over or not, I wasn't going to stop until I got to Kacey's. As far as conserving my energy, if anyone hurt her in *any* way, I wasn't going to hold back. I wouldn't be able to stop, even if I tried.

There was indeed another car in front of her house. The light was on in her bedroom, as well as in the living room and kitchen, but I couldn't see in her windows because the blinds were closed.

"I'm going to park down the street and we can walk up."

My father nodded and pulled out a small black bag from his glove compartment.

"What's that?" I asked.

Smiling, he opened it up and inside were various lock picks of different sizes. "Do you know how many times I've left the keys to the gym at home? Your mother bought me these so I'd always have a way in."

Quickly, we both got out of the truck and ran down the sidewalk, crouching behind a set of bushes at the edge of her yard.

"It'll only take me a couple of seconds to unlock the door," he whispered over to me. "As soon as I do, we don't need to barge in. Let's do it quietly and catch whoever's inside of there off guard."

My father started toward the front door, but I went straight to Kacey's window. Her curtains were pulled down, but they were sheer enough to where I could vaguely see inside. She was on her bed with tears streaming down her cheeks. But that wasn't all . . . she was fucking tied down to her bed. *Motherfucker!*

I tried to lift her window, but it was locked. My father hissed my name, and I was about to go to him when I saw Kacey's bedroom door open and Liam enter. By the look in his hungered stare, and the way he locked the door, I knew what his intentions were.

Kacey trembled on the bed and fought against her restraints, her wrists blistered and red from the ties. The second Liam crawled on the bed and started touching her, I lost all self-control.

He was a fucking dead man.

CHAPTER 43

Kacey

WHEN LIAM ENTERED and locked the door behind him, I knew I was in trouble. I pulled on my restraints and hissed with pain. "What are you doing?"

He crawled up the bed and put his hands on my calves, slowly sliding them up my thighs, lifting my dress along the way. He didn't stop until the bottom of my dress laid on my stomach.

I felt ill. "Get off of me, Liam. Kyle will kill you when he finds out."

"No, he won't, because he knows he's nothing without me," he murmured, kissing his way up my thighs.

My legs were tied too tightly and I couldn't close them or push him off. I was trapped and the combination of wanting to vomit and having my adrenalin pumping was almost bad enough to make me pass out.

"Fuck, you're so hot. I'm going to enjoy this."

When he started unbuttoning his pants, I lost it. "Liam, no," I shouted. "Please, don't do this to me."

Getting to his feet, he lifted his shirt over his head and let his pants fall to the floor. He reached into the pocket of his jeans and pulled out a condom, opening it up slowly, tormenting me. "Just relax, sunshine. It hurts more when you're tense. Although, tense makes you tight, and I guess that's better for me." He shrugged.

Tears poured down my cheeks and all I could think about was Tyler. He would kill both Liam and my brother after this; he would go to jail and things would never be the same.

"Jordan!" I screamed. "Help me, *please*! Don't let Liam do this to me!"

Liam snarled and jumped on top of me, slamming his hand over my mouth. "The only name you're going to be screaming is mine, you bitch. Jordan's not going to help you." He pushed his arousal into my hip and I gagged.

In the next second, the door burst open and Liam was yanked off of my body and thrown across the room. I heard fists pounding into flesh and the gurgling sound of someone struggling to breathe.

I closed my eyes and breathed a sigh of relief. Jordan saved me. I felt my dress pulled back into place and then the cold bite of metal slid against my skin. My wrist was free, the tie cut away. However, it wasn't Jordan who re-leased me from my restraints.

"Kacey." Tyler's strangled voice was full of heart-ache and rage. "I'm getting you out of here." He wiped away my tears.

When I could finally see him, I burst into more tears and held onto him as he lifted me up and carried me to the door. "Oh my God, I was so scared," I wailed. I looked down at the floor and Liam was knocked unconscious, his face a bloody mess.

Tyler's dad already had Jordan apprehended and rushed over, peering down at Liam on the floor. "I thought I told you to leave the roughing up to me, son."

Tyler growled and held me tighter. "That wasn't exactly easy considering what he was about to do to Kacey."

"Then I'm surprised you didn't kill the fucker," his father grumbled angrily. He squeezed my shoulder and turned my chin to face him. "Are you okay?"

I nodded, tears falling down my cheeks.

"Then you two get back to the arena. I'll handle everything here. I think it's time Liam pays for all of his crimes."

"Are you sure you'll be okay?" Tyler asked.

Steven cracked his knuckles and grinned. "You have nothing to worry about, son. Now go."

Tyler rushed us out the door and down the street, where Steven's truck sat cloaked in darkness. He opened the door and set me down gently.

"How did you know?" I asked.

He buckled me up and ran to the other side and got in. "Your brother told Paxton you were sick. When Paxton noticed Liam and Jordan weren't in his entourage, he knew something was wrong.

"I wanted to kill Liam, Kacey. I saw him through your window and I lost it. As soon as my dad unlocked the front door I came straight for you. I don't want to imagine what would've happened if I'd been a few minutes late."

Neither did I.

My hands were shaking uncontrollably and my wrists looked like raw hamburger. I focused on trying to breathe and calming myself down. It hurt to know that my brother was the cause of it all.

"You don't have to go with me, Kacey," Tyler murmured, reaching for my hands. He placed his on top of mine and squeezed gently, making sure to avoid my wrists. "If you don't want to see your brother, you can wait for me in my room."

Shaking my head, I took a deep breath and sat up taller. The thought of seeing my brother cleared my head and gave me new focus. "No, I'm going to watch you fight and I'm going to sit in your corner, with my head held high. My brother likes to break people and we're going to show him he can't break us. This all ends tonight."

By the time we got back to the arena, Tyler had ten minutes before the fight. My dress was part way ripped and my makeup was smeared down my face, but Tyler held my hand firmly in his as I raced along beside him to his room. When he opened the door, I gasped at the amount of people in there.

Paxton and Bree were the first ones up, rushing to my side. Reluctantly, Tyler let me go and Pax took me up in his arms—his skin warm and sweaty from his fight. "Your brother is so fucking dead, Kace. Are you okay?"

"Yes," I whispered. "If Tyler didn't show up I wouldn't have been. Did you win?"

"You know it."

I smiled and held him tighter.

"All right, let me have her. You boys can't always keep her to yourself," Bree scolded.

Pax set me down and Bree immediately brought the tissues to my face and wiped under my eyes. She even had to use them on herself when she looked at me. "We were so worried. When Paxton told us you weren't here . . ."

"Shh. I'm okay now," I consoled her. "I'm safe."

Over her shoulder, I saw Matt and Gabriella, along with one of the Jameson twins. Gabriella smiled at me, her dark hair pulled into a low ponytail and dressed in a royal blue tank top and jeans. Hesitantly, I smiled back.

Matt, looking exactly like Gabriella with the same dark hair and green eyes, shook Tyler's hand and slapped him on the shoulder. "It's time, Rushing. Are you ready to go out there? I'm in your corner tonight."

Tyler smiled, but then looked back at me, his expression uncertain.

"Go," I said, nodding my head. "I'll be out there as quick as I can." I held up my wrists. "As soon as I get these bandaged up."

"I'll do it," Gabriella cut in, coming to my side. "You boys need to get out there, now. Us girls can handle it from here."

Tyler tensed, but Matt grabbed his tape and gloves and started for the door. "Come on, boys. It's time to kick some ass."

All the guys left the room, except Tyler, who took me in his arms and kissed me long and hard. Gabriella and

Bree both turned their heads, giving us privacy. "I love you, Kacey. Wish me luck."

"You don't need luck. I have faith in you."

He kissed me again and disappeared out the door, closing it behind him. Now I was left alone with Bree and Gabriella. The awkward silence was thick enough to choke on.

"Okay, I'm just going to break the ice," Gabriella began. She took my hands and pulled me over to the couch and gently pressed down on my shoulders. I sat down and watched her rummage through Tyler's bag until she pulled out the triple antibiotic ointment and gauze.

Kneeling down in front of me, she turned my hands over and hissed when she saw all of the damage. Bree sat beside me and put her arm around my shoulders.

"I'm going to do this as gently as I can, okay?" Gabriella murmured soothingly.

"Okay," I whispered.

Closing my eyes, I gritted my teeth together as she rubbed the ointment onto my sores and slowly wrapped them in gauze. When both were done, she smiled and got to her feet.

"There, that should take care of it. Tyler can put more medicine on them and rewrap them for you tomorrow."

"Thanks, Gabriella. I appreciate it."

Bree took my hands and helped me up, clenching her teeth at my ripped dress. "I hope Tyler beat the shit out of the guys who did that to you."

"He did," I informed her. "If I wasn't tied up, I would've tried to do it myself."

"Do you happen to have something else to wear?" Gabriella asked.

I shook my head and ran my hands through my hair. "No. After everything that happened, Tyler rushed me out of my house and away from there as fast as he could."

Reaching for her pink duffle bag on the floor, Gabriella picked it up and set it down in front of me. "I know you have no reason to like me and you can say no if you want, but I have something in here you could wear." She pulled out a pair of jeans and held them up. "We're basically the same size, so these should fit. I think my ass might be a little bit bigger, though."

Bree chuckled when I took the jeans and I rolled my eyes at her. Gabriella was actually nice, considering everything between us. It wasn't what I was expecting. Rummaging through her bag some more, she pulled out a couple of tank tops and passed one to Bree and to me. "I know this is kind of silly, but I used to do this a lot with my brother." She pointed to the tank tops. "Hold them out."

When I lifted the black tank top there were words written in the center in bright neon green letters . . . *Team Tyler*. I looked down at the royal blue one she was wearing and noticed that it said *Team Ryley* on it in big, white letters. The tank tops were the same colors of the guys' fighting shorts.

"I would wear the ones for my brother at his fights. Eventually, I had some made for all of my friends, including Tyler. You don't have to wear them, but I figured it would be a good smack in the face to your brother."

Smiling, I held the tank top up to my chest and traced Tyler's name with my finger. "Let's do it."

CHAPTER

44

TYLER

MATT TAPED UP my hands and Ryley shoved a pair of ear buds in my ears, playing nothing but Breaking Benjamin songs, to keep my mind off of Kyle when it was his turn to walk past. Needless to say, I would have to go through three MMA fighters to get to him. I could do it, but Matt, Ryley, and Cole didn't deserve to feel my wrath. Nope, that was all for Kyle.

Ryley fumbled with the volume on the iPod and smiled, mouthing the words to the song playing. His right eye was bruised from his fight and he was still in his blue and white fighting shorts, along with a black T-shirt that had *Team Gabriella* on it—he must have lost a bet. His fight tonight wasn't for a title, but in just a few short weeks, he was probably going to be fighting his own twin brother for it.

"All right, the cocksucker's gone," Ryley assured me, taking out the ear buds.

"Thank fucking God, I'm surprised I can still hear," I grumbled, shaking my head.

"Well, it's a good thing I did, or you would've heard him taunting you when he walked by. It took all *I* had not to go after him."

"Same here," Matt and Cole agreed simultaneously.

Matt handed me my black gloves and I slid them on my hands, fastening them tight. Taking me by the shoulders, he looked into my eyes and nodded his head. "You've got this. I wish your dad could be here to see it, but we all have faith in you. This is your time and you've proved that you earned it."

He slapped me on the back and nodded again before waltzing up to the black curtain waiting for the announcer to call my name. Cole joined him.

"I can't believe everything that's happened," Ryley stated incredulously. "It literally blows my mind how so many people can just be fucked up beyond repair."

Thoughts of Kacey lying tied up on her bed while Liam touched her, flashed in my mind. "You have no idea how enraged I was when I barged in on Liam trying to force himself onto Kacey. The only thing that stopped me from killing him was her. I had to think of what it would do to her."

"Yeah, I can't imagine it either," Ryley replied. "If someone were to do that to—" Abruptly, he stopped and clenched his jaw. I caught his hesitation, but he laughed it off. "All I know is, that someone would be on the brink of death," he finished.

"Uh huh. Why don't you finish what you were going to say, Ryley? If someone were to do that to who? Ashleigh? You can be honest with me, you know."

Ryley huffed and dropped his gaze to the iPod in his hands. "Ashleigh's long gone by now. I've moved on and so has she."

Gabriella was going to be furious with me, but I didn't care. He needed to know the truth. "What would you say if things weren't what they seemed? It appears that women have a knack for hiding the truth to protect us. Why the fuck they do that, I don't know."

Ryley furrowed his brows. "Dude, I have no clue what you're talking about."

Sighing, I placed my hand on his shoulder and squeezed. "I'm talking about Ashleigh. She's not with Colin anymore, man. After the whole baby scare, she left him as soon as they got back to California. From what I understand, she called it quits because she still had feelings for you."

Ryley's face paled, but I could see the anger flash in his eyes. "How do you know all of this? Did Gabriella tell you?"

I nodded. "She told me about a week after it happened. For some reason, Ashleigh doesn't want you to know. Gabriella was just honoring her friend's decision. I guess Ashleigh knew it wouldn't work out since you went right back to your usual self."

Furiously, Ryley ran his hands through his dark hair. "That happened a month ago, Tyler. I can't believe she left him and no one told me! What the fuck am I going to do now?"

"Would it have mattered?" I asked. "Would you have

taken her back after what she did?" When he didn't answer, I knew it was because he was afraid to admit he fell for a girl who broke his heart. "Ryley, whatever's going on with her, you might want to take the time to find out. Yes, it's been a month, but there's a reason she's staying away from you. Take a lesson from my book if you need . . . Kacey kept me in the dark because of her brother. Ashleigh's probably doing the same thing, but has her own reasons. I would find them out before it really is too late."

"Since when did you become all philosophical?" he teased, except the smile didn't quite reach his eyes.

The music blared overhead and the announcer's voice boomed through the microphone. It was time—my time. I slapped Ryley on the shoulder and smiled. "Since Kacey. I can't help it, she brings it out in me."

Ryley rolled his eyes and we both laughed as we walked up to Matt and Cole. Matt held out my robe and I slipped my arms inside, pulling the hood over my head. Kyle was being announced first and if Kacey was already out there in her seat, I wish I could see the look on his face.

"Remember, Tyler," Matt began, "Kyle will go for the legs. He'll try to take you down to the mat."

"And that'll be his downfall. Too bad for him, I've been trained by the best floor gamer in the UFC," I replied with a wink.

"You got that right. Now let's tear this shit up."

Over the speakers, *Had Enough* by Breaking Benjamin exploded into the crowd and they went wild, cheering and screaming my name. It was my turn.

"And the next fighter competing for the Heavyweight title is none other than your local bad boy, *Tyler 'The Ter-*

ror' Russhhiiinngg! This is sure to be one hell of a fight tonight."

The sounds surrounding me felt like thunder booming overhead, the whole arena vibrating in anticipation. It spiked my adrenaline, pushing it through my veins. Cole and Ryley separated the black curtain and I marched out, keeping my head down as I walked toward the ring. Out of the corner of my eye, I noticed the seats where the girls should be sitting were vacant.

Inside, I smiled. I was going to get my wish, to see Kyle's face when he saw his sister in *my* corner. Looking up into the ring, Kyle grinned wide and bounced in place as I made my way up onto the mat. I kept my face blank, psyching him out. His cockiness would be his downfall.

Sliding out of my robe, I handed it to Matt and smiled at him, Cole, and Ryley. They were all in my corner tonight.

"Was your dad too ashamed to come?" Kyle sneered behind my back.

Turning around, I met him in the center of the ring and got into position. I wasn't going to let him make me lose focus. "No, he's been a little busy taking out the trash."

Kyle scoffed, but then I purposely tore my attention away to the empty seats in his section, furrowing my brows. I wanted to make him think I was looking for Kacey.

Smirking, Kyle looked down at his seats then back to me. "Looking for my sister? It's a shame you're still hard up for her. Especially now that she's fucking someone else."

"You're lying," I snapped. "Where is she?"

"Not here with you, that's for damn sure. She said it made her sick when you touched her." Kyle leered at me, taunting me. "How does it feel to know we played you?"

You'll find out.

The announcer stepped in between us pushing us apart. "That's enough, gentlemen. Save it for the fight."

"With pleasure," Kyle sneered, taking a step back.

Ding, ding, ding.

The announcer quickly stepped out of the way and it was time. Just as I expected, Kyle charged first and tried to psych me out with a left hook, but ended up going for my middle. Darting out of the way, I lowered my body and swept my leg across the mat, tripping him. He recovered by rolling and getting right back to his feet.

"I'm impressed, Rushing. You're quick on your feet today."

"Yeah, well, a lot's changed in the past month."

Ever since I'd met Kacey, she made me better—more focused on my goals. I had what it took to win. I glanced down and noticed Bree and Gabriella walking to their seats, followed by Kacey and Paxton. Kacey pointed to her tank top and smiled up at me.

Kyle hadn't seen her yet. He did, however, land a hard kick to my shin, which I immediately reciprocated with a right hook to his face. His head snapped to the side and blood spewed over the mat from his broken nose; I felt the bones crunch when I hit him.

"You're so fucking dead," he growled, swiping the blood away with his hand. It was then I could see in his eyes that he realized I wasn't broken like he'd planned. If I hadn't gotten to Kacey in time, I would've been . . . but thankfully, I did.

Beaming, I grinned wide and beckoned him closer. "Bring it on, cocksucker."

Charging again, Kyle grabbed a hold of my waist and took me down to the mat. He punched me one good time in the jaw and the pain exploded through my skull. Then, I tasted blood. In return, I elbowed him in the side and shoved him away with my foot.

Ding, ding, ding.

We both got to our feet and Kyle spat on the mat, glaring at me. "Round two, it's all going to be over."

He went to his corner and I backed up to mine, only to have someone there I wasn't expecting. "What are you doing here?"

My father smiled and opened up a bottle of water, handing it to me. "Believe me, I didn't think I'd make it, but the detective knew this was a big night for you, and he didn't want me to miss it. I just have to go to the station afterward."

"What about Liam? What's going to happen to that fucker?"

My father looked down at Kacey then back to me. "He's going to be charged for attempted rape and kidnapping, among other things. I'm not going to let him get away with what he did to Kacey." Neither was I.

Ding, ding, ding. It was time for round two . . . the end.

"Go get him, son. You can do this."

Not wasting any more time, I let my smile fade and went straight on the offensive, jabbing left and right, not stopping. My muscles burned like fire but I kept going, ignoring the pain exploding through every inch of my body as my fists connected with Kyle's body. All of the hate, all of the anger, I let it pour out of me and didn't hold anything back. I felt blood splatter on my face and my chest, but I didn't let it stop me.

The next thing I knew, I was on the mat with Kyle's arm locked in an arm bar. I wanted to keep pulling, to break it in two before he could tap out . . . but he was too stubborn to do it.

"Tap out," I growled.

Kyle snarled and continued to fight me off with no effect because I had him locked down. "Fuck you."

I gripped his arm tighter and he hissed, sweat breaking out over his skin. It was time he knew the truth. "You want me to break your arm? Fine, I honestly don't give a fuck. However, first, I want you to take a look at my seats. Who do you see over there?"

Loosening up my hold, I gave Kyle the mobility he needed to see. His eyes went wide when he saw Kacey, getting to her feet with the bandages clearly visible on her wrists. "What the fuck?" he hissed, grimacing in pain.

"I went and got her, asshole. You see those bandages on her wrists? Those are from Liam, when he tried to rape her. Now give me one good reason why I shouldn't rip your fucking arms out. Because, believe me, if it wasn't for her, I'd have already done it."

"You lie!" he shouted. "You're just trying to distract me."

Letting him go, I pushed him away and kicked him in the face. I could've broken his arm and ended the fight, but I wasn't like him. "I don't have to distract you, Kyle. It's the truth. You're headed nowhere fast and you know it."

His features darkening, Kyle rushed me, anger and desperation consuming him. He moved fast and I reacted, but it was like our bodies moved in slow motion before slamming down on the mat. It all happened so quickly. I heard the crack and the screams that followed right after.

It was over.

CHAPTER 45

Kacey

WHEN TYLER HAD Kyle's arm locked down, I knew my brother wouldn't tap out. Deep down, I wanted Tyler to break his arm and get it over with, but he was too admirable to do that—even if he wanted my brother's blood. What I didn't expect was for him to let go.

Afterward, everything moved in slow motion. I heard my brother yell that Tyler was a liar before recklessly charging at him. Tyler's dad shouted something, but then both my brother and Tyler fell down to the mat hard. When only one of them got up, I froze and everything went silent. The paramedics rushed into the ring and knelt down by the motionless fighter.

The only thing going through my mind at that moment was . . . thank God it wasn't Tyler. I did, however, breathe a sigh of relief when I could see Kyle's chest rising and falling with his breaths.

"Kacey," Bree shouted, clinging onto my arm. "Tyler needs you. Go!"

By the time I rushed into the ring, all of Tyler's friends were in there, including his father. My brother had already been taken away on the gurney and Tyler's arm was lifted in the air by the announcer. "And your Heavyweight title champion, by TKO, is none other than Las Vegas' own, *Tyler . . . The Terror . . . Russsshhhhiiiinnn-ngggg!*"

Tyler smiled, but it didn't reach his eyes. His friends lifted him in the air and paraded him around the ring, while the crowd went wild, chanting his name. When they set him down, he immediately came to me and wrapped his arms around my waist, burying his face in my neck. He was covered in spatters of blood, but I didn't care; I held onto him.

"Kacey," he pleaded. "I'm so sorry."

"Tyler, stop. You did amazing. There's nothing to be sorry about." I lifted his head from my neck and smiled up at him. "You deserved to win."

He nodded, his face uncertain. "I know, but I think he's really hurt. We might need to follow the paramedics to the hospital."

"No," I snapped. "If my brother's hurt that's what he gets. It's what I call karma."

"That may be true, but when I told him what happened to you, I could see the anger in his eyes, Kacey. He didn't want to believe it, but deep down he knew it was true when he looked at you. You need to talk to him."

He put his arm around me. "And unfortunately, after

that we have to go to the police station. We need to put Liam away."

Sighing, I walked with Tyler by his side while he waved to his fans and signed autographs in passing. The night wasn't exactly what we'd anticipated, but at least he won the title and I was safe. Things could have been a lot worse.

Tyler had put everything on the line for me, and for that I would do anything he asked me to. Even if it meant talking to my brother.

After Tyler washed up and changed clothes, we went straight to the hospital and were told to wait in the waiting room while they finished up the tests. What didn't surprise me was that Tyler and I were the only ones in the waiting room. None of Kyle's friends were there.

"I never got the chance to say thank you," I whispered, laying my head on Tyler's shoulder.

"For what, beautiful?"

"For the check. I had no idea you'd been looking at properties for us."

A mischievous smile lit up his face when I glanced up at him. "You're welcome. I know you two are ready. I had a lot of time on my hands in California to think about you. That's when I started looking for places. When we get back home there's something I . . ."

"Miss Andrews?"

"Yes," I turned, getting to my feet. A short woman, probably in her mid-forties with really short brown hair approached, carrying a folder. I looked down at her name-tag and it said *Dr. Carol Peters*.

She held out her hand, her face grim. "Miss Andrews, I'm Dr. Peters. I'm the one looking after your brother."

I shook her hand and nodded. "Yes, how is he?"

Tyler stood and came to my side and shook her hand as well.

"It's hard to say right now," she admitted honestly. "The tests show he has a dislocated vertebra in his neck. We don't think it's damaged the spinal cord, but we're going to go in and see what we can do. He's experiencing some numbness from the neck down. Now, I need to pre-pare you. If we can't fix the problem . . . there is a chance he'll be paralyzed."

"Oh my God," I choked. "Will he ever walk again?"

Tyler's face paled and he sat back down in the chair, covering his face with his hands. I knew he blamed him-self, but I had watched the fight. He didn't try to deliber-ately hurt my brother.

Dr. Peters grimaced. "We'll do our best and hope for a good outcome. Sometimes, all it takes is a little bit of faith. If you want, you can go in and see him now, before we take him into surgery. We've already contacted your mother and she's coming in on the next available flight."

Hopefully, my mother would be able to take care of him because I knew I wasn't going to do it. Kyle made his bed and now he had to sleep in it.

Dr. Peters walked away, leaving me and Tyler to our-selves.

I knelt down in front of him and took his hands in

mine. "This isn't your fault. Injuries like this happen all of the time in the MMA. You can't blame yourself. I, for one, don't blame you."

"Are you sure about that?" he asked softly, staring at me with his stormy gray eyes.

I squeezed his hands and leaned over to kiss his lips gently, since my brother split his bottom lip at some point during the fight. "I'm positive. I'll only be a minute, okay?"

Taking a deep breath, I left the waiting room and started down the short hallway to Kyle's room. It was dark and quiet inside, except for the lights and sounds of the machines. Kyle was motionless, his neck held stiff in a brace, but his gaze followed me as I stood beside him.

He started to speak, but I held up my hand. "You don't get to speak right now," I snapped, glaring down at him. "You need to listen to me and listen well. I am *not* going to feel sorry for you because of what happened. All of this," I said, waving around his immobilized body, "is payback for all of the bad shit you've done in your life. Did you think it wouldn't catch up to you?"

He closed his eyes and squeezed them shut. Tears started to blur my vision, but they were from anger. "Open your eyes, Kyle," I demanded.

He did as I said and opened them. For the first time in my life I watched him cry. I held up my hands and ripped open my gauze so he could see the marred flesh on my wrists from the cable ties. "This is what you did to me. You left me in the hands of your scumbag friends and if it wasn't for Tyler, Liam would've—" I choked. I couldn't even finish the sentence. It was too scary to even think about.

"I would've killed him," Kyle rasped. "I never wanted anything to happen to you."

Shaking my head, I closed my eyes and wiped away my tears. "I'm sorry, Kyle, but I don't believe you. You're about to go into surgery and I wish you all the best. Mom is on her way, so hopefully, she'll be able to take care of you and figure out what to do. Because there sure as hell aren't any of your friends out there in that waiting room. It's just me and Tyler."

He kept his gaze on me, his lips trembling. "I'm sorry, Kacey. Please say you'll forgive me."

Swallowing hard, I reached for his hand and touched it briefly, before taking a step away. "You will always be my brother, Kyle, and for that I love you. But right now, I can't say the words you need to hear. It will take me some time. I don't like who you've become and I hope one day you decide to change." I backed away to the door, out of his range of sight.

"Kacey, *please*," he begged.

"Goodbye, Kyle." Quickly, I shut the door and leaned against it with my eyes closed.

"Are you okay?" Tyler asked.

"Yes," I replied as I opened my eyes. "I feel much better now."

Putting his arm around my shoulders, we started down the hall toward the elevators.

"Do we have to go to the police station now?"

"Actually, no. I called the station and they said we could wait until tomorrow."

Once we got to the elevators, Tyler pressed the button and the doors opened. "So what are we going to do then? I'm sure there's some kind of party in your honor for being the Heavyweight champion."

Tyler put his hand on the small of my back and guided me into the elevator. "I'm sure there is, but they're just going to have to do without their guest of honor. Tonight there's only one person I want to be with."

"Oh yeah? And who might that be?"

The elevator doors closed and he pushed me against the wall with his body firmly pressed into mine. "Surely you know," he murmured against my lips. "It's always going to be you." He pressed his lips against mine, and opened my lips with his tongue, going deeper. When he leaned back, I gasped for air and tried to close the distance again.

"You promise?"

Brushing the hair off my face, he rubbed my cheeks with his thumbs and smiled. "I promise, and one day soon I'm going to prove it to you."

I couldn't wait.

EPILOGUE

Kacey

One Week Later

MY BROTHER HAD his surgery, but only time would tell what the extent of the damage would entail. The last I heard, he still couldn't walk because of the numbness. Word traveled fast of his demise and I couldn't go anywhere with Tyler without someone asking questions. His father told us to take the week off, so we spent it at his house, locked away from everyone. It was hands down the best week of my life.

However, the week had come and gone and now we had to get back to work. I still had a job at the gym to do and so did Tyler, even though he was taking a break from training. In just a few short months, he would be the owner of his family's gym, acquiring all responsibility. We were both taking the next step in our lives.

In front of me sat the realty magazines and my budget list. I was pretty good at numbers, so handling the books was going to be one of my many jobs once Bree and I got our restaurant started.

I was too engrossed in the pictures in front of me to notice Tyler standing in front of my desk, staring at me.

"I could sit here and watch you all day, but there's something I need to show you."

Smiling, I shut the magazine and lifted my head. "Oh yeah? Does it happen to be something in the back room that you grew especially for me?"

He chuckled and shook his head. "Not exactly, but I'll be more than happy to show you *that* later."

Getting to my feet, I joined him in front of the desk and he kissed me.

"Have you found any more places you like?"

"No," I sighed.

He led me out the doors to his truck and opened the door so I could get in. My wrists had healed somewhat, but they were still sore and I had scars. It was always going to be a reminder of that bittersweet night.

"So where are we going?" I asked.

Tyler just smiled and started us down the road, throwing a blindfold in my lap. "You'll see, but right now I want you to put this on. And don't ask questions, or peek. If I catch you peeking, I'll have to reprimand you."

"Wow, okay, this just got interesting," I teased, tying the blindfold at the back of my head. I figured I would humor him. With Tyler, there was no telling what he was up to.

About ten minutes later, he put his truck into park.

"Keep the blindfold on, beautiful. I'm going to get out and help you. Don't you dare peek, or I'll bring the wrath down on you."

He got out of the truck and came around to my side. Holding both of my hands, he led me slowly up a couple of steps where, I heard the slide of a lock and a door opening. When I giggled, the noise echoed in the room.

"Where are we?"

Slowly, Tyler untied the blindfold and lowered it. When I opened my eyes, I gasped. It was the place I had *wanted* to buy for my restaurant, but was told someone had bought it. The place wasn't built to be a restaurant, so there was still a lot of work to be done, but it was in a prime location and we had a ton of space to work with. It would be the ideal place to own a restaurant.

"What are we doing here?"

Tyler smiled and walked to the middle of the room. The hardwood floor was dark cherry, the walls a deep beige with an elegant wrought iron spiral staircase leading to the top loft. It was everything I could ever want . . . classy and modern.

When he turned around, he spread his arms wide. "It's all yours, Kacey. Well, yours and Bree's."

"I don't get it. How is it ours? The realtor said we were too late."

Tyler walked toward me and put his arms around my waist, pulling me to him. "You *were* too late, but I used my magic and persuaded the new buyers to sell it to me."

Exasperated, I shook my head. "Yeah, but at what cost? You shouldn't have done that, Tyler. I can't imagine what you spent. How much do I owe you now?"

With a mischievous grin on his face, he led me toward the spiral staircase and I followed him up. "Well, now that's what we need to discuss. I figured you would owe me the money for the place, which I know you already have, but then you would also owe me interest."

"Interest?"

When we got to the top of the stairs, I didn't realize how huge the loft was . . . and there in the middle of it all, was a bed of cream-colored wool blankets with pillows scattered around. Picking me up in his arms, Tyler led me over and set me down on top, covering me with his body.

"Yes, interest," he murmured heatedly. He lifted my gray Rushing's gym T-shirt over my head and tossed it onto the floor. "The removal of this shirt paid for one percent of the interest. Do you want to pay off more?"

Biting my lip, I unfastened my bra and slid my arms out. "How much did that pay off?"

"Hmm . . . let's see," he replied, lowering his lips to my breast. Closing them over my nipple, he moaned, suckling it. "That's another one percent because you taste so fucking good."

While he licked and sucked my nipples, he slid my shorts down my legs and I kicked them off. Now that I was completely bare, he swiftly got to his feet and took off his own T-shirt and lowered his black gym shorts before spreading me wide again.

"So how much does this pay you back?" I asked. I wrapped my legs around his waist and he pushed inside of me, gently.

He kissed me softly on the lips and smiled. "Unfortunately, that's where I have to draw the line. You're only allowed to pay me back two percent a year."

"But that means I'll owe you forever," I gasped and

bit my lip.

Thrusting harder, he bent down and sucked that lip between his, never taking his gray gaze off of me. "I don't see the problem in that, beautiful. It means I've got you for the rest of your life."

Lifting up on his elbows, he reached between my legs and fondled my clit, rubbing it with the pad of his thumb. Arching my back, I groaned as my orgasm started to build and spread throughout my body. Pushing deeper, he knew I was about to come and so he picked up his pace and held me tight, releasing inside of me at the same time I exploded all around him. Breathing hard, he laid on top of me for a minute, and kissed me.

"So what exactly does it mean when you say you've got me for the rest of your life?" I asked curiously. We were together and we loved each other, but we hadn't been together long to really consider our future.

Holding onto me, Tyler flipped over onto his back to where I was now straddling him. He reached behind the pillow, pulling out a small black box, and handed it to me. "I know we haven't been together long, but I know what I want . . . and I want you.

"You're my future, Kacey." I opened up the box and inside was a Las Vegas keychain, with a set of keys on it. He pointed to the largest one. "This one here is the key to this place. Yours and Bree's names are on the deed already."

"Tyler," I breathed as the tears welled in my eyes.

"And this one," he said, pointing to the other, "is the key to my house. I know I don't have a ring right now, but I know in time we'll take that step. I don't want to wake up another morning without you being the first thing I see." He lifted his hands to my face and pulled me down to his lips. "All I want is to hear you say yes . . . that a future with me is what you want. I love you, Kacey."

"I love you, too."

Kissing him gently, I held the keys tightly in my grip and knew without a doubt what my answer would be . . . what it would always be. As the tears flowed down my cheeks, I made love to him again and again, whispering the same word against his lips.

Yes.

The End

**KEEP READING FOR A SNEAK PEEK OF
RYLEY'S REVENGE (GLOVES OFF, #4)
COMING DECEMBER 1, 2014
AND *CAMDEN'S REDEMPTION* (GLOVES OFF, #5)
COMING DECEMBER 29, 2014**

RYLEY'S REVENGE

A GLOVES OFF NOVEL

PROLOGUE

Ashleigh

"ARE YOU IN love with him?" Colin asks.

We'd just walked through the door of my apartment, only long enough for me to sit my bags down and grab a bottle of water from the refrigerator.

We were in Vegas because Colin and Bradley had a baseball tournament. Well, that, and to be with my best friend, Gabriella. That's what I told myself anyway. Deep down, it was because I knew Ryley was going to be there too, fighting. Seeing him again had only awakened what I kept buried inside of me.

I didn't know what to tell Colin as he stood there looking at me with those bright green eyes of his. The eyes which belonged to a man who was everything I could ever want—smart, loving, caring, and sexy as hell. Not to mention he had a body to die for. Colin was our school's star pitcher, and on his way to bigger and better things in the MLB.

I still haven't answered him yet, but if I let the truth come out of my mouth, I won't be able to take it back. Not even a day ago, I was afraid I was pregnant with Ryley's child. It was the scariest moment in my life, but what frightened me more was the look in Ryley's eyes when he thought he was going to be a father. He wasn't ready . . . hell, I wasn't ready.

The only problem was, right after I left him for Colin, he went straight back to his old ways with his identical twin. It's like I was erased from his mind, no longer the girl he fell in love with.

I have too much pride to go back to him, knowing he'll be whoring around with other women. Colin's a good guy and he deserves more than a woman whose heart's divided. I love him a lot, but I'm *in* love with someone else.

"Ashleigh, please," he murmurs, taking my hands. "You've avoided me all day. Did something happen while we were in Vegas?"

I was never good at lying, and Colin's always the first person to know when something's wrong. Sitting down on the couch, I take a deep breath and close my eyes. My stomach is in knots because I know I'm about to break another guy's heart. Colin's my safe place, my guarantee at a normal, functional relationship. I just know that if I stay, I'll never be fully happy. He doesn't own my heart, but he shares a part of my soul.

I have to make a choice. Opening my eyes, the warm tears fall down my cheeks.

Colin doesn't speak because in my actions he already has his answer. He lowers his head and slowly lets go of my hands, running them through his hair.

"I don't think I can let you go, Ashleigh. At least, not without a fight."

Sighing, I wait for him to lift his head, and when he does I lean in to give him one last kiss. "I'm sorry, Colin, but you don't have a choice."

CHAPTER 1

Ashleigh

Present time (One Month Later)

"SO WHEN ARE you coming back to California?" Gabriella asked.

When I get the balls to face Ryley again.

But in all honesty, I didn't know. For the past month, I'd been in Aspen with my family, trying to get away from anything and everything that reminded me of Ryley and Colin. Working in my family's hotel helped. I loved talking to the tourists and getting them all settled in. It was a good distraction.

I'd been afraid Gabriella would've told Ryley by now about my breakup with Colin. So far, she'd kept my secret. Colin, however, refused to give up on me and made sure to keep in touch by calling almost every single day. He'd even visited Aspen twice already. He was my friend before we became lovers, but once you cross that line, it's almost impossible to go back.

"I don't know yet," I admitted. "I'm tempted to stay here for a little while longer. I miss being with my family." It wasn't exactly a lie, but it wasn't the full truth either.

There was something I hadn't told her, or anyone for that matter. I thought maybe running away to Aspen would make my problems disappear, but I was starting to think it was just going to make them worse. For the past hour, I'd done nothing but trace and stare at the phone number on the paper in front of me. I was just too afraid to call it.

Gabriella's laugh echoed in the phone, catching my attention. "Well, all I can say is, you won't believe the shit that's happened here the past couple of days, especially when I was in Vegas for the fights."

Perking up, I held the phone closer to my ear. There weren't any people in the lobby so I had a few minutes to spare. "Oh yeah, like what?"

Anything with Ryley?

Gabriella sighed. "Well, Tyler's super serious over a girl now. And, get this . . . It turns out, she's Kyle Andrews' sister. Who would've thought that, right?"

I gasped. Everyone hated Kyle Andrews. "Oh my God, that's insane. Have you met her? Are you okay with that?"

She snorted. "Yes, I'm okay with it. It was for the best anyway. I miss talking to him though. Anyway, I met Kacey the other day. She's actually really nice—although, a little quieter than me."

"Everyone is quieter than you, Gabriella," I laughed.

"Oh, whatever. Well, now that Tyler won the title,

and Kyle's paralyzed in the hospital, all is right in the world."

"I'd say so," I agreed. Nothing like that ever happened at the hotel; it was quiet and drama free. Only in Gabriella's life was it interesting. "It sounds like you had a lot going on. How are you and Bradley doing? Still just friends?"

"For the time being, we're more like friends with benefits. We've been spending a lot of time together. Colin asks about you all the time though. I actually feel bad for the guy. We did come to the conclusion that something's wrong with you. He's noticed a difference and so have I. I think it's time you tell me what's wrong. And I don't want to hear anymore bullshit excuses. I know how to kick your ass, so don't make me come all the way to Aspen to force it out of you."

Sighing, I held up the post-it note and closed my eyes. If I didn't tell her something, I could definitely see her flying out here to live up to her promise. "I'll tell you as soon as I find out, Gabby. I promise."

"Are you okay?"

"I don't know, but when I do know what's going on, you'll be the first to know. Unfortunately, it might take a couple of days."

"Well, just as long as you get it figured out. I want my best friend back. It's not the same here without you."

I smiled, but the ache in my chest made the burn behind my eyes build. "I miss you too," I whispered, trying not to choke on my tears.

"Make sure to call if you need me . . . or if you just want to talk. I'm about to head out to the gym and get some training in, but after that, you know I'm free."

I nodded like an idiot, knowing very well she couldn't see me. "I will. Have fun with your training. I'll talk to you soon."

We said our goodbyes and I hung up the phone. Still, there was no one in the lobby, so I took a deep breath and picked the phone back up, dialing the number on the piece of paper in front of me. I'd tried calling it before numerous times and always hung up after the first ring.

"Good afternoon, Dr. McCord's office, this is Lisa, how may I direct your call?"

"Um . . . hi . . . Lisa, I'm a patient there. Or at least, I used to be before I moved to California. I'd like to make an appointment. My name is Ashleigh Warren."

"Of course, dear, just give me a second." She typed away on the keyboard and then came back on the line. "Date of birth, please."

I told her my birth date, which happened to be just a couple of weeks ago. Even though I was only twenty-three, it felt like I had aged beyond my years over the past month. Things that used to be important, just *weren't* anymore—not when I had responsibilities looming over my head.

More clacking on the computer keys. "Yes, I see you here. Is this for a yearly check-up?"

Hands shaking, I closed my eyes and cleared my throat. "Not exactly."

"Okay. And why do you need to be seen? Is this an emergency?"

Halfheartedly, I chuckled and lowered my head to the desk, my laugh turning to tears. "In my life, Lisa, yes I'd say it's an emergency." I took a deep breath and blew it out slowly. "I think I'm pregnant."

ACKNOWLEDGMENTS

MY EXTREME GRATITUDE goes out to every single one of you: my family, friends, readers, bloggers, and future readers. You all have made my dreams come true and for that I will always be thankful. I hope you enjoy my yummy MMA fighters because I sure as hell enjoyed writing them. What's not to like about strong and sexy alpha fighters? There will be more to come so make sure you don't miss out.

ABOUT THE AUTHOR

NEW YORK TIMES and USA Today Bestselling author, L.P. Dover, is a southern belle residing in North Carolina along with her husband and two beautiful girls. Before she even began her literary journey she worked in Periodontics enjoying the wonderment of dental surgeries.

Not only does she love to write, but she loves to play tennis, go on mountain hikes, white water rafting, and you can't forget the passion for singing. Her two number one fans expect a concert each and every night before bedtime and those songs usually consist of Christmas carols.

Aside from being a wife and mother, L.P. Dover has written over nine novels including her Forever Fae series, the Second Chances series, and her standalone novel, Love, Lies, and Deception. Her favorite genre to read is romantic suspense and she also loves writing it. However, if she had to choose a setting to live in it would have to be with her faeries in the Land of the Fae.

L.P. Dover is represented by Marisa Corvisiero of Corvisiero Literary Agency.

OTHER BOOKS BY L.P. DOVER

Forever Fae Series

Second Chances Standalones

Standalone (Romantic Suspense)

ALSO CHECK OUT THESE
EXTRAORDINARY AUTHORS & BOOKS:

Alivia Anders ~ Illumine

Cambria Hebert ~ Recalled

Angela Orlowski Peart ~ Forged by Greed

Julia Crane ~ Freak of Nature

J.A. Huss ~ Tragic

Cameo Renae ~ Hidden Wings

A.J. Bennett ~ Now or Never

Tabatha Vargo ~ Playing Patience

Beth Balmanno ~ Set in Stone

Ella James ~ Selling Scarlett

Tara West ~ Visions of the Witch

Heidi McLaughlin ~ Forever Your Girl

Melissa Andrea ~ The Edge of Darkness

Komal Kant ~ Falling for Hadie

Melissa Pearl ~ Golden Blood

Alexia Purdy ~ Breathe Me

Sarah M. Ross ~ Inhale, Exhale

Brina Courtney ~ Reveal

Amber Garza ~ Falling to Pieces

Anna Cruise ~ Maverick